CLAIM ME

TAWNY TAYLOR

Published by Novel Mind Books

Copyright © 2012 Tawny Taylor

ISBN:0615619495
ISBN-13:9780615619491

LCCN:

ONE

Dead had just taken on a whole new meaning for nightclub owner Sylvie Durand -- a much more literal one.

She wasn't afraid to admit she'd been desperate to increase traffic in her failing bar, Carpe Nocturne. But the parade of rescue and police personnel, dressed in matching blue uniforms and wearing identical grim expressions, wasn't exactly what she'd had in mind.

And the night had been going so well too.

All it had taken was one bizarre discovery for the first successful night in her club to come to a strange and shocking end. Terrifying. In fact, if she hadn't been the owner of the bar, she would've been outta there hours ago. She was still shaking all over from finding the dead guy... hanging... in her office... It had been so gruesome. The poor guy looked like he'd been the victim of a vampire attack.

Shudder!

God, it had been so awful. She just knew it would take years and years for the image branded in her mind to fade.

And the smell. Of blood and stuff she didn't want to think about.

Yes, lucky her. Not. She had owned Carpe Nocturne for two miserable months and was really, really hating it already.

Anyone want to buy a bar for cheap?

Only a handful of costume-bedecked patrons remained, hanging around outside the front door after having been questioned and released. They stood wide-eyed, watching the police detectives as they conducted their investigation. Morbid curiosity.

When the police officers decided they were done asking her the same questions over and over, she managed to drag her weary, shaky body toward the exit, intent upon joining the onlookers still crowded around the front of the building. It was a little chilly outside. And dark. But at least the air wouldn't be tainted with the stench of death. A big, huge plus at the moment.

As she stepped through the doorway, a young woman dressed head-to-toe in Victorian garb gave her a weak smile. She was rubbing at the fake blood on her neck, now dried up and flaking off.

Sylvie attempted to give the woman a smile back. She wasn't exactly in the mood to socialize, although she was glad to be among friendlier company. The police officers who'd questioned her hadn't been rude, but they hadn't been kind either. Their clipped tones and deadpan expressions told her everything she needed to hear, more than she was prepared to deal with.

Yes, this pack of costumed strangers, dressed mostly as vampires -- what a creepy coincidence! -- weren't her first choice for companionship tonight. But they were people. Human beings. Alive. And not eyeballing her with the suspicion that she was a cold-blooded killer.

Or course, given her current mental state, even her worst enemy would be acceptable company. The thought of being alone terrified her. She was scared witless. Completely freaked out. The creepy costumes weren't helping, that was for sure. What had made her think themed costume nights were a great idea anyway?

And why hadn't her best friend shown up yet? Sylvie had called her hours ago, left an urgent this-is-life-or-death message on her answering machine.

"Are you okay?" Victorian woman asked.

"Not sure, to be honest." Sylvie leaned back, letting the cold brick wall support her. Her legs were wobbly. Her knees felt tingly and loose, like any moment they'd give out.

Victorian woman gave her an understanding nod. "I can totally relate. Had to be quite a shock finding that dead body."

That's putting it mildly. Sylvie's stomach did a little summersault inside her belly. She swallowed hard against the acid rising up her throat. "Yeah."

"Did you know the person? The one who… you know?"

"No. Have no idea who he is -- was."

"At least that's a good thing. Would've really been awful if it had been a good friend. I've never seen a dead body, outside of the movies. Although I have thought about being a private detective someday. You know, like one of Charlie's Angels," she jabbered excitedly. "I watch old reruns on cable. The original series was so much better than the movie…"

"Nothing too thrilling about any of this, if you want my opinion," she whispered over the woman's ongoing discourse about the shortcomings of a movie she'd never seen. She lacked the energy to continue the conversation. Heck, she lacked the energy to stand erect. Figuring she'd send a subtle message to the yammering red-headed Farrah Fawcett wannabe, she took a step or two to the side. Naturally, Farrah didn't take the hint and closed the distance between them.

A deep chuckle resonated to Sylvie's left as she took a third step.

Why would anyone be laughing right now? What could be so funny about a man who had been murdered in her office? There wasn't a damn thing about this night that was funny. Or exciting. Or cool. It was just plain horrific! The worst thing she'd ever seen.

5

What was wrong with these people? Didn't they have any hearts? A man had died in there! Died. As in dead. Forever. What if he had a family? Children. Oh, God!

Okay, she was done freaking out and overreacting. At least for now.

She turned her head in the general direction of the chuckle. Found the guilty party standing about five feet away, a guy dressed as a vampire, black cape and all. He was talking to a gaggle of women gathered around him, all dressed in Victorian gowns like Farrah Fawcett. They were tittering like a bunch of birds. Fluffing their feathers. Shaking their tails and fluttering eyelashes.

At the moment it wasn't a scene she had the stomach to watch.

Although, after taking a second look, she couldn't blame the women. That vampire wannabe's gorgeous face would inspire just about any red-blooded girl to do a little tail shaking. Even her.

That was, if she had a thing for vamps wearing costumes that played up on devil-made-me-do-it smirks like his.

But she didn't.

Nor did she find the crisp white of his shirt against the deep olive of his skin the least bit sexy. And the tendril of his ebony hair curled over the pulse-numbing swell of his shoulder… that did nothing for her either. Not at all.

Who was she kidding?

When he lifted his eyes, his gaze was incredibly sharp. He reminded her of Hugh Jackman in *Van Helsing*. Dark and mysterious and damned sexy.

She could tell by the way her eyeballs and tongue were drying up that her glance had morphed into a gape-mouthed stare.

What was that all about? She did not gape. She did not stare. *Pull it together, girl!*

His all-too-perfect lips curled into the kind of smile that no doubt inspired women to drop their panties.

Playing the affronted woman of the new millennium, she rolled her eyes and made a failing attempt at turning her attention back to the Charlie's Angel wannabe beside her.

The woman kept talking, rambled on and on about something, but Sylvie couldn't hear her anymore. Now, instead of thinking about the poor dead guy, she was too busy thinking about Van Helsing over there. Him and his "fan club."

Ack! What was wrong with her? A guy had been found murdered in her office. Her bar would be shut down for who knew how long, which meant even more financial troubles were headed her way. As if she didn't have enough of those already! And all she could think about was some egotistical guy wearing cheap velveteen and satin?

Fatigue That's what it was. Exhaustion. And shock. And… and temporary insanity. What was that disease called? Oh yeah. Post Traumatic Stress Disorder.

Is there a psychiatrist in the house?

She needed to go home. When, oh when would she be free to leave? Not that she was eager to go to her empty house, but this standing around, waiting, was driving her nuts. She needed to get out of there before she really did need a shrink.

She stared at Farrah's face and pretended like she was listening.

"Do you need a ride home?" a deep male voice asked.

Without turning to look, she identified the voice as belonging to Van Helsing. It was a gut feeling. She didn't have to look. Little ripples of awareness zipped up and down her spine.

"Thanks, but no," she said. Maybe he was trying to be nice, and she was just overreacting because of her current unstable mental state, but she doubted it. She glanced his way. The evil Cheshire grin was gone, but something sparkled in his impossibly dark eyes. Something that didn't inspire even the tiniest measure of trust. Still, she felt compelled to add, "Not trying to be rude, or anything. My friend's on her way to pick me up. I'd hate to make her drive all the way here for nothing."

"Just as long as you're not driving. You're a little pale." With a tip of his head, he motioned toward her hands. "You're shaking too."

She laced her fingers together, gripped her hands. "Yeah. Kind of freaked out still."

The medical examiner -- or whatever the guy who collected dead bodies was called -- decided that was the perfect time to wheel the loaded gurney through the propped-open front door. Sylvie knew the body would be closed up in something, but she averted her eyes anyway. Her stomach roiled like the inside of a volcano. Thankful for the support of that cold brick wall, she stared down at Van Helsing's well-shod feet and didn't lift her gaze, even after she heard the slam of truck doors.

She felt sick.

Home. She wanted to go home.

A different set of feet came to a stop next to Van Helsing's. "We're all set here for tonight, we've locked up, but we need to ask you to leave the premises secured for a few more days. We'll need to get back in there." The speaker -- and owner of a pair of scuffed, black uniform shoes -- was one of the police officers who'd first questioned her. Couldn't remember his name. Didn't really care. As she lifted her eyes, he handed her a card. "In case you need to get in touch with me."

"Okay. Thanks." She fingered the edge of the card and watched him and the rest of the officers get into their cars and drive off. Farrah and the remaining bystanders, with the exception of Van Helsing, left one by one. Van Helsing hung around while Sylvie put in a third call to her criminally non-responsive and soon-to-be-ex best friend.

Still no answer. What the hell? It wasn't that late. A little after one in the morning. Normally Lisa was up at this hour, stuffing her face with popcorn and watching reruns of *Law and Order*. Where was she?

Frustrated and desperate, Sylvie slapped her flip phone shut so hard it flew from her shaking hands and fell with a plastic-shattering smash on the concrete.

No hope Lisa'd get through now.

"Dammit!" Sylvie bent to pick up the phone she knew was broken to bits but Van Helsing reached it first. Her fingertips grazed the back of his hand as he wrapped his fingers around the target of their simultaneous grappling. A funny tingle buzzed up her body. When she straightened up, her cheeks felt like they were glowing as brightly as Carpe Nocturne's neon sign overhead. She staggered backward, bracing herself against the wall.

He handed her the phone. His lowered eyebrows spoke of genuine concern, but the sparkle still lingering in his eyes spoke of other things. Very intriguing other things, she realized as she looked deeper.

"Are you sure you don't need a ride?" he asked.

"Positive. Thanks. I'll just… drive myself home. I'm not a baby." She pushed off from the wall, letting her legs support her fully. Unfortunately, they were a little too wobbly to do all that great a job at it. She stumbled after her second step, and naturally it was Van Helsing's arm that she reached for as she struggled to keep from falling over and breaking her neck.

At least her spine was spared. No need for a neck brace. But she couldn't say the same for her heel. It snapped off when she twisted her ankle. "Oh, this is just great!" Still holding onto Van Helsing's arm, she reached down and snatched up her wrecked shoe. "My favorite pair. What else could go wrong tonight?" She wanted to cry. Really, really bad.

This was a nightmare. Worse than a nightmare. Thanks to tonight's events, she was on the verge of losing everything she'd worked for. Her home. Her bank account. Her security.

Even though the tears were right there, gathering in her lower eyelids, she didn't cry. She blinked a lot. Sniffled. Blinked some more. Slowed her breathing. "Watch, I'll probably have a flat tire, too," she said through a series of hiccuping half-sobs.

"I'll drive you home. I promise I'm not going to hurt you."

She knew that… Kinda. There was, after all, a very sick murderer running around the city. Who knew what the guy looked like? Could look like Hugh Jackman, with long black hair, a stubbled jaw and a charming smile that made women melt…

No way. Van Helsing couldn't be a murderer. He was the good guy. He only shot vampires and werewolves.

We're talking reality here, not movies.

Even though she had a feeling this man was not a murderer, she still didn't want to get into a car with him. She was too shaken to trust her instincts right now. "I know you won't hurt me. I, er… I need my car tomorrow morning," she explained, having a light bulb moment. "If I accept a ride, I won't have a way to get my car tomorrow."

"Then I'll follow you home, to make sure you make it back safely."

"No. Really." Realizing she was still holding onto his arm as they walked around the side of the building, she released it. There were only two vehicles in the parking lot. Her Honda sat under the flickering light of a street lamp. A few parking spots away, a black sports car of some kind huddled low to the ground. The lamp's light and the full moon reflected off the glossy paint.

He walked her to her car, opened the door, and politely waited while she got in and started it up.

She pulled the door shut, flipped the power locks and rolled down the window. "I'm fine. Really. Thanks. Uh, goodnight."

He pulled something out of his pants pocket and handed it to her. "In case you need to get in touch with me."

A business card. She glanced down but didn't read it. She was too shaken to comprehend printed words. And too distracted by questions to care. Why would he think she'd need to get in touch with him? She tucked it into the front pocket of her purse and smiled weakly. "Thanks." Not waiting for him to get into his car, she put her vehicle into drive, flipped on her headlights and drove toward the street.

She noticed, as she turned onto the road, he still hadn't flipped on his headlights. Curious. She'd half-expected him to follow her, even though she'd refused his offer.

What was he waiting for?

At the first traffic light she came to, she pulled out his business card and read it. Brett Larrington, P.C.

"Oh. My. God! He isn't a murderer. He's just a lawyer. A freaking ambulance chaser." She dropped her head. Her forehead struck the steering wheel hard enough for a shower of stars to glitter behind her closed eyelids. "A lawyer who probably thinks I'll be on the hunt for a good defense attorney real soon." A horn sounded from somewhere behind her car, reminding her she was parked in the middle of the road, blocking traffic. "No wonder he didn't want to leave me. I'm his next meal ticket."

* * *

"Okay, you can come out now," Burke called to the shadowed figure beside the trash container sitting at the rear of the building. "She's gone."

"I don't like this," Isabella, his one and only friend in the world, said as she tugged at the laces running up the front of her velvet gown's bodice. "I hate not being able to use magic. These gowns are a royal pain. And speaking of pain, are you sure there isn't a better way? Do we have to break in? What if she set the alarm?"

"All I can suggest is next time you pick something less… challenging to get out of. You know we can't risk using magic here. And as far as the alarm goes, she couldn't turn it on because the police are coming back in the morning."

"I hope you're right." She stepped out of the dress, revealing a black corset over a white blouse and a pair of black pants. She folded the dress and stuffed it into a bag sitting on the ground. Then she gathered her long red hair into a ponytail high on top of her head. She handed Burke a spare elastic and he secured his hair low, at his nape. "Well, what if the human police come back? I'm sure you can guess what kind of conclusions they'd jump to."

"Doesn't matter. What're they going to do to me?"

"Us," she corrected, tucking the bag into a dark spot behind a stack of empty boxes.

"Us. It's not like they can catch us."

"You don't know that for a fact," she grumbled, fishing through a second bag.

"They haven't so far."

Lifting her head, she gave him a scowl and pointed a lock pick at him. "You're killing me here."

"Just get the door open. Please."

"I'm working on it. You're distracting me." She slipped the tool into the lock, fiddled with it a few seconds then turned the door knob. "Done."

"This is the only way we can collect the evidence we need. You know what happens when we wait. The damn *Excoluni* will be here soon. They'll clear the place of any hint of magic and we'll have nothing. And we both know the human police won't know what to do with this. We don't have any time to waste."

"Yeah. I wish we'd figure out who is doing this so we could go back home, quit running. It's wreaking havoc on my social life."

"I'm trying. I'm trying. I'm no Sherlock Holmes."

"I've noticed."

"Shut up." He softened his words with a smile, knowing Isabella wasn't the kind to take his ribbing personally. Hell, she dished enough of it out not to expect to get a little back in return. They'd been friends forever, since they'd cut their fangs on their first humans. Years ago they'd tried being lovers -- only briefly -- then promptly returned to being friends. Wasn't in the cards for them to be more than that, for a number of reasons.

His only regret was having dragged her into this shit in the first place. This was his problem. If he'd left without saying anything that night, she would be at home right now, living her life as she should. Not running from the *Excoluni* -- the law enforcement organization of the UMN, United Magical Nations.

Thanks to him, Isabella, once a respected member of the UMN, was now a suspected felon and facing the death sentence for aiding and abetting a convicted murderer.

The stench inside the building was almost enough to force him back outside. But he knew his time was short. He'd have to suck it up and get to work.

"I'll wait out here," Isabella said, stepping behind the trash container.

"Perfect. You know the signal. If you see the *Excoluni*, let me know."

"Will do."

He'd already gotten a good look at the victim, thankfully. He'd resorted to frequenting nightclubs within a ten-mile radius of each murder, hoping that one night he might be in the right place at the right time.

For once fate was on his side. He'd not only seen the guy mere minutes before his murder, he'd found the body immediately following, and knew the method of killing. Having shown up at the scenes of previous murders after the human police had removed the body and the *Excoluni* had cleared the place of magic, this was a coup, the first time he'd gotten a good look at a body and crime scene while it was still fresh.

Like the other victims, this one had been a human, not associated in any way with the local vampire clans. There had to be some kind of connection between the victims, but damned if he could figure it out. He didn't have a name for this last one yet, so he had no details about the guy's past life, but the most recent three victims had been a dock workman at a shipping company, a nurse and a delivery driver for UPS. No obvious red flags there. Two men. One woman.

What the hell was the motivation for these killings? They weren't a typical vampire feeding. Vampires didn't have to kill their prey when they fed. And they didn't make a regular habit of taking body parts with them when they were through, either.

If only he hadn't been at the wrong place at the wrong time when that first murder had been discovered he wouldn't be trying to piece this together. He was a nobleman. A landowner. This detective stuff was so far removed from his personal experience. Track down a murderer? Forget it. Negotiate a profitable lease? Now that was something he could do.

It had been all circumstantial evidence, the so-called evidence that had led to his conviction. Just like that, he'd gone from being a vampire who pretty much kept to himself, to a convicted felon, to an escaped convict on the run. Everything he had was gone. His home. His money. His properties. His reputation.

Stolen by fucking circumstance.

Since his night vision was far superior to humans', he needed no light as he carefully searched the room where the murder had taken place. He didn't want to miss anything but at the same time had to take care that he didn't leave any evidence of his visit either. Hadrian Dvorak, the detective in charge of the string of gruesome murders that had been wrongfully tied to his name, would love finding something that would cinch up yet another case against him.

Lucky for Burke, his cotton gloves would hide fingerprints. He'd secured and tucked his hair into the hood of his cape.

He stooped down and searched the peeling, scuffed linoleum tile for clues. Scraps of material. Footprints in the dried blood. Anything that might give him some idea of who was killing the humans. The only thing he was certain of at this point was the murderer was a vampire. And every murder had taken place at a bar.

Dammit, he wished he knew something about detective work. Might actually know when he was looking at a clue.

He saw a little dried mud on the floor. Some smeared blood. A bit of folded paper, partially hidden by a box sitting on a low shelf not far from the trash can.

While the first two wouldn't do him much good because he didn't have access to a lab to analyze them, the scrap of paper looked promising.

He carefully plucked it up. Looked like a folded cocktail napkin. No surprise there. This was, after all, the back office of a bar.

Damn. He'd been too optimistic. Someone had probably simply missed the garbage. He crumpled it up and was about to lob it into the plastic can when he saw the shadow of black writing on one corner. Curiosity got the better of him.

Sure, it was probably nothing. A phone number from some guy hot to get into the bar's owner's pants. He wouldn't be surprised if she didn't get dozens of propositions a night.

Then again, who knew? Maybe it was something? He flattened it out on the desk's top, being careful not to disturb the papers scattered over the surface. A woman's first name and phone number was scrawled in looping feminine handwriting.

Interesting. He was guessing it belonged to either the bar's owner or one of the waitresses, but just for kicks, he folded it up and stuffed it into his pocket. Then he took a look at the papers on the desk. Bills. Most of them late notices. Sure enough, the name matched. Sylvie Durand. Sexy name for a sexy woman. Being careful not to move anything too much, he sifted through the documents.

Evidently Carpe Nocturne was in financial trouble. Hmmmm. He wondered if there was a reason for the murder taking place at a nightclub that was in danger of going belly up. Maybe that was a connection? Though it seemed like a long shot that a vampire would turn to murder to shut down a few local bars.

Too bad for Sylvie Durand. Carpe Nocturne seemed like an okay place to him. Kind of… charming. And the owner… well, she had a few charms all her own. If it weren't for the fact that he was on the run from the law, he'd be tempted to stick around and explore a few of them.

Ruminating about the frustrations of being a criminal on the run, he continued his search, finding nothing else that caught his eye. He headed back toward the exit just as Isabella sounded the signal. She jumped when he whispered, "I'm here."

They carefully worked their way around the north side of the building, knowing Hadrian -- also a vampire -- had night vision as keen as their own. There were two vehicles, he noticed. Not one like usual.

Why the extra men on this case?

He kept quiet about the napkin until they'd made it down the street and into his car, parked about a half block away in a crowded twenty-four hour supermarket's parking lot. He'd moved it there after the bar's owner had left. "I got something this time." When Isabella gave him a surprised glance, he added, "Well, I think. It could be something."

"Oh. Sure."

He started the car and headed north on Main. The apartment he'd rented under the assumed name Brett Larrington was only a few blocks away. "Okay, probably not. But I wasn't going to take a chance. So far, we've searched the scenes of four murders and found nothing. I'm man enough to admit I'm getting a little desperate."

"Desperate? You can say that again," she teased. "In more ways than one."

He frowned. There was no need for that now.

So he hadn't had a lover in a while. That was his choice. It was a voluntary decision -- this last few... decades... of celibacy. He damn well wasn't getting desperate for sex. "What do you mean by bringing that up now? You know why I haven't... why I'm not... forget it." He tried hard to hide the defensiveness from his voice.

She smiled. "Just trying to lighten the mood."

"Didn't work."

"I see that. What'd you get?"

"This." He pulled the napkin out of his pocket and handed it to her then turned into the apartment building's driveway. By the time he'd parked in the lot in front of the building, she'd handed it back to him.

"It's a woman's name. Wrong sex to be the killer."

"We don't know that. Really. Playing devil's advocate here, why couldn't it be a woman? Though I'm not saying this one's the killer 'cause Sylvie Durand is human. The bar's owner, as it turns out."

"It can't be a woman because everyone knows women -- even female vampires -- don't commit murders like this. I watch CSI reruns, you know. They prefer methods that keep them out of reach of the victim. Shooting, poisoning, that kind of thing."

"First, I think you're taking this whole detective thing way too seriously. Second, you need to stay away from television. And third, maybe this killer isn't your normal female vampire. Maybe she's into pain and torture."

"Doubtful. Plus there's the little matter of how she'd get those victims strung up like that. All but one of the victims have been big guys. Over two-fifty. I couldn't heft them up by myself and I'm no sissy. We girl vamps don't have the strength you guys do. I doubt those victims would voluntarily hop up on a chair and let her tie them."

"Never know."

"You're so full of it."

He chuckled. Isabella never hesitated to speak her mind. One of the reasons why they would never be lovers again. As a friend, however, it was tolerable. Most of the time. "Maybe they're submissives looking for dommes to spank them," he suggested, half-joking. Yes, the whole theory of a female murderer was a little far-fetched. But it was fun pushing it, just to rile Isabella. She deserved it for that jab about his sex life.

"No way. In the office of a bar? An office that doesn't even belong to her?"

"Maybe they'd planned to meet and talk? Maybe the killer is a friend of the bar's owner, Sylvie. There are lots of possibilities here."

"Most likely, that scrap of paper was on the desk and fell onto the floor. Or it even could've been in the victim's pocket."

"Sure. But I think I should check it out anyway. The bar was full and all the bar's employees were busy. If the killer knew the bar's owner, he or she might have known no one would be going back to the office for several hours. So, going back to my original theory, if the killer had arranged for a meeting --"

"You're really reaching here."

"I've been convicted of a murder I didn't commit. I'm going to reach." At her understanding nod, he added, "I remember that victim. He sat alone most of the night. Didn't talk to the owner that I recall. But then again, it's not like I sat there staring at him all night. There was a tall blonde who sat next to him, though. She could be our killer. I didn't get close enough to find out if she's a vampire. She could be…" He swiped the paper from Isabella, "… Mistress Z." He waved the napkin then stuffed it in his pocket.

"That's not the name on that napkin," his friend flatly pointed out. "That's your human, Sylvie."

He cut the engine, fisted the keys and opened the door. "I know. Just changing it a bit for dramatic effect. Trying to lighten the mood."

She rolled her eyes as she looked at him over the car's roof. "I wonder about you sometimes."

"Don't. It'll just get you in trouble." He slammed the door, strode up the sidewalk and pulled open the door for her.

As she passed, she gave him another rolling-eyed glance. "Who says it hasn't already?"

He chuckled to hide the wave of guilt pulsing through him. The door behind them fell closed as they stepped into the apartment building. "Touché, my friend. Actually, there's another explanation for this that we haven't thought about yet."

"What's that?"

"Maybe this napkin didn't come from the victim or fall off the desk. Maybe it fell out of the killer's pocket."

"It's possible, I suppose. Unlikely but possible." Isabella stopped at apartment 1A, slid her key into the lock, but hesitated before opening the door. "What're you going to do next?"

He stuffed his hand into his pants pocket and curled his fingers around the wadded napkin. "Oh, I don't know. I think I'll go look up the other Mistress Z on the net. The human one. See if I can find an address. I might be in the mood for a spanking." He winked.

"Now, that I'd kill to see." His friend's laughter followed him all the way up the stairs.

TWO

Sylvie couldn't sleep. Every time she closed her eyes she saw the same thing. That awful image of the dead man, the empty eye sockets, the horrific expression on his face. And then she saw herself as a child, standing under the freeway overpass, the cardboard sign gripped in her grubby hands, her eyes hollow.

In a desperate attempt to distract herself, she watched infomercials for a while. Kept trying to call Lisa. Gave up after getting her voicemail three times in a row. Would Lisa ever hear about it tomorrow! "She had better be near death's door," Sylvie mumbled as she hit the button, cutting off the call before the voicemail kicked in again.

She tried reading, but her brain was too foggy to absorb written words. She flipped through magazines and stared at the pictures blindly. Her fears kept haunting her. That guy's face.

How long would it take before it would fade, even a bit? Dammit, she didn't want to be alone tonight!

She jumped for the umpteenth time when a tree branch scratched her bedroom window. Tiptoed through the house checking and re-checking the locks. Her puppy, Lulu, who weighed in at exactly five pounds, wasn't much of a guard dog but she brought her along anyway. Weren't toy poodles supposed to be good security dogs?

Then again, if that was the case, hers was defective. The little white fur ball kept whimpering and hiding under the nearest piece of furniture.

"A lot of good you'd be if someone broke in. Maybe you'd ruin their shoes," she half-joked, half-scolded, dragging the shivering canine out from under the couch. "This is not the time for hunting dust bunnies." She was almost regretting not having gone for the Rottweiler. Instead of hiding behind a one hundred fifty pound animal with big sharp teeth as she crept through her house, she was carting around a shaking, dribbling poodle.

Front door locked? Check. Windows? Check. Kitchen door? Check. French doors to the back yard? Check. Everything on the first floor seemed to be secure. She headed back toward the front of the house, to the staircase. It was then, as she turned the corner, that she saw something dark pass over the leaded glass sidelight next to her front door.

Her heart stopped. Literally.

Someone was out there! That shadow was way too tall to be a stray cat or opossum.

She dashed back to the kitchen, dropped Lulu on the floor next to her food dish and armed herself with the one and only weapon she could find in her current panicked state -- a broom.

Hopefully the element of surprise would be on her side or she was in big trouble.

Then she tiptoed back toward the front door. Her fingers gripped the broom's wooden handle so hard the muscles in her palms cramped. Her heart thudded so hard in her chest she could feel it banging against her breastbone.

She briefly thought about running back to the kitchen and calling 9-1-1. But what if there was no one out there? Or what if her friend Lisa had come over to check on her?

Please, please let it be Lisa.

Her arms shaking, she peered through the peephole. No Lisa. She went to the living room window to see if there was a car parked in her driveway.

Nothing.

Still holding the broom, she ran from window to window, checking each one. Her yard had a lot of trees and shrubbery. Too many. Up until tonight she hadn't considered the downside of having a house virtually surrounded by dense greenery.

Tomorrow morning she was calling a landscaping company! It was all going, even the lilacs. Too many places for prowlers to hide.

She went back to the front door, paced back and forth a million times until she was so tired she needed duct tape to keep her eyelids open. Finally, unable to keep going, she dropped on her rump on the bottom stair.

The shadow passed in front of the side light once more, sending her into a state of panic all over again. If only the glass panes weren't beveled. She might know what she was dealing with. She lunged for the front door and peered through the peephole again.

The lawyer?

The lawyer!

As if a switch had been thrown, her racing heart rate slowed. It was only the lawyer, Brett Whatever-his-name. She released a huff of air. God, she was a wreck. Freaking out at every little thing.

But as she twisted the doorknob, the welcome relief morphed into anger. The lawyer? How dare he come skulking around her house at this hour! What was his deal? Need to make a payment on that ridiculous car he had? Speaking of cars, where was it anyway? He had to have driven. Unless he lived close by.

Wouldn't that be her luck?

She didn't wait for him to knock. She opened the door and, making sure to wield the broom in the most threatening manner she could, stomped outside and shouted, "What the hell do you think you're doing?"

He was facing the street. And gauging by the way his very nicely-built body jerked when she yelled, he hadn't expected her to open the door yet. He whipped around and, his gaze dropping to her hands, lifted both of his in the universal position of surrender.

Such a strong man in such a weak position. For some reason that gesture looked wrong on him. She had the feeling he didn't need to use it very often.

"I wanted to make sure you got home safely," he explained. "Didn't see your car…"

Fighting a tingle of awareness as her gaze went on a little tour of the landscape that comprised Brett Whoever, P.C., she tipped her head and glared at him. "It's parked in the garage. Like it should be. So get lost. I don't need a lawyer. And even if I did, I wouldn't call you. How fucking low! Trying to solicit new business by doling out cards at the scene of a murder. Can. You. Say. Ewww?" She punctuated each word with a thrust of the broom.

"I'm not here to try to get a client." He crossed his arms over his chest. And thanks to the fact that he was wearing a short-sleeved shirt, she was privy to the sight of a couple really nice biceps.

Drool. And drool.

Still, he was a scummy lawyer, she reminded herself. Out to get his next buck. What else would he be doing at her house in the middle of the night?

"Heh. Yeah," she scoffed. "Like I'm going to believe that. What's wrong? The ad you put in the newspaper didn't get you enough business this month?"

"Plenty's wrong. But not for me." He took a step toward her. It was a pretty large step. Brought him a whole lot closer to her than she wanted at the moment… or maybe not. Yes, too close.

She took a couple steps backward, but the closed storm door stopped her from going any further. The air got a little thicker, harder to inhale. "Yeah… so what're you trying to say?" She lifted her chin, shifted the broom into her right hand and reached behind her with the left, searching for the door's handle. He closed the distance between them before she had her fingers around it. The scent of man and soap and something else she couldn't name swirled around her like a fog. She inhaled deeply, to see if it was really as pleasant as she'd first thought.

Yeah, it was.

Scared, you should be scared! Not sniffing him like a bouquet of roses.

Now, with his threatening -- albeit scrumptious -- bulk blocking her, and her head adrift in thoughts of flowers and biceps, she couldn't step out from in front of the door to open it. Not sure what to do, she released the door's handle and returned both hands to the broom.

His gaze met hers and held it captive. "Please. I realize it looks a little strange, my being here at this hour. But I think there are a few things you need to know."

His voice was so low and soothing and reassuring the little bit of anger she'd managed to cling to vanished. Poof. Gone. She was suddenly tempted to invite him inside.

What am I thinking?

She shoved that idiotic idea aside and yanked her eyes away. For some reason, her brain seemed to get all soupy when she looked him in the eye.

What had she been about to say? *Oh yeah.* "Don't you think a phone call would've been more appropriate? How'd you find out where I live, anyway?"

"That's what I've come to talk to you about." He raised a hand to her face, closed his fingers around her chin and lifted, until she was looking at him again. "You can trust me."

A warm, pleasant feeling, like satin running over her skin, swept through her mind. Equally pleasant tingles danced over her skin, warmed her insides.

Yes, she could trust him. He was strong and mysterious but not scary. He wanted to help her, not harm her.

Very suddenly, she realized she wanted to touch him. No, she wanted to do a whole lot more than that. To taste his kiss. To strip naked, throw herself on the floor and invite him aboard.

The longer she stared into his eyes, the more she wanted to feel his hard body pressed against hers. His mouth over hers, tasting, taking.

Whatever she was about to say faded from her mind.

He slowly lowered his head, tipping it to the side as it came closer, closer.

He was going to kiss her! And she was so very, very glad. She closed her eyes and mentally braced herself.

Nothing.

Confused, her cheeks flaming, she blinked open her eyes. His face was right there. His nose almost touching hers. His lips so close all it would take was a teeny tiny shift forward and they'd be firmly planted on hers, where they should be. Yet for some crazy reason she was frozen in place. Couldn't move a muscle, except for the ones operating her eyelids.

He closed his big hands around her upper arms, backed away from her house several steps, taking her with him, and opened her door.

Dazed, but at least able to move again, she walked inside her house. He followed her, pushed the front door closed behind him and twisted the deadbolt.

"Come. This way." He took her hand and led her to the living room couch. "Sit."

Confused and tired and just plain worn out, she sat. She stared at his face.

It was a bummer to see his expression change. For a second, she'd been sure he'd come to seduce her. There'd been something in his eyes. The simmer of lust burning brightly. Thrilling. Intoxicating, that's what it had been.

But now it was gone and his demeanor was cool. Not cold, but... professional. Suddenly chilled, she pulled the afghan off the back of the sofa and wrapped it around herself.

"I have to ask you about something," he said.

"Oh?"

"Yes, it's about this." He pulled a folded, wrinkled cocktail napkin from his pocket and handed it to her.

Their fingers brushed as she took it from him. She tried to ignore the strange flutter her heart did at the innocent contact and unfolded the paper. Her name and phone number were written on the napkin, in her handwriting. She recognized it right away but wondered how he'd ended up with it. "Yes? I know where this came from. But how'd you get it?"

"I found it in your office."

"That's impossible. My office? When?" She stared at his face, practically memorizing his features. He had high cheekbones. A perfect chin. Cute ears. But it was his eyes that were the most striking.

His eyes...

"Tonight," he answered, vaguely.

She shook her head to clear it. It felt like it was getting clogged with thick, gelatinous ook. "When tonight?" What was he getting at? And what had he been doing in her office?

She lifted her eyes to his again. Why wasn't he kissing her yet? His lips looked yummy. It was so hard following this conversation. She wondered if he'd be insulted if she asked him to put a bag over his head so she could concentrate. Over his whole body would be even better.

"Earlier," he said.

As he paced back and forth, she was left to wonder about a lot of things. Was he really a lawyer? Or was he an undercover cop of some kind? Did he think she'd murdered that guy?

She needed some space, some air. A brain transplant. Hers had stopped working. She'd never reacted like this to a man before. It was damned disconcerting.

She stood up and pushed past him. Cripes, his chest was hard as concrete. Concrete covered with the softest material she'd ever felt. She had to concentrate really, really hard to get herself to remove her hands from their resting place on his pecs. She did manage, eventually, and was able to put at least five or six feet between them. Her head cleared a bit. Relief.

"First, that doesn't make any sense. And second, want to tell me what's really going on here? Because I'm having a hard time believing you're just a nice guy trying to do a good deed. In one night you've snooped in my office and prowled around my house. It's like... three o'clock in the morning. What kind of person goes poking around someone's house at three in the morning? Are you a cop?"

"No. I'm not."

"Then what gives?"

"I'm no one. A guy who wants to find a killer. That's all. But more than that, I'm a guy who wants to protect you."

"Protect me? From what? What's in this for you? If you're not a cop and you're not a slimeball lawyer looking for your next meal ticket, then what the hell are you?" She saw something flicker in his eyes. One corner of his upper lip curled up, just slightly, giving his mien a hint of dark danger.

Dark danger and wicked promise.

A pulse of warmth shot through her body, nearly knocking her to her knees. She covered her face with her hands and tried to listen, really listen to what he was about to say. She had a feeling if she didn't, she'd be sorry.

"I'm your one and only ally. The only person who really knows what's going on." He paused. "Want me to leave? Right now? Or do you want to hear what I have to tell you?"

What was with all the vague double-talk? God, she hated this. Why not just spit it out? What was this guy hiding? For some reason, even though her patience was wearing as thin as the whisper-fine sheer curtains hanging on the window behind her, she lowered her hands from her face and mumbled, "Okay. I'll listen." If there was something she needed to know, it would be a crime for her to miss out on hearing it just because she was either too turned on to care… or too annoyed with the good-looking jackass' Dark and Mysterious Good Guy game.

He motioned for her to sit down again, and she complied. Not because he wanted her to but because she was so tired she was afraid she might keel over from exhaustion at any moment.

He resumed his pacing and she couldn't help noticing the way his backside filled in his pants.

Why was she so distracted? It felt like her mind wasn't her own. Her body too. It was like someone else held a remote control, pushing buttons that controlled her thoughts, her reactions.

Had to be exhaustion. Or stress. What else could it be? She leaned her head back and closed her eyes.

"Back to this napkin," he said. "You said it was impossible for me to have found this in your office. Why did you say that?" His voice affected her like the soft hum of a vibrator. It buzzed through her body, igniting mini-blazes in her groin.

Her eyes still closed, she fanned her face. "Because I wrote that tonight. I know I did. And I gave it to a young woman who wanted to buy a car."

"You gave her your home phone number?" His accusatory tone grated like fingernails on a chalkboard. Doused a bit of the heat boiling her blood, cooling it to a more tolerable simmer.

She opened her eyes, giving him a dose of squinty mean-eyes. "Yes, I gave her my home phone number. I have voicemail. It made sense. As a matter of fact, right now I'm glad I didn't give her the bar's number. The bar'll be closed for the next several days and my cell phone bill was horrific last month. Not to mention, my cell's kind of dead now."

He nodded slowly, his expression uber-serious now.

She wished that naughty twinkle would come back.

"Where were you when you gave it to her?" he asked.

"Behind the bar, giving Shelley the bartender a hand. She was slammed. When I was serving a guy a Heineken, I overheard this blonde talking to a friend about needing a car. I bought the Honda about six months ago, and I haven't been able to find a buyer for my old car. So I slipped her my number and told her to call me tomorrow."

He stopped directly in front of her. For some reason her gaze decided it needed to pay a visit to the terrain located just south of his belt. Oh. My.

"Any possibility you took the napkin back into your office for any reason?" she heard him ask.

"No. I was standing at the bar," she heard herself answer. "I remember handing it to her." She jerked her gaze from the bulge in his pants. Nice bulge it was, but she knew her staring had to have extended beyond a polite two or three seconds.

If it did, he seemed unfazed, outside of a slight red tint to the sides of his neck. "Did you invite the woman into your office for anything?"

"No, I didn't go into my office until later, when I discovered the man… until… you know." She wrapped the afghan more snugly around herself. Damn thing had too many holes in it. When he just stood there, looking all lost in important finding-a-killer thoughts, she added, "What? Tell me."

He rested his hands on the arms of her chair, leaned forward and licked his lips.

Her girly parts rolled out the red carpet.

"Before I tell you what I suspect," he murmured, "humor me with one more question."

"Okayyyy. Then will you tell me what's going on? I'm really… tired." *Not! Tired of being teased, yes.* She shifted in her seat. Her pussy was really getting warm. She could feel the slick wetness coating her panties.

He lowered his head a little more and she closed her eyes, expecting him to kiss her.

"Is there any chance the woman you gave the phone number to might have given it to the guy who was found dead in your office?" he asked.

Still no kiss? Argh! "I don't know," she snapped, revealing her frustration. "I mean, I didn't see them together. But I was busy. There were so many people." What did he expect? She'd stood facing a wall of men and women demanding beer for hours before running back to her office for a pen. Got tired of having to borrow one from the waitresses every few seconds. Nobody paid with cash anymore.

Now, would he kiss her, for God's sake? She blinked her eyes open just in time to catch him grimacing.

"If that's the case," he said, backing away from her, "then we need to consider the worst."

"Which is?"

"Which is… you handed your phone number to a murderer."

All of a sudden, Sylvie didn't feel so well. Her stomach lurched and she made a dash for the bathroom. She made it to the toilet a second before the heaving started full force.

A few minutes later, she emerged from the bathroom, tears still blurring her vision, her stomach empty. She'd brushed her teeth and washed her face but still felt yucky. And shaky and sick. And bone weary. But a little more clear-headed, for some reason.

"Are you okay?" He looked concerned, and she was extremely grateful he'd decided to risk her calling the cops to come and tell her about the napkin.

God, she might've given her phone number to a murderer!

Of course on the bright side, it seemed the murderer had dropped it. That gave her some hope a psycho killer wouldn't be knocking on her front door tonight.

"No, I don't think I'm okay," she answered. "I haven't dealt with stuff like this in a long… I mean, what should I think? I gave her my phone number, yes. But does that mean she wants to kill me? Or does that mean she wants to buy my car? And she lost the paper. So am I safe? Or does she have a photographic memory?"

"Want to take a chance?"

"No, not really."

"Okay. Then I think you should pack. You can stay with me for a few days, unless you want me to get you a hotel room somewhere."

She thought about it for a minute. Hotel room. Alone. Versus a safe and secure home with a guy who looked like he could whoop some serious killer-chick ass?

Did she trust this guy? His story about being a good guy who just wanted to help her was more than a little shady, but she felt deep in her gut that he wasn't out to harm her.

But to play it safe, she could call Lisa and leave a message, letting her know where she'd be staying. She fished in her purse for Brett's card. "I'll be right back. Uh. There is one thing. How do you feel about poodles?"

He looked like a guy who'd just been told he needed to have both testicles removed with some fishing line and a dull butter knife. "Great. I love dogs," he said weakly.

THREE

Brett's apartment wasn't exactly your typical bachelor pad, though it wasn't nearly as showy as the car he drove. The furnishings boasted simple lines. The colors were muted -- tans, browns. They gave her an instant feeling of calm tranquility. She felt safe.

"This is very nice," Sylvie said as she followed him through the living room.

"Thank you." He led her down a narrow hallway, pointed to the right. "This is the bathroom." Then he stopped at the first door on the left. "And this is the guestroom. I hope you'll be comfortable here." He pushed open the door to reveal a gorgeous room decorated in a slightly darker version of the living room's color scheme. The bed was covered in rich-looking fabrics and piled high with pillows.

Heaven!

She sat, gave it a quick bounce test. Soft. Just the way she liked it. "How could anyone be anything but comfortable in here? It's nicer than a five-star hotel."

He looked pleased. His smile made her feel all soft and girly and warm. "Excellent," he said, his voice like a low purr.

Oh, how she wanted to rub up against that dangerous feline.

Lulu circled a few times then curled up for a nap in her lap. No doubt it was the heat radiating from certain body parts that inspired her dog to settle there. Her face warming, her heart hopping around in her rib cage like a toddler on a sugar buzz, Sylvie ran her hand down Lulu's back. "Th-thanks."

He stepped out of the room. "You're welcome. If you need anything else --"

"Wait!" Before he got too far, she set Lulu down, hopped off the bed, ran to the door and caught his wrist. Their eyes met and she swore someone had cranked up the heat to ninety. "No, I mean thank you. For everything. I haven't been exactly cooperative tonight. I jumped to all kinds of conclusions and suspected the worst --"

"You were frightened."

"Yes," she heard herself whisper as she stared at his mouth. Those really were the most amazing lips she'd ever seen on a man. She wondered what it would take to convince him to kiss her.

Suddenly, she wasn't holding his wrist, he was holding hers. He pulled and she fell against him. She gave a shocked squeak when he looped an arm around her waist and turned, stepping forward until her body was sandwiched between the hallway wall and his amazing body.

What a wonderful place to be! Sweet, hot desire pulsed through her center in rhythmic waves.

He lowered his head, and her insides broke into a cha-cha. "I don't know what it is about you. I can't... dammit, I can't resist." His mouth came down on hers in a crushing kiss. His tongue pushed at the seam of her lips until she parted them. Then it stroked and tasted and took.

Instantly lost in the need his tongue and lips stirred in her, she lifted her arms and looped them around his neck to hold on. An urgent heat shot to her groin and she found herself rocking her hips back and forth in a feeble effort to cool it.

It felt like her blood was on fire. Literally. Her insides were scalding, burning up from the inside out. She kissed him back with all the need and heat she had. She met each thrust of his tongue with one of her own. Still it wasn't enough. It would never be enough.

Make love to me. Now!

A stuttering heartbeat later, she staggered forward, dizzy and confused. He broke the kiss? He had released her? Why?

He was staring into her eyes. It was quiet, except for the wild huffing of her breathing and the thump of her racing heartbeat in her ears.

She'd never, ever felt like that from a single kiss.

His eyebrows hanging low over eyes full of confusion, he took another step backward. At the same time he lifted his hands to her shoulders. One index finger traced the neckline of her T-shirt. "What is it?" he asked.

"What's what?" Still out of breath -- had the oxygen been sucked out of the room? -- she glanced down at the finger running down the deep vee of her shirt. If it kept on its current path, it would land in the cleft between her boobs in about five seconds. Four, three, two, one. Bingo! She held her breath and watched him lick his lips.

"Why do I feel this way? Like I'll perish if I don't…"

"Don't what?" she whispered, taking a step forward. She needed to be closer to him, to touch him. To taste him. The impulse was worse than any craving she'd ever battled before.

He gathered her hair into his fists and lifted them to his nose. His expression was wicked hot as he audibly inhaled then released the tresses, letting them fall over one shoulder.

She tried to watch as he walked a tight circle around her. She lost sight of him when he stopped directly behind her.

He gasped.

Little bursts of heat sizzled up her spine when he traced a circle on the nape of her neck. Goosebumps coated her upper body.

"This?"

"What?" Her neck? Was something wrong? She started to turn around, but he halted her with two strong hands on the back of her shoulders.

"I've heard. But I never knew for certain…"

He sounded shocked, like he'd just discovered the secret to eternal life or something. On the back of her neck?

She hated to ruin the mood, but what the heck? "Mind sharing what's so fascinating about my neck? Do I have a mole? Ringworm? What?" She slapped a hand back there and felt around with her fingers, half expecting to feel a bump, a lump, an extra appendage.

He pushed her groping hand aside. "No one I've known has found…"

Getting more curious by the second, she jerked away from him and twisted. Big mistake, moving so quickly. Her head whirled, or rather the world spun around her head. She grabbed his arm to steady herself. "Found what?"

He looked at her like she was either Pamela Anderson or a Greek goddess come to life. "You're an *Origo*."

"You mean an original? I like to think so. But I've never had anyone react with quite so much… amazement before."

"Not original. *Origo*. You are one of the chosen. A human who is mate to not one but two vampires."

"Oh. Oh!" Did she hear him right? Did he say -- gulp! -- vampire? Oh, man. Brett, Van Helsing, whoever he was, believed in vampires? He was cuckoo. "Sorry to tell you this, but vampires don't exist. Outside of movies and costume parties, that is."

"Oh, yes they do." In the time it took for her to blink, Brett's clothes changed. He was back in his sexy black vampire getup. The black cape and white billowy shirt. His hair was untied, falling in silky waves down to his shoulders.

What the heck?

"Didn't you know?" Eyeballing her like a starving man would a juicy grilled steak, he licked his lips. "Tonight at your club. There were hundreds of vampires. And other fantastic creatures too."

What the heck?

"Ohhhhh! You mean the *costumes*?" She laughed humorlessly. "You thought they were real? Uh, they weren't. It was a *costume* party. A theme. You know? Kinda like Mardi Gras." How silly of him to think there'd been real vampires at her bar.

Ridiculous.

Impossible.

Bizarre.

"Perhaps that was what you planned. But I can tell you with a great deal of certainty that the immortals outnumbered mortals by about ten to one."

"No way. You're joking." She did a quick one-eighty and... ran smack dab into him when she took a step forward. How? "How the heck did you do that? You were over there!" She pointed behind her. "What's going on? Who are you?"

"That's an easy one to answer." His gaze swept up and down her body. "I'm Burke Langton." He smiled, revealing a set of chompers straight out of a vampire film.

There was absolutely no way he could fake those. A friggin' vampire! This guy was a vampire? Vampires were real? "I'm one of your Masters."

Sylvie swore her jaw struck the floor it fell so hard. If it wasn't for Burke... Brett... whoever's lightning quick vampire reflexes, her butt would've been the next thing to hit the floor.

* * *

Burke dragged Sylvie against him and kissed away every protestation that made it past her throat.

He'd known there was something special about her. It had struck him right away, the moment he'd stepped into Carpe Nocturne. Before he'd seen her, smelled her, heard her voice, he'd felt her. Deep inside. Even with the distraction of trying to find the murderer, he hadn't been able to shake the lust stirring in his loins, heating his blood.

And now. Now that he had her here, in his home. So close. He could barely resist the urge to fuck her. It was more powerful than the fiercest hunger he'd ever experienced, worse than the night of his Awakening.

The need to take her burned. He knew he couldn't resist. Wouldn't resist.

She was his. He had only one thing to worry about. He could not feed from her. At this point, to do so would mean certain death.

He swept his arm under her and carried her into his room. Too impatient to bother with the door, he merely kicked it in, regretting his impatience only because of the fear he felt charge through Sylvie like an electric current.

He vowed right then, even if it killed him, he would go slow. For her sake. He would not take her yet. Not as long as she feared him.

When he set her on the bed, she looked up at him with wide, fear-filled eyes. The tang of her terror, mixed with the sweet scent of her arousal, created a bouquet that awakened the hunter within him. Never had he wanted a woman so badly. It was all he could do to cling to the whisper-thin threads of humanity that remained within him.

"What're you going to do?" she stammered.

He stared into her eyes and reached for her mind. The psychic connection he'd discovered earlier was still there, stronger actually. He sent her reassuring thoughts. "I'll do nothing you don't wish me to do."

Her face flushed.

He waved his hand, and her clothing flared in a blue flame and then disappeared completely, leaving his delightful Sylvie lying unharmed but naked.

She instantly crossed her arms over her chest and scooted back.

He sensed her mind was filled with mixed reactions -- fear and wanting, shock and understanding. It would not be difficult to bring her to full acceptance, to have her burning for him as much as he burned for her. Without magic. Although a little bit might come in handy.

She liked this, craved it. A mixed tonic of fright and arousal. He sensed it. He knew it, even if she wasn't fully aware of it yet. He could see even the darkest parts of her mind, where she hid her secrets, the ones she didn't want to know or accept yet.

"Sylvie." He waved his hand again, magically binding her wrists up over her head.

She shrieked, looked up at her bound wrists, pulled and twisted, arched her back as she tested the restraints. As she struggled, her hard nipples jutted into the air. He longed to taste them. "What are you doing?"

"I'm giving you what you want. What you've always wanted."

She stilled, but only long enough to send him a glare. "How could you possibly know what I want? You don't know me at all. We met only a few hours ago."

"I know you better than you know yourself, my darling." He kneeled on the bed beside her, gently brushed aside a lock of hair that had fallen over her face. She smelled so good. Sweet like ripe apples and spicy like curry. His balls were tight. His cock hard. All he could think about was the slick heat between her legs.

"You're freaking me out here. I'm not your darling. What's going on?"

"Like I said, I am your mate. Your Master. One of two, actually. I do not know who the other one is. But if he comes near you, we will both know." He held up his forearm for her to see. There, the sign, a mark identical to the one he had found on her neck, had appeared. Like a tattoo. An intricate circle with a symbol in its center he had never seen before. That symbol would be the mark that would identify Sylvie's other Master.

He was eager to discover who it was. Only when their triad was complete could he feed from her and conclude the Binding.

Only then would he be able to say she was truly his.

"I don't understand. What does a tattoo have to do with anything?"

"You have one too. It's identical to this and marks you as mine."

She tipped her chin up and gave him a fierce glare. "That's silly. I don't have a tattoo. I know that for a fact. I don't like tattoos, not that yours is ugly."

He waved his hand and one of her arms sprung free. Two mirrors appeared in his hands. He handed one to her. "Look." He positioned the mirror he was holding behind her so that she could see the reflection of her neck.

She gasped, dropped the mirror, and pressed her fingertips to her mouth. "How? What's going on? I don't understand."

"If what I've read about an *Origo* is true, it was only a matter of time. We would have found each other eventually. We would have been driven to search until we did." This time he used no magic to fasten her wrist back in the restraint. It was far too pleasurable to do it the natural way -- with his hands. Her skin was warm to the touch. Smooth and sweetly scented.

He leaned over her, dragged in a deep breath to pull in as much of her essence as he could. It was as if he had never smelled in his life, as if he'd lived in a colorless, tasteless, scentless world before and now it was all new to him.

She was so beautiful. So perfect. From the gold that glittered in her wavy locks to the flecks of grey in her pale blue eyes.

His.

"You have been searching, haven't you?" he asked, as he ran a finger down the side of her neck. He could hear her pulse beating there. It beckoned him, but he knew he had to resist. Sweet torture.

She shuddered and closed her eyes. "Searching?" she whispered.

Leaning closer, he whispered in her ear, "You sensed I was out there. Somewhere. Waiting for you. Searching for you." He dipped his tongue into her ear and received a quiver as a reward. Encouraged, he kissed a trail down her neck. "You ached to find me. To find your dark lover. The one who would set loose all your fantasies." He could smell her passion building. Could taste it on the tip of his tongue as it stroked her skin.

"Oh…"

"Legend says there is no greater passion than that between the *Origo* and her Masters. Do you wish to find out the truth?" He knew the answer before she spoke the word.

"Y-yesss."

He reached between her legs and, finding her slit hot and wet and ready for him, pushed two fingers inside. She screamed and thrust her hips forward, forcing them inside. Her silky canal tightened around his fingers.

"Yes, oh yes!" She opened her legs for him. "More. Please, more." Her chest was rising and falling quickly. Lifting her tits high into the air with each inhalation. He had to taste them first, before he moved down to her pussy. She was like the most decadent dessert. Every bit of her more delicious than the last. He hungered to sample every inch of her skin. To explore every part of her. He knew the hunger would not ease until he did.

His fingers gliding in and out of her pussy in a slow but steady rhythm, he took her right nipple into his mouth and suckled. She arched her back, pressing her full breast into his face. Eager to increase her pleasure, he nipped at the hard tip. Hot juices spilled from her pussy, coating his fingers.

"Please, please," she begged as she met every thrust of his fingers with a tip of her pelvis. "Stop torturing me. Fuck me."

"First, I must taste your juices. You cannot deny me."

"Oh God."

He moved lower, pushed her knees back until she was open to him. Salivating at the thought of what wonders he would experience, he parted her swollen labia and lapped away every bit of her juices. More. He wanted more. He thrust his tongue into her vagina and sucked, drinking in her flavor. Her essence. But the more he tasted and smelled, the more he wanted.

"No! No, please. No more. Fuck me."

He could feel the hunger building inside her. Could smell the climax that was just beyond her reach.

It was time. "Yes, my sweet. I will take you now." With a wave of his hand, his clothes were gone. He moistened the head of his cock in the juices still pulsing from her slit then in a single thrust drove himself deep inside.

A roar of raw lust rose up his throat and he was unable to hold it back. The sound of her cries of pleasure drove him mad, to the point where he was fucking her hard and furious. He lost complete control and couldn't hold back for another moment.

He reached between her thighs, found her clit and stroked it with his thumb, knowing it would bring her to climax. But only after his cock was bathed in her hot juices and her pussy was spasming around it in its sweet rhythm of release did he take his own. His cum pulsed from his balls, blazed down the full length of his rigid cock. He groaned in agony and gratitude both as he sealed his claim to his sweet bride. His seed spilled into her cunt.

Her eyelids fluttered closed just as he felt the Change pulling at his bones and tendons, turning him into the beast he really was. Her fingers wrapped around the chains of her restraints, she whispered, "Yes, my Master. Yes." She lifted her legs, hooked her ankles around his back, holding him deep inside until he was spent and his cock had slackened, and the Change had reversed.

In awe of her beauty, of the depth of her acceptance, he freed her wrists of their bindings and pulled her to him as he lay down.

He had discovered that which he hadn't thought existed. He had discovered his true love. His mate. His bride.

Now, all he needed was to find her other Master before his will failed him and he took that first bite.

FOUR

Sylvie woke up sometime later, sore, groggy but deliriously happy.

That was it. She was ruined forever when it came to sex. She had never -- never! -- had sex like that before, not that the studly man sleeping beside her had done anything too crazy. Sure, she'd never been tied up before and that was something she'd wanted to try. But last night… it had been so intense. So much more than a little bit of kink and a couple of leather wrist cuffs.

It was as if he'd made love to her mind. To her very soul.

Oh, God! What a night!

And if she'd had any doubts that Burke was telling the truth about vampires, they were long gone now. With the mere wave of a hand, he'd fried her clothes off her body, chained her up… not to mention the magic he'd performed on her body. Oh, no. There could be no question. Even though she'd spent four years in college studying natural sciences, and her entire life denying the existence of anything that couldn't be seen, heard, or touched -- from God to the Loch Ness monster -- she knew for certain that vampires were very, very real.

And very, very sexy.

The world had just tipped on its side. Everything she'd ever believed to be true was now subject to doubt. Had her mother, a self-professed psychic, been right all this time?

It was really too bad she couldn't ask her.

Shoving aside a wave of regret, she took a peek at the clock. It was noon and she was staaaaarving. She scooted to the edge of the bed, hopped to the floor and shivered. It was cold. Like, refrigerator cold. No way could she run around naked in here. Resigned to the fact that she'd have to make do until her hunky vampire woke up and magically whipped up some new clothes, she dashed to the closet.

As she sifted through clothing that was at least five sizes too big for her, she wondered if he could make her some designer duds. Maybe some DKNY. Their clothes were so classy. And so expensive.

With her limited clothes budget, the closest she'd ever gotten to owning anything by her favorite designer was a pair of sunglasses she'd picked up on eBay for forty bucks. Even that had been a bit of a stretch. Normally, when it came to eyewear, she went for ten-dollar specials at Fashion Bug.

She settled for a pair of sweatpants and a T-shirt. The pants barely stayed up, even with the waistband's string pulled as tight as she could get it. The shirt hung to her knees but at least she was warm. Evidently, vampires liked their homes to be the temperature of a restaurant's meat locker.

She didn't want to think too long and hard about that bit of irony.

After locating Lulu -- closed up in the spare room -- and taking her out for her morning duty, she brought her inside and set her on the floor. Lulu gave her the doggy cold shoulder big time, no doubt because last night had been the first night ever that she'd slept alone.

En route to the spare bedroom to retrieve Lulu's bowl and food, she checked the thermostat. Fifty degrees? It was set at fifty degrees! She'd hate to see Burke's electric bill come summertime.

Her curious side sated, she gathered up Lulu's cans of food and headed for the kitchen to satisfy both their hunger. However, Sylvie realized rather quickly that Lulu might be okay, but if she was going to eat, she was going to have to order something in. There wasn't a thing in the fridge. In fact, it wasn't even turned on.

The cupboards were bare too.

Duh! Vampires didn't eat food.

"Well, poop." Her stomach grumbled, letting her know it did not appreciate the long wait between meals. "I'm working on it," she said aloud as she headed back to the bedroom to get her purse. There had to be a restaurant around there that delivered. After retrieving the only credit card left to her name that wasn't maxed out, she headed back to the living room to try to locate a phone and phonebook. She was leafing through the restaurant section when Burke whispered in her ear, "What're you doing?"

She jumped like a cat spooked by a German shepherd. "Oh God! Will I ever get used to that?"

What had made her say that? Who said she'd be given the chance to get used to anything? No one had made any reference to a long-term thing. Talk about jumping the gun! Thoroughly embarrassed, she poked his glorious chest and backpedaled. "I mean, you're so sneaky."

"Mmmm…" He gathered her hair in a fist, draped it over one shoulder and ran a fingertip down the back of her neck. "I'm not trying to be sneaky."

"Maybe not. But you move soooo… fasttttt…" Man, it was hard holding a conversation with a vampire kissing your neck! "You're over there one moment and right here the next. It startles me."

"I'll try to keep that in mind," he said between kisses.

"Good." She let her head fall back when he slid his hands up under the T-shirt. "Ohhhh."

"Come back to bed." Hands kneading her breasts, fingers tormenting her nipples, he hooked his forearms under her armpits and stood, lifting her with him. And before she exhaled, before she even realized he'd picked her up, they were in the bedroom, him lowering her onto the bed.

Her girly parts waged battle with her stomach, demanding satisfaction at the expense of food. When he bent down and kissed her like he had last night, the battle came to an abrupt end.

Food? Who needed food?

She was content to keep her mouth busy with more pleasurable purposes for the moment. It was being plundered by a certain man's pushy, invading tongue... and damn happy about it too. Some other parts of her anatomy were also feeling the joy. She sighed into their joined mouths.

He broke the kiss and with a bizarre hand motion made the clothes she was wearing vanish. Naked again, but not cold. Oh no, not in the least. Not with an extremely gorgeous vampire dragging his tongue over one nipple, then the other, his fingers teasing and tormenting. As a matter of fact, in short order she was feeling more than a little overheated.

Oh, what this man did to her body!

"You don't know what you do to me," he murmured between nips.

He had no idea what he did to her either.

"I want you. I want you now. I'll want you again as soon as it's over. It's agony." He slid one hand down between her legs and thumbed her clit.

Oh... now that was agony!

More. She wanted more. She wanted his cock. Now. She couldn't speak. She was too lost in the sensations he was stirring in her body. The intoxicating scent of man. The sound of his voice as he whispered wicked promises in her ear. The taste of his kiss lingering on her tongue. The urgent need building deep inside her body.

She bent her knees and opened her legs wider in a silent invitation to take her. But he didn't. He remained kneeling at her side, on the bed, smoothing one flattened palm up and down her torso while he tormented her clit with his other hand.

"I know what it is you secretly hunger for. What you haven't even admitted to yourself." He sat back on his heels, looked down upon her with eyes partially hidden by heavy eyelids.

She believed what he said. He'd proven so much already. Last night had been so... incredible. So intense. Beyond words. "Yes?"

"I will show you." He made that bizarre gesture again, and poof, the bed was gone and she was somewhere else, or so it seemed. In an entirely different room with some very unusual furniture.

The huge canopied bed was gone. The dresser. The fine artwork. The soft tan walls. They were now in a room that was the same size, with the same dimensions, but the walls were painted the dark blue of a night sky. The furnishings were not the kind a girl would expect to see in a bedroom. But they were the kind Sylvie had seen on the Internet.

She was in a real live bondage dungeon.

He held her hand and helped her up onto a wooden table-like thing. He traced a circle around her breast with a fingertip. "It takes time for a submissive to learn to trust and respect her Master so I don't expect you to trust me after only one night. But try to remember that everything I do is for your enjoyment. I take no pleasure until you have been satisfied."

Giddy anticipation made her nerves all jumpy. She nodded, looked into his eyes, searching them for reassurance. She really needed it at the moment. So many things had happened in the past twenty-four hours or so.

First, she'd found a dead body in her bar, then she'd learned the murderer might have her phone number -- and possibly her home address -- and then she'd learned there were real vampires in the world.

And now this? She was actually lying on her belly, on a table, letting a real live vampire, who happened to have abs male models would turn green with envy over, tie up her arms? And it was making her really, really hot.

Could the world get any stranger?

Once he had her arms secured up above her head and out in a wide "V", he went to where the closet had been in the other room and pushed aside the rolling track door.

It was a virtual bondage paraphernalia treasure-trove. She watched him pull out a metal bar with leather straps attached to either end, a dildo, a little whippy looking thing.

Uh. What was he going to do with that? She was a whole lot more nervous when he stepped up beside her holding that whip in his fist.

"As your Master, it is my responsibility to protect you."

Despite the rising heat pulsing through her body, she found herself mentally backpedaling. Had she asked him to be her Master? Wasn't there some rule about that? Shouldn't he have given her some kind of talk first? Told her what the rules were?

"I will not do anything to harm you." He stepped out of the line of her sight, which was limited by her position.

The muscles of her back tensed when something touched her, right in the center of her spine. The light, tickling touch went up, stopped between her shoulder blades and then went down. It stopped at the base of her spine, just above her rear end.

"You are so beautiful. So perfect."

Was he looking at her ass as he said that? Couldn't be.

"Look at that ass. Dammit, it's perfect. Round and soft."

Okay, he was blind.

"Lift your ass for me," he said in a low voice that sounded like an animal's growl. "Kneel and get it up in the air."

"Uh…" Was this what she wanted? To be teased and tormented in a dark room with a sexy vampire who made her squirm just by looking at her?

She'd been on those bondage sites, stumbled upon them while surfing. But she'd stared at those pictures because they were so shocking. Not because she'd wanted to do that stuff.

Right?

If not, if she thought that stuff was so strange, why was every nerve in her body tingly? Why did the sharp edge he'd given his voice send little blades of pleasure through her? And why was she shaking all over, anxious to see what it would feel like to have him smack her ass with that whip thingy?

How would he know what she wanted? Especially if she hadn't even admitted it to herself?

"Up on your knees," he barked.

She shuddered as heat pooled between her legs. My God, this really was turning her on! In a big way!

To hell with the questions. She had the feeling the answers would come. In time. At the moment, she just wanted to let it all go, all the doubts and questions. She wanted to lose herself in the experience. To try something that suddenly she was sure she'd be sorry to miss.

It was foreign to her, speaking the word "Master." It sounded funny to her own ears. Not nearly as sexy as it did coming from those perfect *bondage babes* on those websites she'd trolled. But she forced herself to say it anyway as she struggled to reposition herself. "Yes, Master." It was difficult to move because her arms were tied up and out, fastened by three-foot chains to two rings bolted to the wall. But by gripping the chains in her hands and pulling, she was able to get her upper body up off the table and work her way onto her knees.

She felt so vulnerable in that position -- her hands tied, her fanny up in the air. Vulnerable but also sexy.

"Yes," he murmured.

There was a touch to her bottom. A little tickle that made her muscles clench and pussy heat. She huffed out a little whimper.

"This is what you've wanted, what you've dreamed of. For a long time, since you were a child. Do you remember? Remember how you would lay in bed at night, daydreaming about a strong man who would steal you away to a big, dark castle?"

How did he know about that?

He kissed the small of her back. Out of reflex, her spine tightened, arched to thrust her bottom up higher into the air. She held her breath. He was going to strike her. But when? And how hard? The anticipation was making her jittery. Her heart was drumming a speedy beat in her chest.

"I know because I've seen your secrets."

She believed him. There was no other way he could have known about her daydreams. She'd never told anyone. Never written them in a journal.

"Because I know your secrets, I must do this."

There was a soft sound, a whistling whoosh. And then the smack of leather against skin.

He'd struck her on the right side of her ass. A sharp, stinging pain whizzed up her spine. She yelped and curled her spine, tucking her back end down.

"Oh no. I will not have that. Ass up."

Her arms trembling, adrenaline pumping through her body, she tipped her hips, pushing her bottom back up into the air. The pain was dulling to a tingly burn already, yet she couldn't help tensing every muscle in her body in preparation for the next strike.

It came a few heartbeats later. This time on her left side. Searing pain razored up her spine and exploded in her head. Her ass burned hotter, like an iron. She cried out, "Oh God!"

"Do you feel it yet? The buzz of endorphins flooding your brain? It's better than any drug mankind will ever create."

She did feel something, a heady rush like nothing she'd ever experienced before. Her nerves were on edge. Her senses so sharp every scent, sound, touch felt ten times more intense than normal. She felt like she was strong enough to toss around a Mazda Miata like it was a toy. She laughed. "Yes, oh yes! I do feel it." Her pussy was burning with the need to be filled. He ran his palms over her stinging backside, teased her anus with a prodding fingertip. She wrapped her hands around the chains securing her wrists to the wall and tossed her head back. "Oh yes. Fuck me."

"No, no. It's much too soon. The last time I went too fast. I will go slow. For you." He stroked her slit with what she guessed was the head of a dildo.

Inside! Would he please bury that dildo in her pussy? She tried to rock back on her knees to force the toy inside but the chains secured to the wrist cuffs stopped her. She groaned in frustration.

"It's the anticipation that makes it such a powerful experience, don't you agree?" he whispered. "Your heart is racing so fast it sounds like a purr. Your breath rushing in and out of your lungs. Will I strike you again? Or will I thrust this dong deep into your pussy?" He pressed harder until just a tiny bit of it slipped into her vagina.

She tensed, silently begging for it to go the rest of the way in.

"No, you're not ready yet." He pulled it out.

Teasing bastard!

She whimpered again and tried to look back, to give him a healthy dose of mean eyes but the stupid chains restricted her movement too much. It was impossible for her to twist her upper body to look at him. That fact, coupled with the rumble of his voice as he spoke only made her gnawing need that much more urgent. "Burke... oh, God."

She'd never been tormented and teased like this. Her past lovers had all been about the orgasm. A little bit of foreplay to warm her up, followed by ten minutes of fucking, and then it was over. If she came, it was only because she'd taken the matter into her own hands -- so to speak. She had no qualms about reaching down and stroking her clit while they hammered away. Sure beat lying there like a blow up doll, stiff and lifeless, and ending the night completely unfulfilled.

This man. This vampire. What he was doing. It was... amazing.

Maybe it was the vampire in him? The dark predator. In the wild, predators sometimes liked to tease, to play with their prey. So it made sense a vampire -- the ultimate predator -- would do the same.

"You like to touch yourself. I want to watch."

The wrist straps fell away from her wrists and she fell forward, nearly toppling from the table. A set of powerful hands closed around her waist. She turned to give him a smile of gratitude for keeping her from falling and cracking her skull open on the hard tiled floor.

She froze when her gaze met his. She was sitting on the wooden table, her legs dangling over the edge. He was so incredibly gorgeous. His face so sexy and masculine. His eyes were such a dark brown they almost looked black.

One corner of his mouth lifted into that naughty smile of his. The one she'd noticed last night. "I have such plans for you tonight, my sweet. This way." He picked her up by the waist and held her until she somehow managed to get her feet under herself. He motioned toward a wooden chair set off in the corner. A bizarre metal contraption of some kind stood in front of it. There was a long metal rod protruding from the front of the machine, the end of it a half foot or so from the chair's seat.

She had a feeling she knew what this was. She'd seen one on the Internet.

Would a fucking machine really do it for her? Or would she be left wanting for the real thing? She knew she was about to find out.

"Sit. Feet up on the edge of the seat. I want your pussy wide open."

She was quivering so much from the anticipation she could barely get herself situated on the chair. The smoldering look he gave her as he slid the thick dong over the metal rod and positioned it at her pussy, oh God. She was going to melt.

"Now touch yourself while the machine fucks you. I want to see how hot it makes you. I want to smell your cream. To see it running between your ass cheeks and glistening on the dong."

It was doing that already!

She slid a hand down to her pussy. The other she used to steady herself on the chair. And while the thick dong fucked her oh so tortuously slow, she rubbed her clit.

It was pure heaven.

Thick dong filling her pussy. Waves of pleasure pulsing through her body. It wasn't so much the mechanical motion of the machine as it was Burke's dark eyes watching. There was this feral look in them. Wild and dangerous. His expression was what drove her crazy.

Now at her side, he growled and lowered his head to feast on a nipple. As if she wasn't already in heaven!

"Yes! Yes!" Orgasm was just a few strokes away. She could feel the telltale heat spreading through her. The tension pulling at every muscle, right down to the soles of her feet. Coming. She was coming!

"No!" The machine cut off and the dildo halted mid-air, just shy of plunging into her pussy again.

No!

There was a twitch but no spasm. No orgasm.

Now she wanted to growl. Teasing bastard! She gritted her teeth, literally, and concentrated really, really hard on not screaming at him. Ooh, it was hard!

So was his dick, she noticed when he did his little hocus pocus thing and his clothes vanished. The growl lodged itself in her throat, kind of morphed into a purr as it worked its way up her throat and out through her lips.

He pushed her shoulders back, until her spine was pressed into the back slats of the chair, then he kissed her to the point of delirious begging. After kneeling on a mat that appeared out of nowhere, he drove his cock into her.

Yes! At last! Oh yes. She squeaked into his mouth, wrapped her arms around his neck and clung to him. And just so that he wouldn't get away, she wrapped her legs around his waist.

That deepened his thrusts, which was just fine by her!

Fast and hard, exactly the way she liked it. Exactly the way she needed it. With every thrust, his groin rubbed against her clit, creating just the right amount of friction to catapult her back to orgasm-land.

A wave of heat spread out over her body and she tensed in anticipation of the first spasm.

Please, don't stop now. No more teasing.

"Come now!" he shouted.

He didn't have to say that twice. She dug her fingernails into his shoulders and pulled back, tightening every muscle in her body. Finally, sweet release. It pulsed through her body in quick spasms that made her jerk and scream. As his shout filled her ears, she felt his shoulders move under her hands. They changed somehow, but with her eyes closed, and the bliss of orgasm still rippling through her body like waves in a pool, she didn't care. All she cared about was holding on to the feeling for another second. And another. And another.

It ended. Eventually. She felt weak and tired, but also very, very satisfied. When she opened her eyes, they were back in his bedroom, sitting on a chair in the corner.

That magic stuff was really something. Very cool. Very sexy.

He was practically sprawled over top of her. Heavy and warm, his skin slick with sweat. She closed her eyes and sat there, enjoying the closeness, and the giddy, happy feeling that came from having the most incredible sex in her life.

As if he hadn't spoiled her before, now there was no doubt. No man would ever measure up to Burke the vampire lover. No way. No how.

Which left her wondering -- how long could she expect to keep him around? Were vampires the love-them-and-leave-them type? God, she hoped not.

Burke stood, took her hand in his and pulled. "Come, my sweet. We must sleep now. At sunset, I must leave. I must find the murderer before he kills again."

Sylvie lay beside him, tired but restless, and no longer hungry. Most surprising, she'd been so preoccupied by Burke's very distracting lovemaking abilities, she'd all but forgotten about the murderer. What would happen tonight? Would someone else die? Maybe even someone she knew?

FIVE

This had to work. He'd followed the spell to the letter. Found the right human. Killed him exactly as it was written in the *Book of Shadows*, took the ingredients in the right order.

"It's time." He stroked his love's hair.

She lay on the stone altar in the room's center, her eyes closed, her skin cold, her body lifeless. "This time it will work. I will have you back. I can't live another night without you." He lifted her hand and kissed its back then held it to his cheek.

How he missed the sound of her voice. The feel of her gentle touch. The taste of her kiss.

Two cycles of the moon. She'd been stolen from him two cycles ago. It felt like it had been an eternity. He was empty without her. Hollow and cold and… dead. "I did everything right this time. I will not fail. I cannot fail."

He gently placed her hand on her chest and turned to the large circle drawn on the tile floor in ash. Last time he'd made a mistake. He'd rushed the killing and that had been why the spell had failed. But not this time. This time he'd done everything exactly as it was supposed to be.

He read the *Book of Shadows* one last time, to make sure he was following the spell to the letter. Yes, perfect. His love would be returned to him in just a few moments! His suffering would be over. At last.

He placed the bowl of human blood in the circle's center then drew the star within the circle with the ash. He set the other items on each point of the star -- heart, tongue, finger and two eyes.

He closed his eyes and began the incantation. Instantly, the magic crackled in the air, sizzling like bolts of static. He spoke the words of the spell in the ancient tongue, "*Socusi donomini. Letre dos golomine.*" Almost done. He turned to face his love and extended his arms. The magic charged through his body, fiery hot like bolts of lightning. It swept up his legs, whirled around inside his chest and then blazed down his arms. He quaked with the power of it. The power of all the demons in Hades. Laying his hands on his love, he spoke the final words, "*Yumada renise dolin dagado!*"

Wham! The magic blasted through his hands and leapt into his love. She jerked and thrashed as the dark powers charged through her body, reanimating her dead form. The gaping wound in her chest fused before his eyes. She shifted from beast to the beautiful woman he'd known and loved.

Silence.

He sagged against the altar, rested his head on her chest.

A shaky hand stroked his hair.

He had succeeded, once again.

Please, please let her stay alive this time.

As he turned his head, she blinked open her eyes and smiled. "Master."

He stroked her cheek. Soft as velvet but still cold. He traced her full lower lip. His hand shook as hope and joy swept through him. "Yes, I'm here, my sweet. I did it. I brought you back to me. We will be together forever. I won't let anything happen to you again."

She took his hand in hers and cradled it to her cheek. Her skin was warming. He could feel it. She blinked and a single tear ran down her cheek. "Thank you, Master."

"Feed. You must feed." He turned his hand to offer his wrist. "Feed now and live."

"Yes, my Master."

The pain of her bite was sweet agony. He closed his eyes and let the bliss sweep through his body. Lust, profound and urgent, gathered in his loins, sparked by the pleasure of her feeding.

He needed to fuck her. Needed it more than he needed his next swallow of blood. But not yet. It was too soon to know for certain if she would live or if he'd failed again. Very soon he would know. Within minutes. Only when he knew for certain that she would live could he satisfy his need for her.

These next few minutes would be pure agony.

Her hunger satisfied, she released his wrist and slowly sat up. "Will it last this time? Or will it be like before?"

"I did everything exactly as the book said. How do you feel?"

"Weak. Tired. But getting stronger." She raised a hand to her forehead. "Kiss me. Even if I must go back... even if it doesn't last, I want to die with the taste of your kiss on my lips --"

"No!" he shouted, shaking her shoulders. "You will not die again. You must fight!" He pulled her roughly to him, crushed his mouth to hers and kissed her. His tongue stroked, twisted, tasted and took, as his hands stroked and pinched and pleasured. She moaned and the sound echoed in his head, reverberated in his chest.

He had his love back!

And then she jerked. Her head fell back and her form shifted from beauty to beast. She screamed as the torture began once again, the agony of death.

How could he have failed? "No!" he shouted. "No, no, no!"

"Master," she whispered, just before life left her again. "Do not try another time. I beg you."

"I'm sorry, my love. So sorry for your pain. But I will not stop. I cannot stop. Do not ask that of me." He swept her lifeless body into his arms and held her. The pain of loss tore through his being. "I cannot stop. Next time I will succeed. I cannot live without you. My love."

He gently laid her on the altar and cursing the devil for the pain of his loss, turned to the *Book of Shadows*. "What mistake did I make?" he yelled as rage burned in his gut. "What did I do wrong this time, dammit?"

The answer had to be in the book. But where? What had he missed?

* * *

"Don't you ever, ever do that to me again!" Lisa scolded, dishing out a one-two smack to Sylvie's shoulders. "You had me scared. To. Death!"

"Me? What about you?" Sylvie gave her friend a warning glare. That girl had better keep her hands to herself! If she didn't, gorgeous, slinky black dress or not, Sylvie was going to have to take her down. "I called how many times? Left how many messages? Why didn't you answer? Did you even listen to them?"

Lisa's face turned the shade of a tomato.

Sylvie turned sideways, wedged herself between two guys sitting at the bar, hunched over martinis, and waved at the bartender. "Ah! So you were doing something I wouldn't approve of. And so you decided to avoid the lecture you knew was coming by avoiding me altogether. Well, that's just fine! I could be dead right now, no thanks to you and your sex life."

The guy facing her gave Sylvie a curious glance, then turned to do the same with Lisa.

"Say it louder, why don't you?" Lisa grumbled.

"I just might. What kind of best friend leaves their friend sitting alone at the scene of a crime? Huh? Just so she can have sex?" She shouted that last word, just because Lisa deserved it. A few more males in the crowded upscale club took notice and they were all sizing Lisa up. Sylvie was satisfied to see her friend was really squirming now. Served her right. "Don't you at least screen the calls? Check your Caller ID, so that if it is something important, you know?"

"Yessss. Normally, but --"

Sylvie ordered two cosmopolitans, paid and then turned to her friend and smiled. Time to lighten things up.

Lisa gave her a weak smile back. "Done hating me now?"

"Yes. You know me. I can't hate anyone for too long." She turned when the bartender set the drinks on the bar, picked them both up and handed one to Lisa. "Here. On me."

"Thank you." Lisa took a sip. "So, where were you last night? I tried calling this morning that number you left. A lot of times. No one answered. What happened?" Lisa headed for the only open table in the place. Dropped her purse on the tabletop and set down her drink. "Seriously, I was worried."

"I know you were." Sylvie sat across from her friend while simultaneously scanning the crowd for Burke. She knew he wouldn't wander far. He was too worried about her safety to do that.

Unless something bad had happened. To him. To someone. Where had he gone?

"I'm sure you'll be reading about it in the newspaper by tomorrow," Sylvie said. "There was another murder."

Lisa's eyes widened. "Oh no…"

"Yep. At Carpe Nocturne. And get this. The guy was killed in my office and Burke thinks the killer is this woman I talked to about my car."

Lisa cupped her hands over her mouth and inhaled an audible gasp. "No. Way! What're you going to do? Wait." She dropped her hands. Her eyebrows dropped a smidge too. "Uh. Who's Burke? A cop? I thought you said you were staying with a guy named Brett."

"Well… not exactly."

"What does that mean, 'not exactly'?"

Sylvie considered telling her friend the truth, but she quickly decided that would be a foolish thing to do. Like herself, Lisa only believed in what she could see, hear, touch. She'd never in a million years believe there were vampires living outside of the imaginations of film writers and romance authors. At least not without more substantial proof.

"His real name is Burke, not Brett. And he's a… private detective."

"Ohhhh." Lisa daintily sipped from the narrow cocktail straw. Licked her bright pink lips. Her eyes flickered, focused on something behind Sylvie.

She knew that look. Lisa had spotted some man meat. "What's he look like?" Sylvie teased.

Lisa smiled dreamily. "Tall. With long brown hair. And a body to die for." She tipped her head slightly. "I think he's staring at you."

"At the back of my head?" Sylvie raised her hand to check and see if her upswept hair had come undone. "Is there something sticking up?"

"No. You look fabulous. Didn't get a chance to say anything earlier. That is a hot dress! Where'd you get it?"

"Uh…" She couldn't tell Lisa the truth -- that Burke had magically conjured it up out of thin air. But where else could she say she'd gotten something that was clearly way out of her budget? Black and slinky, with an open back that plunged nearly down to her ass crack, it was nothing like anything she owned. "Bought it on eBay," she lied. "Although, I didn't know how low-cut the back was going to be."

Lisa momentarily looked at her. "It is low. But it looks amazing on you. Like it was custom sewn."

"Thanks."

Lisa's eyes brightened. She fiddled with her straw. "Oh my God, he's coming over here."

"Could it be because you gave him that fuck-me smile?" Sylvie teased, looking around again for Burke. Still nowhere to be seen. She was starting to get worried.

"Hello, ladies." The guy -- who Sylvie had to admit was extremely good looking -- rested an arm on the back of Sylvie's chair. "Can I buy you a drink?" he asked the back of Sylvie's neck.

Why was he speaking to her back?

She turned, to see if his hand was doing anything funny, or if he was perhaps checking the time.

No watch. Huh.

Feeling a little weird, she self-consciously lifted her hand to her nape. It was only when she felt the slightly raised ridge that she realized what he was staring at.

Instantly her gaze dropped to his arm. Covered, dammit.

She tried to remember what Burke had said about that crazy tattoo stuff, about the mark on his arm, and what it had meant. And whether other vampires could see it or not. But damn if she could remember much of anything, outside of how his kiss had tasted.

Speaking of kisses, the guy standing next to her sure looked like he wanted a kiss. She licked her lips, getting them pucker ready.

Since when did she think about swapping spit with total strangers, mere moments after setting eyes upon them?

Insanity, that's what it was.

"Thanks," Lisa said, her face aglow. "I'll take another cosmopolitan. This one's about gone."

The man nodded then turned to Sylvie and gave her a look that made her panties instantly wet. "And you?"

"Nuh -- no, thanks. I'm good." She lifted her still full glass with a shaky hand, maneuvered the straw to her mouth somehow and sucked hard until her dry mouth was full of liquid. It all went down in a big gulp. Hit her gut like a block of ice. Cold and heavy.

He watched her, his eyes sparkling with… something. She wasn't really sure what they were trying to say to her. "Are you sure?" He nodded to her glass. "It's empty."

"Oh. Yeah. So it is." Her face was flaming red, she just knew it. "But, no. No thanks. I'm the designated driver."

Someone kicked her leg and she jumped.

She looked at Lisa, who was giving her *that* look -- the one that told her she was making a really stupid mistake.

"Okay," he said, sounding a little put out. He gave her a half-smile and stepped back.

The room's oxygen supply finally seemed to normalize.

"I'll be back in a minute," he said.

"Okay. We'll be right here waiting," Lisa sing-songed, giving him a little wave. The second he was out of sight, Lisa leaned forward and said, "Are you friggin' crazy? What's wrong with you? That guy was gorgeous, and he was so into you. What would it hurt to have one more drink? You can out-drink half the Navy."

"Yeah, well," Sylvie said, shifting in her seat. God, it was hot in here. Why wasn't the manager turning on the air conditioning? Was he an idiot? Or was he trying to get people to drink more by making them sweat? "I need to keep on my toes tonight."

"You insulted him."

"He'll get over it, I can tell. Heck, he's probably at the bar hitting on some other babe in a backless dress."

"No, he's not." Lisa pointed behind her. "He's on his way back. With my drink."

"Oh, great." When he was out of her line of sight, she could think clearly again. And she was worried about Burke. Where the heck had he gone? Didn't he see this guy practically drooling over her? Didn't that bother him? She was, after all, his... what had he called it? Original?

"So quick!" Lisa said, batting her eyelashes as the guy handed her the fresh drink.

"Got lucky. There wasn't a line at the bar." He looked at the chair next to Sylvie. "Mind if I sit?"

Sylvie really wanted to say "no," she really did. She wanted to get up and go hunt down Burke, find out where he'd gone. Make sure nothing was wrong. But for some reason, she just plain couldn't move. She couldn't deny this man. She couldn't do anything but mutter, "Sure."

Her body warmed. Sensual awareness pricked her spine, like little needles. It was both an uncomfortable and extremely pleasant sensation.

"The name's Miko," he said, offering a hand to her. "Miko Dvorak."

"Sylvie." She tried to give his hand a quick, non-committal shake. It didn't turn out that way. Her eyes met his and then there was this crazy connection, just like there'd been with

Burke. He twisted his hand around, so their fingers were twined and his thumb was stroking the side of her hand. And oh... her girly parts were jumping up and down with glee and planning a party.

Burke! She jerked her hand away, broke the connection between their eyes and stood up. "I... need to go to the ladies room. Be right back."

Her celebrating parts put up a scream of dissention, but she carried them away on wobbly legs to the bathroom, scanning every corner of the bar's interior for Burke as she walked.

She found him, half hidden by the disc jockey's booth, which was empty.

He cringed when she walked up to him.

"Are you hiding?" she asked as quietly as the bar's noisy interior would allow, spinning around to see if she'd led anyone to him. No one seemed to have followed.

"Yes. Kind of. They're here."

"Who?"

"The *Excoluni*. They're here, looking for me, which means I can't keep a close eye on you if you're more than a couple feet away. The place is packed. This is too dangerous. We should leave."

"But what about catching the killer?"

"How can I do anything hiding back here?" The frustration in his voice made her want to forget about the danger and help him any way she could. "I don't want to go," he continued, "just in case there is another murder. This is the only bar in the area that the murderer hasn't hit yet."

"Then we'd be foolish to leave."

"No, we'd be foolish to stay if you're the next chosen victim."

"We still don't know that. For all we know, that slip of paper has nothing to do with the killer. Besides, if I was the intended victim, why would the killer come here? I've never stepped foot in this place. And why wouldn't she have tried killing me last night?" When Burke had no answers to her questions, she felt her smile turn smug. "You see? I'd say the odds are in my favor.

The paper with my name and phone number had nothing to do with the murder."

He stared thoughtfully at the booth's control panel for a moment. "You have a point. But I don't like taking these kinds of risks with other people's lives. I've done enough of that already." He sighed. "Has anyone been watching you tonight? Anyone but me? Do you feel like you're being followed?"

"No…" Even she could hear the wavering in her voice. Darn! He had almost lightened up.

His expression turned fiery. Before she realized what had happened, he was out of the booth and standing next to her. He lunged forward and caught her shoulders in his hands. "What aren't you telling me?"

"Uh. Okay. There's this guy…" *This mysterious, sexy guy who was making me hot with a mere whisper.*

Man, if Burke could read her mind, the shock he'd get!

"What guy? What'd he do?"

Her cheeks burned. "Nothing. Really."

His eyebrows dropped. He wasn't buying it.

"He offered to buy me a drink. That's all. I swear. Nothing creepy or out of the ordinary. We are in a bar, you know. And by all appearances, I'm unattached…" Feeling uber-guilty, like she was cheating on Burke or something, she let her words trail off. There was nothing to feel guilty about. They hadn't made any commitments to each other. An offer to buy a drink was nothing to be shocked or alarmed over. Although her reaction to the guy was. Perhaps. Okay, most definitely. "I didn't accept the drink," she added weakly.

He stared into her eyes. "You're still keeping something from me."

Maybe he could read her mind. Or maybe she was just a really bad liar. She pulled her gaze from his and took it to safer territory -- the wall behind him. "No. Not really. Like I said, he just came up and offered to buy me a drink." For some reason, she left out the part about him staring at her neck, and her suspicion that he might be the other vampire in her supposed triad. She had a feeling her instincts were wrong about all that stuff and she didn't want to rile Burke up even more at the moment, make any of this out to be more than it was. Now was not the time. Besides, he was looking like he'd pop a few blood vessels at any moment, thanks to the stress he was already shouldering.

He had a killer to catch. That had to be his focus. There was no reason to distract him with secondary non-important stuff at the moment, like her raging libido.

He pulled on her upper arm and started toward the back of the building. "That's it. We're leaving."

"No. Wait!" She yanked as hard as she could, determined to get free of him. If there was one thing that annoyed the crap out of her it was being manhandled. "First, I'll decide when I'm ready to leave. And second, you're overreacting." When he refused to release her, she lowered her voice until it was a deep, threatening growl. "Get your hands off me and I'll explain."

Mid-stomp, he whirled around and gave her a glare that made her heart stop for a full second. "Are you trying to get yourself killed?" he hissed.

"Puhleez. You're being melodramatic. No one is trying to kill me."

"What's going on?" Lisa asked from somewhere behind her.

"Go away," Burke barked.

"Don't talk to my friend like that." This guy was way out of line. Sylvie stomped on his foot with all her might. "Back off!"

Caught by surprise, he loosened his boa constrictor-like grip on her arm long enough for her to get free. She caught Lisa's hand and made a beeline for the empty dance floor, knowing he didn't dare follow her with the Ex-co-whatever searching for him.

She stopped in the dead center to catch her breath.

A song by Coldplay started thrumming from the bar's speakers and hordes of people crowded around them.

Great, so much for her plan to stand where she'd be in plain sight.

"Who was that?" Lisa asked, sounding both mystified and impressed, like she'd just met Vin Diesel or something. She handed Sylvie her purse.

Hugging her purse to her chest, Sylvie wriggled and shuffled her way between gyrating bodies, figuring she'd head back to their table. "It's no one. This guy I met last night. He's turning out to be a real pain in the butt."

"Wait a minute."

Sylvie stopped at the edge of the dance floor and turned. "What?"

Lisa studied her for a moment. A knowing smile spread over her face. "That's the private detective you were talking about. You slept with him?"

Her cheeks started burning all over again. This place was hotter than blazes. "Yeah. Well, that was a mistake. Granted a fun mistake... but a mistake."

"My God, he was hot! What a body." She gave Sylvie a pat on the shoulder. "I officially forgive you for not being home last night to take my call."

"Gee thanks." Sylvie sighed and looked at the DJ booth, which now appeared to be inhabited by someone else.

"So, why're you running from him?"

"Because he's a controlling ass. He got all grabby and bossy. I hate that!" *At least, outside of the dungeon.*

"I hear that. No biggie. You win some. You lose some." Lisa poked her in the rib. When Sylvie turned to look at her, she pointed toward the opposite side of the room. "You've always got hottie number two. Look, here he comes. Damn, girl. I want to know what you're doing to get all these gorgeous guys to chase you around. Share the wealth, would ya? Toss me a scrap. Anything."

"I'll let you know what I'm doing as soon as I figure it out myself."

"And look at that. He took off his jacket. Wow, does that man know how to fill a shirt properly. Mmmm mmm!"

"I'm beginning to think you ladies are running from me," Miko said by way of a greeting. "Dance with me." It wasn't a question. It was a demand. Not waiting for her to respond one way or the other, he looped an arm around her back and pulled until her entire front was smooshed up against his. He took her right hand in his and started a slow, seductive sway.

"I'll just be standing over here," Lisa said, backing off the dance floor.

SIX

Sylvie tipped her head to get a close-up look at Miko's face. Bad move. Bad, bad move. The air left her lungs somehow when she wasn't paying attention. Either that or someone had turned on a gigantic vacuum and sucked it all out of the room. After dragging in a few desperate gulps, she managed to mutter, "Don't you think this music is a little fast to be dancing like this?"

"No." He pressed on the small of her back, making her front even more smooshed. Her nipples had taken notice of the contact and were poking at him through the thin fabric of her dress. His hand wandered north, over the gathering of fabric to her exposed back. Goosebumps immediately coated her upper body, despite the fact that the room was beginning to be as hot and muggy as a sauna.

He bent his head and whispered, "I know what you are."

What she was? That statement was a mite confusing. "Oh?" she asked, following his lead as he swayed to a much slower beat than was pounding through the air and shaking the walls.

He nipped her earlobe. "You're an *Origo*." Releasing her back, he bent his elbow and lifted, showing a mark on the inside of his forearm. It was identical to Burke's. "My *Origo*." Clearly not in any hurry to have her leave, he returned his arm to its previous position, snuggled her against him and in a snazzy move a la Gene Kelly twirled her around.

Dizzy from the motion, dizzy from the heat blazing through her body, dizzy from whatever, Sylvie clung to him and tried to keep her feet under her and her brain from melting into grey goo. She felt like she was losing both battles.

Her feet felt like they were hovering above the ground more often than planted firmly on it. And her brain? Well, that was short circuiting like crazy, or so she assumed. Because it was telling her to do some downright shocking things with this man.

Like throw him to the ground and have her way with him. Or rather, throw herself to the ground and beg him to have his way with her.

What had gotten into her? Was this *Origo* thing some kind of magical connection? Because while she would admit she'd never been a prude, she'd also never reacted to a man the way she had to Burke and Miko. Her body temperature spiked with just a look from either of them. Burke with his long, dark hair, lopsided grin and smoldering gaze. And Miko with his slightly lighter hair and stunning good looks. He looked like he'd just walked off the red carpet -- or the pages of a men's fitness magazine.

"Do you know what you do to me?" he murmured, his mouth grazing the side of her neck. He released her hand and lifted his to the back of her head, pulled the clip from her hair and tangled his fingers in it as it fell heavy over her shoulders. "I can hear your pulse. Right here." He swirled his tongue over a sensitive spot on her neck and she jerked against him, instantly rigid. "I can smell your desire." He audibly inhaled. "Sweet. Intoxicating. You're wet, ready for me. Makes me want to take you right here."

She meant to give him some kind of sarcastic comeback, but the best she came up with was, "Eerk!"

Taking her right then and there didn't sound like such a bad plan, come to think of it.

Yep. Brain was gone. She put out a silent SOS vibe to Lisa, hoping her friend might by some miracle answer it. Granted, she couldn't get Lisa to answer a simple phone call the last time she'd needed her.

But if someone didn't come and shake things up within the next thirty seconds, she knew with absolute certainty she was going to do something stupid. Like beg him to take her home with him.

Unfortunately, no one came, and she was left to stand there, stumbling over her own feet and whimpering while Miko nibbled and licked her neck like she was a lollipop. With each flicker of his tongue, little pulses of heat rippled through her body. They spread out from her center, these happy little ripples, yet for some reason, more heat seemed to keep building deep inside.

She realized quite suddenly there was a reason for that. She was grinding against his leg.

So not cool!

"Hey, Dvorak! There you are. Quit with the chicks…" some unidentified male voice said to the left of her.

She turned to look, found she was standing beside yet another huge, muscular, extremely good looking guy.

"Sorry, Miss. But my friend's gotta cut this dance short."

"Not now," Miko said in a low voice that reminded Sylvie of Burke's growl. It was very predatory, almost inhuman, which made sense, since vampires weren't exactly humans.

His friend blinked. "Yes, now. Right now. What's wrong with you?"

"Nothing's wrong with me. Just go away." He gave his friend a shove.

The man squared his shoulders and lifted his chin, giving Miko a piercing stare. "As your superior, I command you to come with me this instant."

Sylvie swore she heard Miko say, "Fuck off," but if he did, he said it low enough for only her to hear.

He loosened his hold on her, but didn't release her completely until after he said, "I need to find you again. Tell me how to find you."

Despite the fact that her tongue felt swollen to at least twice its normal size, she managed to utter two words, "Carpe Nocturne."

He leaned down, barely brushed his mouth over hers and turned to leave.

He was no more than a couple feet away when she heard someone say, "Look who we have here. It's Langton. What're you doing? Hunting your next victim?" She spun around so fast, she nearly fell over.

Miko's supposed boss was glaring at Burke. And Burke was giving him an equally evil look right back.

Despite the festive atmosphere all around them, the eardrum-splitting music and gyrating bodies, Sylvie could literally see the tension in the air between the two men. It was like a dark shadow, rippling like heated air above the asphalt in July.

"Are you going to come quietly or are we going to have to take you by force?" Miko asked, stepping forward.

They wanted to take Burke? Did they really say that? Why? What was this all about?

She wanted to do something but didn't know what. And then someone, or something, caught her by the neck and yanked hard, forcing her to stumble backward. An arm circled her neck, and something sharp pierced her skin, just below her ear. A little tilt to her eyes, and she verified it was a knife blade. A really sharp looking knife blade.

"Let Langton go or this woman dies," a female voice said behind her. It was a woman holding her? Had to be the strongest woman this side of hell.

Who the heck was she? What was she trying to do? And what the hell made her think those two vampires gave two fangs whether she ran that knife blade through Sylvie's throat or not?

The one guy gave her a cool look and shrugged his shoulders. "She's nothing to me."

"But she is to me," Miko said solemnly.

A few sets of eyes fell on him at that bit of news, one of them belonging to Burke.

"I couldn't tell you before because…" He sighed before continuing to explain to his boss. "She's my *Origo*. My mate."

The gasp she heard didn't come from the boss. It came from Burke. As she watched, he grabbed Miko's wrist with his left hand and twisted, forcing the man to reveal the underside of his forearm.

"Well, that explains a lot," Burke said, studying the black symbol that matched his own, which she knew was on the arm he held behind his back. "A whole hell of a lot." For the first time in eons, his gaze met Sylvie's. Something flashed in his eyes.

"Let him go," the woman repeated.

"Fuck, I can't!" Miko's boss snapped. "He's a convicted felon."

"You have to!" Miko snapped back. "You know what will happen if she's killed, Hadrian. You know what'll happen to me."

"Have you taken the bond?" The man called Hadrian studied Miko for a minute. "No, you couldn't have. They won't kill her, anyway."

"Who says I won't?" the woman holding Sylvie said in an icy voice.

Sure convinced Sylvie. She stiffened.

"They're murderers. Why wouldn't they kill her?" Miko challenged.

"Because she's their friend."

"She's not my friend," her captor said. "I've never met this bitch before. I'm a cold-blooded murderer, right? It would take so little effort." The woman pressed the blade into Sylvie's skin. It pinched and she flinched when a rivulet of warm wetness dribbled down her neck. "Oh, dear. Looks like she's bleeding."

Precisely three seconds later, all hell broke loose. It went something like this -- Hadrian jumped at Burke. Miko jumped at Hadrian and Burke just started swinging at both of them. Three vampires fighting. It was a bizarre if not confusing sight. They moved so fast, it was like she was watching a movie playing back at the wrong speed. Or like a cartoon fight, where there was this cloud of smoke and arms or heads popping out every once in a while.

As quickly as it started, it was over. Burke staggered out from the cloud, followed by Miko. Hadrian was lying on the floor. She found herself hoping he wasn't dead, or Burke's problems -- which already seemed to be pretty huge -- had just gotten a whole lot worse. Whoever Hadrian was, it appeared he was some kind of VIP. Someone with ties to the police. Nothing good could come from killing a guy like that.

The woman's grip on Sylvie's neck loosened a smidge but not enough for her to break free.

Hadrian stirred, pushed himself up on one arm and rubbed his head. "Fuck!"

Miko shoved Burke. "Get out of here. Now."

Before Sylvie knew how it had happened, Burke had her in his arms and was running for the door. Everything flew by her in a blur, like she was driving down a bumpy road at eighty. He stopped outside at his car, opened the back door, hurried her in, then slammed it.

In the back seat, she twisted around and caught Hadrian and Miko running from the bar's front door. Hadrian stomped his foot as Burke gunned the engine and the car rocketed down the street.

Well, that wasn't exactly the way she'd expected the evening to go. She'd been seduced. Held hostage. And then rushed from the building, with a couple of pissed off men on their tails.

She wondered what would happen next. She lifted her hand to her neck, found a little sticky wetness at the base, where her neck met her collarbone. She checked her fingers. Sure enough, it was blood. That... woman had cut her!

What the heck was going on? "Burke?" she said.

"Not now."

What, not now? Was she a child whining for a cookie?

"Excuse me?" she said.

"Don't you ever lay your hands on her again," Burke said in a low growl, evidently directing his anger at the woman sitting next to him in the front passenger seat.

"I'm sorry," the woman said. "I was trying to help --"

"Not her! I can't see someone hurting her without... without wanting to do something drastic."

"Ohhhh. Oh!" The bitch who'd cut her twisted in the passenger seat and gave her a smile around the seat's back. "I'm Isabella. Sorry about your neck." She reached back with her right hand. "I... uh... didn't realize you and Burke... I mean... Nice to meet you."

Who was Isabella? Obviously she knew Burke. But how well? And why was Sylvie burning up with jealousy, even though he was so obviously steamed at her for the stunt she'd pulled at the bar?

She took Isabella's hand in hers and gave it a polite but unenthusiastic shake before releasing it. "Sylvie Durand," was all she could manage to utter. She raised her hand to her neck again, to see if she was still bleeding. Felt like it had stopped.

"It's a shallow wound. It's clotted already. Sorry. I had to do something, or Burke here would've been on his way to face the executioner if I had just stood there..."

Sylvie listened, half-comprehending what Isabella was saying. She was partly distracted by her efforts to remember where she'd seen the woman before -- she looked vaguely familiar -- and partly preoccupied by her attempts to figure out where Burke was taking them.

He wasn't driving back to his home, or back to hers.

"Where's he taking us? Burke?"

Isabella turned forward for a second then looked back again. "The *Excoluni* saw our license plates. They'll be at our apartments before sunrise. We're going to need new identities. Again."

"What's an *Excoluni*?" Sylvie asked.

"Dammit!" Burke said, smacking the steering wheel. "Dammit, dammit, dammit! I need to stop at an ATM, get as much cash as I can. Before my bank account's seized. I won't be able to get it all. There's a daily limit. And there's no way I'll risk going back to my apartment to get the stash I hid there."

"Bank account seized? For what?" Sylvie felt as lost as a movie-goer who'd walked into the middle of a mystery film. But tons more frustrated and scared. "Someone want to tell me what's going on before I freak out?"

"I'd start from the beginning, but I figure that's for Burke here to tell you. Maybe later," Isabella said. "For now, I can tell you we're being hunted by the *Excoluni*, the police force of the UMN, for murder."

"Y-you? And Burke? Murder?" Sylvie heard herself stammer.

"I didn't kill anyone," Burke said. "Yet."

"Neither have I," Isabella explained. "But we're being blamed for the murders of several people, one of whom died last night. At your bar. We're trying to catch the real killer."

It was then that Sylvie realized why Isabella looked so familiar. She was Farrah! "You were at Carpe Nocturne last night, talking about *Charlie's Angels*."

"Yes. That was me. I thought you realized that already."

"Well, gosh. You look so different." Sylvie took a good long look at Isabella's face and hair. Isabella had looked pretty in an innocent sort of way last night, wearing her midnight blue Victorian gown, her long deep-red tresses cascading down her back. Tonight, she looked tough and dangerous, like a spy chick. Her hair was pulled tightly into a ponytail at the back of her head. She was wearing all black. Snug pants, form-fitting knit top. Sylvie half-expected her to whip out some spy gear.

"Call our contact," Burke said as he maneuvered the car into a bank's parking lot. "I'll be right back."

Half-listening to Isabella place a call on her cell phone, Sylvie watched him as he walked to the front of the building, to the glassed-in enclosure holding the ATM. He was walking stiffly, like he was either in pain or so ticked off there wasn't a muscle in his body that could relax. She hoped it wasn't the first and suspected it was the second.

He was heading back to the car by the time Isabella had ended her call. "I got all I could. It isn't much. We'd better get what we can from your account too."

"Okay." Isabella handed him the cell phone. "He's working on our new papers. We can go pick them up in a couple of hours."

"Good thing it's early."

When Isabella got out, Sylvie climbed out of the cramped back seat and took her spot in the front. She focused her attention on Burke.

He sighed and dragged his fingers through his hair, pulling out the elastic holding it at his nape. "I'm sorry I'm being such a bastard right now. I just didn't need this. Any of this. It took so long to get to where I was. And now…" He shook his head, leaving the sentence hanging there, unfinished. He raised his fist and she thought he'd put it through the window. He didn't.

She wanted to do so many things -- comfort him, console him, help him. But mostly she wanted to bombard him with a million questions. Obviously, he wasn't just a nice guy trying to protect her. He was a guy who had problems. Lots of them. He was a guy on the run from the police… or so she assumed. She had no idea what or who the UMN was.

Instead of doing anything useful, or helpful, she merely nodded and lifted the corners of her mouth into something she hoped resembled a smile. Their eyes met. That crazy connection zapped and buzzed in the air between them. She reached a hand out to touch him, but he jerked away before she'd done more than pat him.

"No. Don't," he said softly, grimacing as if she'd just scorched him with a branding iron.

"Wow. Sorry." She heard the hurt in her own voice, but she hadn't been able to stop it from coming out. Despite all the confusion, the questions, the men chasing them, she felt a strange and unexplainable draw to this man. And any distance, whether it was physical or emotional, hurt. Bad. Physically. It took the form of this burning deep in her gut. The pain made it hard to breathe. To think. To do much of anything.

It was so weird and horrible and fascinating.

"We're both feeling it, the pain of the *Iugum*, the Binding. It's because we've found the third member. The *Iugum* is calling to us. It will get worse."

The third member. Miko. Could she be with two men? Be their lover? Would she desire them both? Serve them?

Love them?

Was that possible?

Isabella returned to the car, and without complaint took the backseat, leaving Sylvie beside Burke. "I got all I could too, but between us, I doubt we'll have enough to pay for the new identities."

"Dammit. We'll have to go back to my place after all." He pulled a U-turn in the middle of the two-lane road, heading the car back the way they'd come.

"No. It's too risky."

"What choice do I have? No money, no IDs. No IDs, no hotel or apartment or jobs or food for Sylvie."

"Don't worry about me. Sounds like you've got enough to worry about yourselves," Sylvie said, trying to be helpful.

Burke shook his head. "You're in my care. I will provide for your necessities. Besides, we cannot risk you using your credit cards, either. They may be able to track our movements and find us."

"Okay." Feeling torn, she clutched her purse to her chest. Thanks to all the commotion, she still hadn't gotten to the bank to make the deposit on last night's bar sales. Even though the night had been cut short, and a fair amount of the bar's sales had been paid by credit card, she was still holding onto almost five thousand dollars. It was enough money to pay off all the vendors she owed money to, including the utility companies, and catch up the payroll.

But this was life or death.

She sucked in a deep breath, flipped open her purse and pulled out the envelope, already filled out and sealed. She swallowed a huge lump that had lodged itself in her throat. "You can have this."

Driving, Burke glanced at the envelope she was offering him and shook his head. "No. I can't take your money."

"Please. I've thought about this. I want to help."

"No." He gently pushed her hand back toward her own lap. "Last night, when I searched your office, I saw more than that napkin."

She had no doubt what he meant by that. He'd seen the piles of bills on her desks. The ones with red lettering all over them, threatening all kinds of horrific penalties if payment wasn't made immediately.

They were important. The meat guy needed to get paid. So did the wine vendor, the electric company, the waitresses and cooks. But dammit, what good would the money in her purse do any of them if those two Exco-whatevers found them? Would she be named an accomplice? Was she now wanted for aiding and abetting felons?

Oy! She didn't want to know the answer to that question at the moment. "I insist."

"No. You need that money. We're going back. For mine."

Isabella placed her hand on Sylvie's shoulder. It was a soft touch, a silent show of support and gratitude.

After studying the stubborn set of one adorable man's jaw, Sylvie returned the envelope to her purse. He'd won the argument but she'd win the war. She'd just have to approach things with a different strategy.

All men had their weak points. She'd find Burke's.

And she'd find a way to help him clear his name.

SEVEN

He would have his answer. *Finally.*

The pain of living this way had become unbearable. He missed her so much. Needed her more than anything. The price he'd had to pay to find the answer was a dear one, but well worth it.

The document was fragile. Scrawled in a barely discernable variation of the Ancient Tongue on a piece of dried human skin. The skin had then been rolled onto a bone that once belonged to a powerful wizard. The magic, which protected the document, shimmered in the air as he slowly unrolled it. The faintest zapping sensation, like tiny pinpricks, traveled over his fingertips.

It was the most amazing thing. And what it would give him was the one piece of the puzzle he'd lacked, the answer to why his past attempts at raising his beloved had failed.

He would not fail again.

He read the document for the third time, double-checking to make sure he had all the necessary ingredients for the revealing spell.

Who'd known each spell in the *Book of the Shadows* had its own key? Lucky for him, a mage had owed him a fairly large favor, or he would never have known.

It paid to know people in high places.

He drew the circle on the floor with ash, set the candle in its center and lit it. Then he read the spell on the scroll aloud, poured the virgin's blood onto the ground. Setting the scroll down, he slowly tipped the burning candle, adding the molten wax to the puddle of blood.

Slowly at first, then quicker, the blood congealed. It turned into a thick black gelatin, forming words on the ground.

But the words were nonsense. Utterly meaningless, even in the Ancient Tongue.

Had he been taken for a fool? Furious, he thought about throwing the still burning candle into the mess, but ran to gather a pencil and paper first.

It never paid to act in haste.

He copied down the entire message then completed the final cleansing step to clear away the results of the spell.

He took a moment to read what he'd written on the paper. Was it some kind of code? A puzzle he had to solve?

He supposed it would be foolish for a mage to hand over a spell this powerful if there were no protective measures in place.

That had to be it. A code. A puzzle. He was excellent at both.

"It won't be long, my love," he said to his beloved, still lying in her resting place on the altar. "It won't be long at all. The next time I cast the spell, you will be mine for always."

* * *

Burke Langton parked the car in the middle of a drugstore's parking lot. He turned to Sylvie Durand -- his *Origo*, his mate -- and was immediately rendered a near cripple by the pain of the *Iugum*, the Binding. It had increased a hundredfold since leaving the bar.

Fuck!

Of all the Insurgis who had to be Sylvie's other mate… of all the fucking Insurgis! Why did it have to be Miko Dvorak, brother and second in command to Hadrian Dvorak?

While he knew in the back of his mind there was the possibility the situation could work to his advantage, right now, while his blood was burning like acid and his body ached for what it could not have, he didn't care. All he cared about was completing the Binding. The pain would be gone. And if the legends were true, he'd not only find completion, but he'd also experience the one thing that was impossible for him now -- love.

The emptiness, the hollowness, he'd lived with all his life would be gone.

His suffering would not end until the Binding was complete. The ache would steadily increase until it either killed him or drove him mad. Would he catch the killer in time? Before he lost his grip on sanity? Before he lost his life and soul?

And what about Sylvie? He knew she was a resilient woman, with a strong will and spirit. But how much suffering could she endure? Would he be forced to take his own life just to free her from the torture?

She licked her lips as she looked at him, searching his face for the answers he'd been too unwilling to answer yet. His cock stiffened as his gaze fixed to her mouth. To feel those lips down there, gliding up and down his shaft. Her tongue swirling around the head.

He stifled a roar of frustration. He needed to get moving. Now. Get some money and find them a place to hide until their paperwork was done, allowing them to travel freely, register in a hotel, rent a car.

He needed to ease the burn a little. Fucking her would do that, lessen the pain. For both of them. But only temporarily. There was only one permanent cure. And it was impossible without Miko.

"Stay here and stay together," he said. "I'll be back in a few minutes."

"What if you don't come back?" Isabella, his dearest friend, asked.

"I'll be back. Just stay out of sight. And don't go anywhere." He knew he'd regret it, but he leaned over and brushed his mouth over Sylvie's. It hardly qualified as a kiss, but the effect would have knocked him on his ass if he hadn't already been seated.

Dizzy and lightheaded, he fumbled with the door handle, pushed open the car door and after standing on legs that felt wobbly for the first time ever, he gently shut it to keep from making too much noise. It wasn't too late yet, not even eleven in the evening. But the suburban neighborhood was quiet. Dvorak had no doubt tracked down his address and was trolling the area, looking for him. He'd have to be careful.

He stuck to the darkest shadows as he walked to his building. Once again, he found himself thankful for the fact that his apartment complex didn't have street lights. It made for plenty of shadows. The moon, mostly hidden behind an inky cloud, produced only the faintest bluish glow, barely enough light for even a creature of the night to see.

He made it to his building with no trouble. As he neared, he was relieved to see there was no sign of visitors. No cars. No lingering glitter of magic. No sounds. Moving slowly and carefully, not to make a sound, he rounded the side of the building. Still nothing.

Could he have been wrong about Dvorak? Had he failed to get a clear view of the license plate?

He could only be so lucky!

He slipped inside, and made his way up the stairs, his every sense alert to anything that was out of the ordinary. Nothing, except the pathetic whimper of a poodle.

Oh the gods, he'd forgotten about the dog.

He hated dogs, especially girly dogs like poodles. And this one had made it clear it didn't exactly have the greatest regard for him either. But dammit, he couldn't leave the thing there to starve. There were some things that even he knew were plain wrong.

He considered leaving her be until he was ready to leave but changed his mind. It seemed, from its reaction, that it was sensitive to the scent of the Insurgi, the Immortal. Therefore, if there were any *Excoluni* members nearby, the little thing might go yipping and nipping after them. At least that would get them out in the open and give him a fighting chance at getting out of the apartment with his money.

Sounds like a plan.

Walking soundlessly, each step taking far longer than he wished, he made it back to the bedroom, flattened himself against the wall and opened the door.

The poodle, yipping at an eardrum-shattering volume and pitch, went straight to the door.

At least it was trained well. And nothing had distracted the animal. It wasn't exactly a clear signal that the apartment was empty, but it eased his worries a bit.

Unable to let the poodle outside to conduct its business yet, he went back to his room to handle his.

Working quickly, he pulled the suitcase out from under his bed, went to the closet and removed the hidden panel. Didn't take more than a few minutes to gather the cash from its hiding place, pack it in the bag, gather a growling, snapping dog and head for the door. It took a whole lot longer to convince the fur ball to shut up and stop trying to take off his digits so that he felt safe enough to head outside.

He was smack dab in the middle of the building's front yard when the headlights hit him.

"I've got you!" Miko shouted. "Stop!"

Blinded by the glare, Burke ran as fast as he could, in the opposite direction of Isabella, Sylvie and the car. As he tripped and stumbled over lawn ornaments and low-lying shrubberies, he put up a silent prayer to the gods that the women hadn't been found.

The dog stiffened but showed the rare wisdom not to start yapping. At a full run, Burke headed around a corner at the end of the block and into the small patch of woods that cut the apartment complex into two. He stayed in the woods, dodging trees as he ran, until he had gone to the end. He stopped just before stepping out onto the paved street.

He saw no sign of a car coming. Heard nothing behind him. No snapping twigs or rustling leaves. Had Miko given up so easily? Although it would have been nice, Burke didn't believe that for a minute.

Being extra careful to stay in the shadows, he walked down the residential street, heading back toward the parking lot where he'd left the car. It was a long friggin' walk, especially while carrying a squirmy, dribbling poodle. The little beast was the most nervous animal he'd ever seen. Lost its bladder control at the slightest noise. Sure helped him, though. It was a particularly substantial leak that alerted him to the fact that there was a car coming up behind them with its headlights off.

Burke was able to duck behind a hedge and hide until Miko had driven by.

"Yeah, you spoke too soon, asshole," he murmured to the taillights of the car.

It was too dark to tell if there were any other people in the car with him, but Burke was guessing there weren't.

Twenty or so minutes later, he crept into the parking lot. He was hugely relieved to see the car was parked where he'd left it. And he guessed, by the subtle shift of shadows inside the vehicle, that Isabella and Sylvie were still waiting, probably getting anxious and impatient, not that he could blame them. By his estimate, it had been at least forty-five minutes since he'd left them.

It was a wonder they hadn't wandered off to go looking for him. He knew Isabella had probably been tempted.

One thing that bothered him as he approached the car was how careless they were being. Even though he couldn't see them per se, he could see their forms shifting. He'd told them to stay quiet and still, to avoid calling any undue attention to themselves. Looked like they were practically holding a party in there.

And then he realized what was going on. It was the legs and trunk of a non-female body emerging from the vehicle that shed some light on the situation. The car parked next to his, engine running, headlights off, gave him a fairly reliable clue whose legs and torso they were.

"Fuck!" he whispered, cutting a sharp right to hide behind a crop of trees in an empty lot. "Should've known you wouldn't quit so easy."

"Why would you think something as stupid as that?" Isabella said behind him.

He jerked. The dog tinkled -- again -- dousing the front of his clothes. It then decided to yap its fool head off at Isabella.

Burke dropped the suitcase and tried to muzzle its mouth with his hand, but it bit him. He swallowed an angry growl and was about to go for a second attempt when Sylvie jumped up from behind a shrub and snatched it out of his arms, whispering, "Shhhhhush, Lulu! Before you get us caught."

"You're... Who's in the car?" Confused and relieved, Burke turned back to the car to see if Miko had heard them.

Okay, the guy was standing next to the car, his gaze leveled right at them.

He'd say that was a yes.

"Fuck. Gotta run. Fast!" He pointed east. "That way!" Snatching up the suitcase, he bent down, hit Sylvie mid-stomach with his shoulder and scooped her off her feet. Still hugging her dog to her side, she dangled over his back as he ran, kicking her legs, insisting he put her down.

Not that he could take the time to explain it now, but there was no other way. Humans moved slow as snails compared to immortals. If he let her run, they stood absolutely no chance of escaping.

Ignoring Sylvie's continuing rant, and her dog's continued assault on his shoulder, he turned north, cutting through some lawns to go back toward the woods. That narrow patch of forest wound down several miles, to the county line. It was their only hope of staying out of sight.

They stopped running about three miles in. He set Sylvie down on her feet and prepared himself for the verbal assault he was sure to get. She gave him a pretty nasty glare but didn't say a word. She hugged her quivering animal to her chest and stumbled beside him as they walked. When she tripped over a tree root, he caught her hand to keep her from falling.

She answered his gesture with a faint smile. "Thank you. For getting Lulu."

"You're welcome."

Neither of them released the other's hand.

It seemed he'd been forgiven.

One disaster averted, several actually.

Now he just had to figure out where they'd go next. With no car, they could only go so far. And with daylight coming in the next few hours, they needed to find someplace safe to hide, or he'd be dust.

Literally.

EIGHT

Sylvie knew she was holding his hand. There wasn't a cell in her body that wasn't vibrating like a bee trapped in a glass jar. What was left of her gray matter was telling her she should cut ties now, while the cutting was good. Those two, Burke and Isabella, were in some serious trouble with a law enforcement organization she knew nothing about.

At this point she figured she could talk herself out of any legal trouble her affiliation with them might have brought on her, but if she stuck with them much longer... there was no telling what might be assumed.

Oy, the tangled webs, blah, blah, blah.

Ironically, her troubles had started because she'd tried to do something new and exciting to get Carpe Nocturne in the black.

That was another thing. She needed to get in touch with the police and find out when she could open Carpe Nocturne back up. Because she'd had to close early Friday, she'd now lost almost two days' revenues, and although Sundays weren't her biggest day of the week, money was money. Things were beyond desperate at this point.

But damn if she could get herself to let go of Burke's hand, let alone wish him luck and hightail it away from there. Whether it was the vampire-bonding thing or her Catholic upbringing, even the thought of leaving him made her feel guilty as hell. It was like she was abandoning him.

She was getting really tired now. Beyond tired. Her feet were killing her. Her legs were sore. Her back was achy. Her eyes felt like they'd been alternately rolled in crushed glass and petroleum jelly. She did a lot of blinking as she walked. And a lot of wondering.

Where the hell were they headed? They weren't far from Lisa's house.

"Where are we going?" she asked.

"We need to find shelter before sunrise." Burke stopped walking when they reached the end of the woods. He looked right and left, down the street. She admired his profile. Until she'd met him, she'd never even held a conversation with a man who looked like that, let alone had sex with one.

How things had changed in the last twelve hours or so. In some ways for the better. In some ways for the worse.

"My friend doesn't live far from here," she suggested. "I'm sure she wouldn't mind some company. She works days, so it'll be quiet once she leaves. That is, if you don't have somewhere else in mind."

Burke smoothed a hand down her arm then nodded. "That sounds good. Real good."

"It's this way." She pointed to the north. "She's bound to be freaking out by now anyway, after what happened last night."

Burke continued to hold her hand as they started north, keeping to the shadows. Little buzzes and zaps of erotic awareness zinged up her arm and straight to her groin. Her cheeks heated.

"Is there any chance she might've gone back to your house after we left the bar last night?" Isabella asked, falling into step on her right side.

"Maybe. Why?"

"We'd better keep a lookout as we get closer," Isabella suggested. "Someone posted at your house might've followed her home, thinking she might lead them to you."

"Oh." Sylvie looked at Burke. "If that's the case, maybe we should go somewhere else."

He shook his head and gave her a reassuring smile. It wasn't the most gleeful expression she'd ever seen but it eased her worries a smidge. Also amplified the tingles and zaps. "It'll be okay. You can go in alone and then sneak us inside."

"You want me to sneak you in?"

Burke stopped walking and took her arms in his hands, giving them a firm squeeze before changing his touch to a slow, erotic caress. He looked into her eyes and she saw the heat of suppressed longing in his eyes. A spark of wanting flashed through her. Her mouth dried. "It'll be better for everyone, especially your friend, if she doesn't know we're there."

She nodded. "Okay." She didn't like the idea of lying to Lisa, but she could kind of see his point. Already there was a good chance she was neck-deep in trouble. Why drag her best friend into the quicksand with her?

It was choosing the lesser of two very nasty evils.

It took them about a half hour to walk to Lisa's house. Sylvie told Isabella and Burke she'd tell Lisa she was letting Lulu out and then sneak them in the back door. Despite the fact that she knew she'd see Burke in a little while, she had a really hard time leaving him. It felt like a part of her anatomy had been sliced from her body when she took a few steps away from him.

This Master-slash-mate stuff was hard on a girl.

Feeling both dull from exhaustion and sadness, and also jittery from fear, she walked up Lisa's front walk and knocked on the door.

It took a long time for Lisa to answer. She looked like death as she opened the door. Her short hair stuck out at odd angles and dark circles made her eyes look sunken in.

"Where the fuck have you been?" Lisa snapped, scowling.

"Long story. Can I come in?"

"Yeah, sure." Lisa stepped aside to let Sylvie in then slammed the door shut. "So, spill. What's going on? Something's going on. Something weird. Tell me now or I'm going to… to do something drastic." She scratched Lulu's head and cooed,

"How's my girl? How's my girl?" as she took the shaking animal out of Sylvie's arms and inspected her. "My goodness! You're a wreck." She gave Sylvie another look. One of her trademark I'm-not-going-to-quit-hounding-you-until-you-spill-it looks. "What happened? First, you made me go to that yuppie bar last night. And then you were fought over by not one but two absolutely gorgeous men. And then some chick who looked like Anna in *Van Helsing* stuck a knife to your throat and dragged you off." Her voice rose with every word she spoke until she was shouting and practically shaking as bad as Lulu. "I've been worried to death!"

Sylvie had never seen Lisa so hysterical. Hysterical friends were absolutely no help. "Listen, I realize things are kind of crazy right now but I need you to keep it together. For both of us. Okay?" When Lisa responded with a nod, she asked, "Did you go to my house last night?"

"No. I was going to but then the police told me they'd handle it --"

"The police? You went to the police?"

"I talked to the undercover cops who were at the bar when you got kidnapped. That good looking one who'd bought --"

"Shit!" Sylvie shouted. The noise made Lulu twitch in Lisa's arms. She peered out the front door's peephole. So far there wasn't a fleet of unmarked Ex-co-whatever police cars crowding the driveway, but she knew chances were good Miko would head to Lisa's after losing them outside of Burke's apartment complex. "Shit, shit, shit! Please tell me they didn't take your address."

"Um… Yeah. They did. Why? Don't police officers usually take someone's personal information when they report a kidnapping?"

"Gotta go. Will you do me a favor and keep an eye on Lulu for a few days?"

"Uh, sure, but --"

"And the bar. Will you call the detective on this card and ask him if it's okay to open the bar?" She unzipped her purse, pulled the detective's card from her wallet and handed it to her friend.

"And whatever you do, don't talk to those other policemen again. They're not real police."

Lisa glanced down at the card Sylvie had handed her. "But what about --"

"I'll get in touch with you as soon as I can. Thanks." She gave Lisa a quick hug and pulled open the door.

She stopped dead in her tracks. Miko was standing on the front porch.

Her libido went wild when their eyes met, sending frenetic bursts of heat through her bloodstream. She staggered backward and bumped into someone or something behind her. The air leaked from her lungs until they threatened to collapse.

"I'm glad to see you're okay," Miko said, stepping into the room and reaching for her.

Every minute part of her body -- especially the girly ones -- wanted him to touch her. Yet she threw her hands up, blocking him. "Don't." Her voice sounded a whole lot firmer than she'd expected it to. She glanced behind her to see who she'd backed into.

"I'm sorry," Lisa said, still holding Lulu. "I called before I let you in. I was scared. I thought I was doing the right thing --"

"Your friend was worried about you," Miko said.

Sylvie spun around and nodded, trying not to notice the spark in his eyes. The swell of his shoulders. The flat plane of his stomach. "I... uh, kind of got that."

"I was worried about you too," he said. "It nearly killed me to watch you get dragged away by that bastard, Langton." His words eased her nerves and weakened what little remained of her resolve to keep some distance between them. "If he'd hurt you... I would've killed him," he whispered.

Oh God, she was in the middle of a huge mess. A huge mess that involved two men she couldn't resist no matter how hard she tried. Her body, her mind, her will, none of them belonged to her anymore. She was being tugged this way and that. It was both frustrating and thrilling at the same time.

What to do? "He didn't hurt me. I swear." She looked into Miko's eyes, searching them for the answers she desperately needed. He was her second Master. What a shocker that had been when Burke had flipped his arm over to reveal the mark. Though she shouldn't have been so surprised, considering her reaction to him.

She instinctively knew she could trust him not to harm her, but how much could she trust him otherwise? Should she tell him the truth -- that Burke didn't kill those people? Would he believe her? Was he unable to harm Burke, since they were in some weird, magical way bound to each other? Did Miko know about Burke? That he was the other Master? Should she tell him?

So may questions. It was all so confusing.

At least at this point one question had been answered. It seemed she wasn't being tied to Burke and Isabella by the authorities. If anything, it seemed they viewed her as a victim.

That part was good. Right?

Too bad all she could think about was dashing out there into the dark to help Burke and Isabella. Well, that or throw herself on Miko and beg him to haul her off to the nearest bedroom.

She should be relieved he didn't see her as a criminal. She should be staying with Lisa until the killer was found. She should be contacting the real police department and getting the clearance she needed to open Carpe Nocturne.

"I must protect you. He could come back."

If only he knew.

As if he'd read her mind, Miko snatched her wrist and gripped it so tightly her bones ground against each other.

She knew she should be angry, furious, absolutely livid at his barbaric treatment, but she wasn't. She was totally turned on. Her pussy was warming up in preparation for some fun. Her nipples were hardening into tight peaks. Desire was rolling through her body in relentless, swelling waves. Regardless, she tried putting on a good act. She gave him her best mean-eyed glare and twisted her wrist. "Let go of me."

"You're in danger."

"No, I'm not. I'm perfectly safe here with my friend. And my dog."

As if on cue, Lulu let loose with a less-than-threatening snarl that sounded more like a burp.

He raised a single eyebrow at Lulu. One corner of his mouth curled up, pulling it into a lopsided smile that made her knees wobbly. "That... ball of fluff?"

"She's tougher than she looks."

He reached out with his free hand to pet the quivering animal, and Sylvie stiffened.

"Don't!" she said, recalling Lulu's reaction to Burke.

He didn't flinch. "Why not? She's such an adorable little thing." He patted the top of her head and, being the attention whore she was, Lulu wriggled in Lisa's arms in an attempt to get closer. "Not much of a guard dog, though."

"Tell me about it," Sylvie deadpanned. Evidently, Lulu didn't have it in for all vampires.

"Time to go." He gave the dog one last scratch behind the ears then turned to the door and pushed open the screen door. There was no doubt she was heading to parts unknown with her second Master.

Some parts of her put up a loud cheer of excitement.

But the small portion of her brain that was still functioning reminded her that posed a huge problem for Burke and Isabella.

"Wait! I... I need to let Lulu out first." Catching him off guard, or so she assumed, she easily wrenched her arm free and snatched Lulu from Lisa. She headed toward the French doors leading to the backyard with Lisa hot on her tail, rattling off a million reasons why she didn't need to worry about Lulu's more basic needs at the moment.

Turning, she gave Lisa a meaningful stare. "I insist. I'm already asking a lot from you."

Lisa might not have completely understood what she was trying to say, but she backed off. "Ooookay."

Sylvie stepped outside, set Lulu on the ground and searched the dark for Burke and Isabella. She heard nothing, and it was too dark to see. After turning to make sure Miko was still inside and out of earshot, she whispered, "I'll leave the door unlocked, but I'm not staying here. Miko is inside. He's insisting on taking me with him. If I try to leave, you'll have nowhere to go."

"Dammit." The male voice came from a nearby bush.

She stepped closer to the source of the voice. "There's nothing I can do. I have to think of your safety first. With me gone, he'll have no reason to come back here. You can hide in the basement. There are a couple of bedrooms down there. No windows. It'll be perfect." If she hadn't been so upset at the moment, torn between her new and unexplored feelings for Miko and her loyalty to Burke, the fact that she was whispering to an evergreen might have been funny.

"It's okay," Burke said, stepping out from behind the bush. He pulled her into an embrace that felt so warm and wonderful she never wanted to leave. She held him tightly, wishing she could literally crawl into his skin and fuse with him forever. He stroked his flattened hand down her hair. "It's okay. I know what you're feeling, what you're struggling with. It's the way it's supposed to be. It will get easier. When I'm gone."

"Gone?" She tipped her head to look at his face. When he didn't meet her gaze, her heart grew as heavy as a bus. It sank to her gut. "Gone!" He was going to leave? Forever? No. Not forever. "No, this is just goodbye for now. See you later."

"Go to your Master. You'll be safer with him." He gently pushed her away.

Tears burning her eyes, she backed from him, snatched up Lulu and went inside, making sure to leave the door unlocked.

What a strong and sweet man. He'd pushed her away for her own good, for her protection. She knew that. It didn't make her feel any better about leaving him, but it sure did make her respect for him swell to enormous proportions.

Her heart heavy, she turned to Lisa, handed her Lulu and went to Miko. "I'm ready now. Let's go."

Miko took her hand in his and led her outside to his waiting car.

* * *

Battling the most unpleasant emotion he'd felt in a long time, Burke stood in the shadow of a tree and watched Sylvie leave with Miko. It wasn't jealousy. He was sure of it. He could feel nothing but joy for Sylvie. She'd found her second Master. That could mean completion, the Binding, if it weren't for the fact that he was a ranking *Excoluni* officer. No, this pain was more a sense of loss and frustration. The Binding could not be completed until the true murderer had been found and his name was cleared.

He knew the agony would grow. He'd be compelled to go to her, to find her. It would be difficult to fight the compulsion. But he had to think of Sylvie first. Miko would protect her from the killer. He would provide for her.

"I can't believe you sent her away," Isabella said, stepping up beside him just as Sylvie's friend cut the lights in the living room and, with dog in tow, left the room. "I know that had to hurt."

"It's for the best."

"You're going to suffer."

"So be it. There wasn't another option." He reached for the door.

"How will you keep from going after her?"

"I don't know." He turned the handle, motioning for Isabella to follow him into the house. "Let's get inside before the sun rises or none of that'll matter."

NINE

Miko couldn't believe he'd found her, his *Origo* Sylvie. Safe. She was safe. Unfortunately, the fever her nearness spiked wouldn't allow him to relax, even though daybreak was mere minutes away.

He knew he wouldn't be able to sleep until he'd had his fill of her, regardless of how weary and tired he was.

He hadn't believed what he'd seen back at the bar. Until he'd felt the symbol rise on his inner arm, he'd always believed *Origo*s were the stuff of legend. He'd never seen one. Never read of one. It was one of those things that had been passed from generation to generation by word of mouth. No one actually knew anymore if it was based on truth or fiction.

Except now he knew for certain.

He wondered how much his mate understood. He wondered if she'd found her other Master. If she had, her Master would follow her, search for her. If the legends were true, her Master would be powerless to stop himself.

He peered at her after parking the car in his garage. She was sitting silent, her hands clasped together in her lap, her expression glum.

She needed gentle reassurance. Patience and understanding. The fire burning through his veins would make it hard for him to be patient, but he would try his best.

He had been put through the most rigorous *Excoluni* training. It tried a man's self control and strength on every level. Yet, he suspected it would be nothing compared to the challenge of resisting the urge to take Sylvie before she was ready.

A Master serves his submissive first. Her needs must come before his own. Always.

Those words had meant a great deal to him. He remembered them whenever he took a new submissive to his dungeon. But now their meaning took on a new importance. They were more than polite reminders. They were the key to his sanity.

He shut off the car and gave her one last look. She was staring down at her hands. Still. She hadn't moved since they'd left her friend's house. "Are you sure you aren't hurt?"

"I'm fine. Just… very tired." She gave him an empty smile.

Guilt pricked him. He should wait, let her rest. Tomorrow night would be soon enough. "Remain here. I'll get the door for you."

She sat obediently and waited for him to walk around to the passenger side and open her door. And she politely thanked him when he offered her a hand as she exited the vehicle. He was overjoyed when she left her tiny hand in his as they walked into the house.

"This way. You may sleep in the guestroom tonight."

She gave him a slightly brighter smile. "Thanks."

It nearly killed him but he allowed himself the pleasure of only a small kiss on her forehead before leaving her. Even that brief contact of his mouth to her skin left his cock painfully erect and his balls heavy.

The needs of a submissive must always come before the needs of her Master.

"Goodnight, Miko," she said, meeting his gaze for the first time since they'd left the bar.

He mentally reached for her mind, to psychically send her soothing thoughts. What he found, however, as he gently prodded her mind had the opposite effect on him.

She had found her other Master.

He was Langton. The murderer.

"Rest," he heard himself murmur. "We will talk later."

* * *

Sylvie woke up some untold hours later. She felt better, although she wasn't exactly in the mood to sing a cheery tune.

Miko, being the thoughtful guy he'd revealed himself to be last night, seemed to have anticipated her every need. Her room was warm, her bed comfy. And there was a tray sitting on the nightstand with a pot of piping hot coffee and a dish covered with a metal lid to keep the food warm. She salivated at the scent of bacon but made herself wait to eat until after she downed her first cup of coffee.

It was positively delicious, better than the stuff she paid a small fortune for occasionally at the local coffee shop. Sigh. And sigh.

She could get used to this treatment.

She wondered how Burke and Isabella were doing. Had they been able to sneak into Lisa's house? Were they safe?

The phone sitting on the nightstand on the other side of her bed jangled. She set her coffee cup down and scooted across the bed, tipping the receiver to peer at the caller ID.

Lisa.

She scooped up the receiver and answered, "Hello?"

"Hey. Just calling to make sure you're okay. We didn't get to talk much last night."

"I'm a little better. I think I slept a week. What time is it?" Sylvie asked, searching the room for a clock.

"It's almost five."

"Five? Holy crap. Five at night?" She emptied her coffee cup in a series of frantic gulps and refilled it. "Did you talk to the detective?"

"Yeah. He said you can open up tomorrow."

"Excellent. I can't afford to stay closed any longer than necessary. I'm in deep shit."

"I told you I'd help --"

"No," she interrupted before her friend offered yet again to bail her out of financial trouble. Living in poverty sucked. Using people you loved sucked even more. She had nightmares about her past, about being homeless and scared and cold. But she wouldn't stoop to taking money from her friends. No way. "I told you I won't take a loan I can't pay back."

Her friend's sigh sounded as tired as Sylvie felt. "Can you get to the bar tomorrow?"

"I don't see why not."

"Okay. Call me if you need me."

"Will do. Thanks."

"Gotta go. Bye."

Sylvie hung up the phone and devoured the absolutely delicious breakfast Miko had left for her. Cheese omelet, bacon, sausage, fruit salad. The man was a god, although the hearty eating was not going to do her figure any favors.

Stuffed to the point of shame, she took care of some personal issues in the attached bathroom then poked around the closet to see if he'd been so kind as to whip up a new wardrobe for her while she was sleeping.

Good-golly, he had.

I'm in love.

Yes, it was a little shallow falling in instant love with a man who had magically produced some food and clothing, especially after saying farewell -- temporarily or not -- to Burke last night. But she'd been stressed lately. She was due for some shallow indulgence.

Okay, maybe her justifications were a little lame.

Actually, she'd thought long and hard about this whole thing last night, or rather this morning. She'd laid in bed, her eyes closed, her thoughts her only company. And she'd worked through some things.

She missed Burke, no doubt about it. A part of her physically ached after leaving him last night. That pain hadn't eased even a tiny bit, and she figured it probably wouldn't until they were together again. But pain in any form was an old friend to her in some ways. It never left her, not as long as she could remember. So, it was pathetic, but the pain of leaving Burke added a little to the already enormous burden she carted around every day. Like a dull throbbing headache. She just kind of got used to it and moved on. Always had to keep going. That was life.

Whether she was truly ready to accept it or not, Miko was a part of her life too. He might be a virtual stranger to her now, but deep down inside she knew he was destined to become an important part of her future, as big a part as Burke. Eventually they would all be together. It was just a matter of time.

She was ready. Ready to face Miko. To face the hunger that had been plain in his eyes last night. He'd been kind by denying himself last night, kind and patient. She knew he wouldn't be able to resist today.

She knew something else as well. She knew she'd want him as much as he'd want her. Regardless of any preconceived notions of what love and relationships she'd had for the first twenty-something years of her life, she'd accepted the fact that these men did something to her that no human ever would. And she decided to allow herself to embrace it. She wouldn't fight the overwhelming desire any longer.

They needed each other. All three of them. They would not be complete until their circle had been closed. There was no reason to be scared or guilty. Despite what she'd grown up believing, wanting, needing -- even loving -- two men was possible. She could do it. There was room in her heart for both Miko and Burke.

Perhaps she would love them differently. She didn't know yet. But she knew for a fact she would love them with everything she was.

She passed up the tailored blouses, slacks and skirts and went to the lingerie. A short black sheer nightgown caught her eye. It was uber-sexy in an understated, sophisticated way. As she expected, it fit her perfectly, covered everything it needed to while enhancing what it should. It was the outfit to greet her new Master in.

If she was going to spend the rest of her life as a submissive to two absolutely drool-worthy vampires, she was going to do it whole-heartedly. And with style.

Was there any other way? Really?

At the faint metallic sound of the doorknob rattling, she lowered herself to her knees, rested her hands on her thighs and waited. He was coming to her. She hoped he would be pleased.

Her heart racing, she kept her gaze lowered and watched a set of well-shod feet step inside and pause. Did all vampires have a thing for expensive shoes?

Silent, he pushed the door closed, walked to her and stopped.

She wasn't sure if he expected her to look up at him or not. She took a chance and glanced up.

He was looking down upon her intently. He nodded. "I see your other Master has taught you well."

"He hasn't had much of a chance, really. We were together for such a short time before we were separated."

"How long?"

"Less than two days."

"I will keep that in mind." He circled her and she felt her face flush with excitement and embarrassment. The sheer material didn't hide much, and she'd never felt particularly comfortable with her body.

"The clothing suits you perfectly. You look lovely." His voice was rich and warm and comforting.

Some of her self-consciousness faded. The heat gathering in her belly didn't though. If anything, his sweet compliment cranked it up a notch or two. "Thank you." The sight of him in his black trousers and unbuttoned white shirt cranked it up another six or seven.

He was in some ways very different from Burke. But in other ways he was similar. He was every bit as handsome. Every bit as muscular. Every bit as sexy. How was it that she'd been chosen to be with two absolutely gorgeous men?

"Do you miss your Master?"

She hadn't expected that question. Not now. Not when they were about to… do whatever they were about to do. She tipped her head up again and looked him in the eye.

"I suspect I know your answer but I want to hear you say it," he said.

"Yes. I do miss him. Even though we were together for such a short time, there was something there. A connection. It was very strong -- is very strong."

He nodded. "It's something only an *Origo* and her Masters can know. How quickly and intensely the bonds form."

"Does it bother you? That I miss him?"

"No. It is as it should be. We are three parts of one. Burke, you and me." He took her hand in his and gently pulled, urging her to her feet. When she stood, he ran his fingertip along the lace trim at the nightgown's plunging neckline. "I feel the ache of his absence too. It's more compelling than I expected it to be. Complicates things a bit." He licked his lips.

How would he taste? Would the first kiss be as sweet as Burke's? Would he kiss her roughly, his tongue darting in and out of her mouth, his lips firm? Or would the kiss be soft and sensuous? Staring at his mouth, she murmured, "How?"

He pushed one narrow strap off her shoulder. Her breath caught in her throat as he lowered his head. "I want to feed from you. I need to feed from you. But I can't." He nipped her skin and she flinched at the sting. "I have to resist. I can have you in all ways but that. Without the Binding complete, I can't take even a taste of your essence. Yet that is the one thing I will be compelled to do. The hunger is the worst kind of agony." He nipped again, this time lower on her shoulder. "I am sworn to bring him to justice. If he is executed for murder, I will never be able to feed from you. And the hunger will only grow and grow." As if to illustrate or make his point, he dragged his tongue down the side of her neck. She was instantly coated in goose bumps.

She closed her eyes. This man had barely touched her. A couple of nips, a lick. Yet the moment was soooo erotic. It was difficult to remain standing, to remain still.

Her arms hung at her sides, her hands balled into tight fists. Her knees felt a little lose and wobbly. These vampires sure did know how to tease a girl. She both appreciated that fact and hated it.

He raised his head and met her gaze. "You feel our hunger, don't you?"

She nodded. There was a burning in her gut. It wasn't so bad she couldn't stand it but it was there. She expected it was a hundred times worse for them.

He grasped her chin and stared into her eyes. She knew what would happen if she looked deep into the darkness. As expected, her pussy spasmed. Her nipples hardened. Her breathing grew shallow. Her blood sizzled in her veins.

She wanted him. She wanted him now. Her Master.

She whimpered. A gush of hot juices seeped from her pussy. "Miko."

"Come. I will take you to my dungeon." He brushed his mouth over hers, the brief contact making her lightheaded. More. She wanted a lot more. He was a cruel Master. A cruel Master in the most delicious way.

He took her hand in his and led her out of the room, down the stairs and into a well-furnished bondage dungeon. As expected, the room was dimly lit. The walls were painted a deep red. The furnishings were all constructed of darkly-stained wood, polished to a rich gloss. Table. Kneeler. Swing. Various other pieces she couldn't name. They were both beautiful and intimidating at the same time.

"Do you like to feel powerless, at your Master's mercy?" he asked, looking at her as if he knew the answer already.

"Yes, Master."

He nodded. "Undress."

"Yes, Master." Her hands trembling a little, she lifted the nightgown over her head and handed it to him. Then she stepped out of the matching panties.

Fire in his eyes, he led her to an apparatus that looked like an upright cross attached to the front end of a narrow bench. There were ropes secured to either side of the cross. "Sit." He pointed at the bench. She sat with her back to the cross. "Now lean back."

She did as he asked, sitting back until the upper part of her spine rested against the center post of the cross. He walked around the back, lowered the crossbar, lifted her arms and tied her hands up over her head. The position made her breasts stand out. She felt sexy and powerless.

"Look at my sweet little *Origo*." He gave her a wicked smile. "You're wet." He secured two more ropes to the crossbar then stepped to one side and lifted one of her legs.

"Yes, Master."

He tied her leg up and out, one rope just above her knee, another at her ankle. Then he did the same thing with her other leg.

She was as open and exposed as she could be. She was hot. Trembling. Anxious to see what he'd do next. Her nerves were all on edge. Her muscles tight. Waves of hot wanting coursing through her body.

"Would you like me to fuck you, my pet?" In a blink, his clothes vanished. Everything.

His body was glorious. Perfectly proportioned. Thickly muscled.

"Yes. Please, Master. Fuck me."

He moved to the end of the bench and straddled it. "I don't believe you're ready yet." Moistening two of his fingers with his mouth, he sat. The head of his cock was inches from her pussy. Inches. Yet he was clearly not going to fuck her. Not yet.

She wanted to plead. She moaned instead.

He ran his damp fingers over her vulva, spreading her juices and his saliva up over her clit. "I never take a woman before she's ready."

How much readier could a girl be?

Her face flamed when he thumbed her clit. Her eyelids felt like there were lead weights tied to them. She let them fall closed and let the sensations he was stirring in her carry her away to a dark, secret place. A place where she could let herself go and just feel, explore, be.

Sliding two fingers into her pussy while continuing to stroke her clit, he murmured, "Just before a woman comes, there's this scent she gives off. It's the most wonderful fragrance. It drives me crazy."

His intimate strokes were driving her crazy. The way his fingers curled slightly so that his knuckles rubbed that very special place inside her. The way his strokes to her clit sent rhythmic pulses of heat through her body. The way his words stirred her wanting to even greater heights. "Oh God," she said on a sigh.

If he kept this up, she'd come within moments and it would be over. She didn't want that. Not yet. Not really. She wanted it to last and last. Even though her body was careening toward a quick and powerful release.

"Stop. Please," she begged. She wouldn't come without him inside her.

"Yes," he said, plunging his fingers into her one last time. "You're ready now."

She felt his fingertips digging into her hips as he lifted them. The large head of his cock prodded at her opening. In one swift thrust, he buried his thick cock inside her hot pussy. She moaned her gratitude and wrapped her fingers around the ropes securing her wrists.

Tightening her inner muscles to increase both their pleasures, she rocked her hips to meet each of his thrusts. He drove into her slowly, deliberately. He nearly pulled completely out before driving deep inside again. It was the most delicious fuck. Beyond words or thoughts.

Releasing her hips, he teased one of her breasts with one hand and stroked her already burning clit with the other.

This was more than a fuck. It was a complete joining. A fusing of minds and bodies and souls. For a split second, as her body trembled at the brink of completion, she felt his presence within her. He was there. Filling her. Claiming her. Putting his mark on her soul.

She belonged to Miko and Burke.

Orgasm came in a flash. It quaked every muscle in her body. She heard herself cry out but didn't feel herself speak. She heard him too, as he joined her in ecstasy.

He drove into her hard, pounding in and out of her spasming pussy. She tossed her head from side to side and rode the waves of bliss, wishing they'd never end.

But eventually, the pulses slowed. The sensations faded. He pulled out, untied her and held her gently in his arms.

She smiled against his chest and kissed his slick, smooth skin.

The man was a virtual stranger and yet she felt so special and treasured and secure. She didn't know if she'd ever get used to the feelings the two men stirred.

"Come now. It's time for us to decide what we should do about Burke." He helped her to her feet.

TEN

"What do you mean?" She twisted her body at the waist to look back over her shoulder.

"I want to see that you're comfortable first. Then we'll talk." He motioned for her to keep walking, upstairs, down the hall, back to her bedroom. "As much as I delight in the sight of you like this, I want you to be wearing something warmer. It's chilly. I don't want you to catch cold." While she stood staring at his back, wondering at exactly how he'd become such a thoughtful man, he searched her closet for what he considered appropriate clothing. He emerged smiling, a pair of knit jogging pants, a tank top and a matching jacket in his fists. "These will do." He handed them to her then settled in the huge cushy chair in the room's corner. With a sweep of his hands, he was magically dressed, wearing a snug T-shirt and a pair of black pants. He rested his elbows on the chair's arms and steepled his fingers under his chin.

She was acutely aware of his gaze on her as she dressed, even though she sensed his mind was somewhere far away. Yes, they'd just had the most mind-blowing sex a few minutes ago, and she was ready to go another round.

These vampires were turning her into a sex fiend and she was oh so grateful.

Once she had located some fresh panties and a bra, she donned her clothes and accepted his invitation to join him in the chair. It was nice sitting on his lap, being held so protectively. His arms were strong and sure. His touch soft and firm at the same time. He pulled her against him, until her side pressed up against his scrumptious chest. Her head decided it needed a shoulder to rest on.

She let loose with a genuine sigh of contentment.

"I'm facing a difficult situation here. I have to choose. Between my career and my sanity." Miko's voice was thick and heavy. It rumbled through her body like a low voltage electric current.

She didn't want to seem flip, but she knew which choice she'd make. In a heartbeat. Then again, she'd never had her dream career, the one she'd always thought she would have when she grew up. What kind of choice would she make if she had?

She tipped her head to study Miko's profile. He had a strong forehead and chin. A long, narrow aristocratic nose and a perfect mouth. He was a delight to look at.

"I've wanted to be an officer of the *Excoluni* for as long as I can remember. My father retired from the force years ago but I remember being a kid, having a father I was so damn proud of. He was the best." He breathed in for the first time since she'd sat on his lap. His chest rose then fell when the air left his lungs in a huff. He shook his head. "I can kiss my career goodbye if I help Langton."

"But what if he didn't do it?" she whispered, sensing the frustration and turmoil Miko was struggling with.

His gaze met hers. It was probing. Intense. "You're saying he's innocent so I'll help him."

"No, I'm saying it because I believe it's the truth."

His eyebrows dropped to their lowest point. "You don't know the details of the case --"

"True, but you have to admit I share a very unique and personal bond with the man. I would know if he was the killer.

I'm sure I would. He didn't kill those people. The man in my bar, in Carpe Nocturne. He didn't kill the others either. I believe what he said, that he was at the wrong place at the wrong time." When Miko didn't respond, she added, "He's trying to find the real killer so he can clear his name."

Miko shifted his gaze away from her again and nodded slowly. He pressed an index finger to his lower lip. "What has he found out?"

She couldn't help staring at his mouth as she answered, "Not much of anything that I'm aware of. The only connection he saw between the people was the setting -- the bars. Outside of that, he couldn't find anything tying the victims together." She hesitated. Should she tell him more? Would it put Burke at risk? Or help Miko see Burke didn't know the victims? She had to take the chance. "That's why he'd been spending nights in bars. He was hoping to be at the right place at the right time."

Again, Miko's eyebrows dropped. His tongue slipped between his lips and left a dab of moisture on them before disappearing back inside his mouth again. He caught his lower lip with his teeth. "He hasn't told you everything. He hasn't told you that all the victims share a connection to him, a vague one, perhaps. But a connection."

Whatever she was about to say flew from her head like a caged bird let loose. No, Burke wouldn't have kept something that important from her. "Uh… what kind of connection?"

Miko gently lifted her off his lap and stood. He turned, gripped her shoulders in his fists and stared down into her eyes for what felt like an eternity. The silence was heavy. She dropped her gaze but he caught her chin in his hand and lifted it until she looked at his face again.

"I commend your loyalty. It's unfortunate that your Master has put you in this position. This isn't the way it should be." His eyes softened as they swept over her face.

Despite the fact that his warm expression was doing all kinds of pleasant things to her insides, she sharpened her gaze. "I believe Burke," she said crisply. "I believe in his innocence." She needed to convince Miko. She needed him on their team.

"The first victim was the nephew of a gentleman Langton was in negotiations with," he barked. When she stumbled backward out of reflex, he caught her wrists and held them until she steadied herself. In a lower voice he said, "I apologize." He shook his head. "Dammit, I want him to be innocent as much as you do. But it's hard to ignore the evidence."

"What evidence? So, the first victim was related to some guy Burke was doing business with? What does that prove?"

"The deal fell through and a few nights later, the man's nephew was found slaughtered. What would you think if you were investigating the case?"

"And you assumed Burke did it? For what reason? Revenge?"

He crossed his thick arms over his broad chest. The position made him look big and strong and a little intimidating. Rigid and determined.

How would she ever change his mind?

"That deal would've made him billions of dollars. I've seen people kill for less."

"I can't believe Burke would kill out of revenge. Or for money. What about the other victims? How many have there been? The others can't be close relatives of business associates too."

"There have been four murders so far. The second one was also related to an individual Burke had had business dealings with, a cousin."

Did Burke know this? Had he kept the facts from her? Shit. She was starting to feel like she was losing ground, not gaining it. She mentally scrambled for a foothold. "But didn't Burke live in Europe somewhere? And weren't the murders here in the United States?"

"They've all been here, in the Detroit area, yes. Then again, so was Burke. The coincidences are compelling."

"And all of the victims were related to someone Burke has done business with? What about the third one?" she asked with a sinking feeling. She didn't want to doubt Burke's innocence, but the coincidences were stacking up. The mountain they created was a smidge condemning.

"Yes, all three were related to someone Burke has had difficulties doing business with. We're still working on the connection with the fourth victim, but I'm sure we'll find something."

She nodded, appreciating why the *Excoluni* had narrowed their focus to only Burke. The victims hadn't been chosen randomly. They were loosely linked to Burke through business associates, which meant the real killer had to know more than a little about his business activities. That had to narrow the field to a few people, in addition to Burke himself. "How many other people would know about Burke's business dealings?"

"Not many. He keeps his personal and professional business to himself. I'm sure you've noticed that about him already. To my knowledge, he's never employed a large staff."

One person sprang to mind, a person who was close enough to know details about his activities. And one who had confessed to being blamed for the murders. It was hard picturing Isabella as the kind of individual who'd gouge out an innocent man's eyes, but she supposed it was possible. "What about his friend Isabella?"

"We've thought of her, but there's no obvious motive, and without some kind of evidence linking her to the crimes, we have no reason to suspect her. Unlike Langton, she wasn't in town at the time of the first murder. She has a solid alibi."

"Then she isn't wanted by the police?"

"Not for murder. Only for aiding and abetting."

Obviously, proving Burke's innocence wasn't going to be easy. "Did he have any enemies? People he owes money to? People who felt they'd been screwed in business? People who were jealous?" She had an equally hard time picturing Burke being anything but fair in business transactions, but she'd long ago accepted that people sometimes saw things in very twisted ways. Perhaps someone felt they'd been cheated and decided to seek revenge on Burke?

"He has no enemies, at least none that we've been able to identify."

She slumped into the chair, rested her elbows on her knees and dropped her chin onto her fists. "But doesn't it seem too obvious for an intelligent guy like Burke to risk killing relatives of his business associates? Wouldn't he know that sooner or later the connection would be discovered?"

"In a way, yes. Then again, the victims weren't sons or daughters. They were nephews and nieces. Cousins. More distantly related. We felt he chose those individuals for that reason, to put some distance between himself and the victims."

She looked Miko in the eyes. She wasn't going to change his mind. "You're convinced he's guilty."

He studied her for a moment. His gaze was warm and yet intense and assessing at the same time. "I have to accept the facts."

"Where does that leave us?"

He sighed. "At an impasse, I'm afraid."

"Then what's the point of this conversation?"

"I wanted the chance to explain why I have to find Burke… and why I have to turn him in."

* * *

In all his many centuries of life, Miko had never been in a more frustrating position. Why did he, a sworn officer of the *Excoluni*, have to end up in a *Triumvirate* with Burke Langton, a convicted killer? If it hadn't been so physically painful, it would've been funny. He'd always been able to appreciate irony.

Not in this case.

The disappointment and frustration he'd seen in Sylvie's eyes only amplified his agony. Like his mate, he ached for their circle to be complete. They would never perform the Binding. They would never be whole.

Worse yet, the guilt of keeping one very significant piece of information from Sylvie was sitting heavy on his shoulders.

He had to tell his brother about Sylvie, and about her second Master. Because he was an officer first, he had to take himself off the case. He could not fulfill his obligations. And he would take Sylvie with him, back home. Putting as much physical distance between them and Langton was the only chance they had of easing the burn of their wanting.

He discussed his plans with the security guard he kept on staff before leaving to meet his brother. He gave the guard a thorough description of Langton, cautioning him that there was a good chance Langton might try to sneak onto the property to see Sylvie. Then, only minutes after nightfall, he drove off to meet his brother at a nearby professional park, where they'd set up a temporary headquarters in an empty warehouse.

Hadrian scooped up a stack of papers, stuffed them in a dusty old book and greeted him with a wave of a hand, motioning toward the chair on the other side of his rusted metal desk. As he dropped the book into a desk drawer, he held a phone cradled between his shoulder and head. Miko could hear the tone of the caller's voice as he sat, but couldn't make out exactly what the caller was saying. It was the Director of *Excoluni* Operations.

Clearly, he wasn't happy with their lack of progress in Langton's case.

"Yes, sir," Hadrian said at last, meeting Miko's gaze. "We have a solid lead on Langton and I'm hoping to have him in custody tonight." After listening to a few more minutes of barking, Hadrian replaced the phone in the cradle. His shoulders dropped several inches. "We have to nail him tonight. Vrabec is about ready to haul both our asses back home and demote us."

"I know how to get Langton, although I don't know where he is."

Hadrian's left eyebrow rose. "What do you have?" He leaned back in his rickety metal chair, a piece of garbage they'd picked up for a song from a thrift store nearby. It creaked as his weight shifted.

"I have his *Origo*."

Hadrian's right eyebrow joined his left at the top of his forehead. "Is that so? Who is she?"

"The bar owner from Carpe Nocturne. Remember the blonde?"

"The one who's your...? Wait a minute!" Hadrian shot forward. "You're the second Master in his *Triumvirate*? Langton's? That woman was his --"

"*Origo*. Yes."

"And yours?" he asked. His gaze dropped to the desk drawer for a split second before rising again.

Miko nodded. "Yes, she's my *Origo*. Which is why I'm here today. I am asking officially to be reassigned. I cannot in good conscience complete my assigned task in this case."

"Have you... completed the *Iugum*?"

"No, of course not. That would require Langton to be with us. I haven't seen him. Sylvie was abandoned when I found her."

"I see. Then, no. I cannot grant your request. You heard Vrabec. There isn't time to get another officer here. You'll have to stay and finish the job."

Miko shook his head. "You're making a mistake by keeping me here. I can't say what'll happen if Langton and I end up in the same room together, especially if Sylvie's with us."

"Then you'll just have to make sure that doesn't happen. Where's the woman now?"

"At my house."

"Good. We'll use her as bait to get that snake Langton to crawl out from whatever hole he's hiding in."

"How? He knows I won't hurt her."

"He knows you're her second Master?"

"Yes."

"Then she'll need to be moved. So that he won't be able to count on your protection." He crossed his arms over his chest and tapped on his lower lip with an index finger. He'd always done that when he was thinking, even as a kid.

Miko knew the instant his brother had a plan in place.

Hadrian smiled. "I know exactly what we're going to do."

ELEVEN

Sylvie hadn't gotten completely over her frustration with Miko by the next evening. He'd taken her to some empty apartment on the other side of town and left her there, with a single suitcase of clothes. He left her alone for a full twenty-four hours. With nothing but a few frozen Lean Cuisines in the freezer, a few bottles of her favorite cola, a half-gallon of Moose Tracks... and four blank white walls.

Twenty-four hours was a long time to stew and worry and think. To fume and rant about men and their controlling ways. To work herself up to a healthy rage about their inability to see what was most important in life.

Not to mention to try every window and door in the place to see if she could get out.

No such luck. He'd locked her up like an animal! Grrr!

Although she did have to admit after about twelve hours, she'd simmered down. The urge to pound some sense into the vampire had eased... somewhat. For one thing, it simply took too much out of her to remain pissed off that long. And second, she understood the position Miko was in. He had to do what he had to do and clearly his personal situations had to take a backseat to his professional obligations. While she didn't appreciate being locked up, he'd sort of explained the reason for it. She was in danger, and he didn't want her going to Carpe Nocturne. She guessed he was afraid of coming to check on her too often, in case the killer was following him.

Okay, so if they thought Burke was the killer, why, oh why did everyone think he was after her? Clearly they knew something she did not.

Knowing Miko couldn't come to her during the daylight hours, she'd forced herself to sleep then. When she awoke at dusk, she showered and put on fresh clothes. She nuked a frozen dinner and ate it. Wiped out the rest of the ice cream. Then, she returned to her spot in the one and only piece of furniture in the place, an old recliner sitting next to the living room window, and sat. She stared out the window, watching the cars roll by, wishing someone would come to see her. About a half hour into her second staring-out-the-window session of the night, she perked up when she saw what looked like Miko's car drive by.

A few minutes later, the doorknob rattled and she heard the jingle of keys outside.

She stood up and faced the door, not sure if she should give Miko a friendly smile or a mean-eyed glower. As the door swung open, she went for a calm and sedate semi-smile.

He nudged the door open with a knee and picked up the grocery bags he'd evidently set on the floor in order to free his hands to unlock the door. "Sylvie, I'm very sorry it's taking so long." He kicked the door shut behind him and carried the bags to the kitchen. "I brought a peace offering. You don't deserve to be locked up like this," he added as he started unloading the groceries from the bags. More frozen dinners. Some fruit. Some snacks.

She snatched up a bag of corn chips and ripped it open, popping a cheese flavored chip into her mouth. "If that's the way you feel, then why can't you let me go?" she asked as she chewed. "I'm not a two year old. I can take care of myself."

"You don't know who you're dealing with." He shook his head then turned to put a fresh half gallon of ice cream in the freezer.

She had to smile at his back for having thought to bring more of her favorite dessert, even if it wasn't going to do her thighs any good. She stuffed her hand back into the chip bag and pulled out another chip.

"It shouldn't be much longer," he added as he shut the freezer door. "I'm hoping we'll catch Langton tonight."

"But what makes you think he can hurt me? Frankly, I don't believe it's possible. If he's the killer, I don't think I'm the next victim."

"I can't talk about this. I've told you everything I can right now."

She crossed her arms over her chest. Ooh, this was making her mad. She had a nightclub to run! She had bills to pay! And she was sick and tired of being a pawn in someone else's game. "Which is nothing," she spat. "I'm weary of this. I need to open my club, before I lose it to the bank."

Miko set the packages of food he was holding on the counter and reached for her. She lunged backward, scrambling to get away before he caught her. The vampire vibe would render her brainless within a second if he touched her. As it was, with him standing so close, it was getting harder and harder to keep her wits about her.

It was so not fair that those two vampires gave off some energy or hormone or whatever that made her dumb and horny in no time flat. Even as she was trying get away from him, she was thinking about how she'd get him out of his clothes.

She was a slave to her hormones.

She had a new appreciation of what male humans dealt with, especially teenage males. She'd heard more than one man say he thought about sex constantly when he was a teenager. Now she was in the same boat, particularly when she was in the same room with Miko or Burke. The minute they were near, her mind dropped from important stuff and settled into the Lust Zone.

Was there a cure?

Miko's lowered eyebrows and thinned mouth said everything his words didn't. "Sylvie. Come here."

She knew she was acting like a crazy woman, staggering away from Miko the way she was. But she needed space. The urges inside her were becoming overwhelming already. Whether it was the firm tone of his voice, or the way his eyes twinkled when he looked at her, or the fact that she'd been away from him for over twenty-four hours, she couldn't say. All she knew was she wanted him. In a bad way. Her anger at him for locking her up like a naughty kid was all but forgotten.

It shouldn't be that easy! She'd wanted him to suffer for it.

She met his gaze and her will crumbled like warm feta cheese. "Yes, Master."

He ran his hands down her arms then held her hands in his. His thumbs tickled the backs of her hands. His gaze caught hers and held it captive. "Not that I feel I should explain this to you, but I want you to know I'm acting in your best interest. I will not allow you to walk into a dangerous situation blindly. I can't take that kind of risk. It is true, as your Master, Langton would not harm you. However, I still have reason to believe you could be in danger."

She heard the conviction in his voice, saw the concern in his eyes, and had to accept he was genuinely worried. It had been a long, long time since anyone had cared so much about what happened to her.

Why did the movies portray vampires as terrible beings with no hearts, no souls? Clearly both men had hearts if they were that caring. She'd seen human males show less concern for their wives and girlfriends, now that she thought about it.

"I want you to understand how grave this situation is," he said, still holding her hands. "You may not even be safe here, which is why we have several undercover officers watching the apartment around the clock. I will not let anything happen to you. But you should still do your part. You must stay alert. And stay away from the window. I don't want anyone to see you." He released her hands. His shoulder brushed hers as he walked past her toward the window. He pulled the shades closed then turned to face her again. "I promise this will all be over soon and you'll be free to go wherever you wish."

She stared into his eyes for a while then dropped her gaze to her hands, which were clasped together in front of her. There were so many questions buzzing around in her head, like a swarm of houseflies. But one question stuck out from the others. It demanded an answer. "I need to know… exactly what happens to us if Burke is executed? Because of this strange bond, I'm afraid…" She let the rest of her words trail off. How to put into words the terror she felt at even the thought of losing Burke forever? Her eyes started burning and she blinked to ease the sting.

Miko sighed, took two long strides to reach her then pulled her into a tight embrace. One of his arms circled her back while his other hand stroked her hair. She wrapped her arms around his waist and practically melted into him. He smelled so good, like fresh spring air. He was warm and strong, his voice soothing. The total effect was heating her insides to a pleasant simmer.

She tipped her head up to look at his face. He was gazing down at her. His mouth pulled into a gentle smile when their eyes met. Her breath caught in her throat.

"I'm not sure what to expect. I hope we won't have to find out firsthand."

Her mood launched into the stratosphere. "Does that mean you're going to help Burke?"

"Not exactly."

That brought her spirits back to earth in a hurry. She was nearly motion sick from how fast they fell. "Oh." She let her forehead rest against his chest.

"I must do my job to the best of my ability. New information I've discovered has raised doubts about whether Langton is the murderer, which is why I haven't stopped searching for the truth, whatever it might be." He gently lifted her chin until she was looking him in the eye again. "I've never sent an innocent man to the executioner, no matter what kind of pressure I felt from my superiors."

"You're being pressured?"

"It's part of the job."

"In other words, if Burke is innocent, you'll find the real killer, but if he's guilty you won't stand in the way. He'll pay for his crimes."

Miko nodded. "No matter what the consequences to us. The law must come first."

That was all the reassurance she could ask for. Miko would find the real killer. It would be only a matter of time before they were all three together. Complete. And the aching would ease.

She decided to show her gratitude to her Master in the way she knew best. She spread her fingers wide, tangling them in his hair and pulled on the back of his head until his mouth met hers. The kiss was consuming and passionate. Her tongue parried with his in a fierce battle as their bodies melded together.

One instant, she was clothed and the next completely nude. The material of his shirt rasped against her nipples and they hardened into tight peaks.

Now on fire with raw, urgent lust, she moaned into their joined mouths and swayed backward. Still, he didn't let up. While his tongue and lips did magical things to her mouth, his hands explored her body. Her neck, her breasts, her stomach.

Breaking the kiss, he scooped her into his arms and turned. In a snap, the empty room was filled with bondage furniture. He carried her to a kneeler and set her down. "I will not see you again until we have caught the killer."

While positioning herself on the kneeler so she was facing Miko, she swallowed a plea that he reconsider that unwise and extremely selfish move and nodded. "I understand."

Had he no idea how much she hated being separated from him?

He smiled at her. "You please me. In so many ways. It makes me want to please you in return." While she watched in awe, he pulled his shirt over his head. He'd obviously done that for her benefit, knowing how much she enjoyed watching him move. His arms, shoulders, chest. Otherwise he would've snapped his fingers like he had the last time.

The skin of his upper body was deeply tanned and smooth, with a narrow line of hair running from his bellybutton down to the waistband of his pants, where it disappeared underneath. She knew where that sexy line led and was salivating at the thought that she'd soon be feeling his cock gliding in and out of her.

"Would you like to suck my cock?" he asked as he unzipped his pants and slowly pushed them down over his hips. His thighs were thick and muscular, also tanned and smooth-skinned like a body builder's. His body was like a work of art.

She nodded. She wasn't the most skilled at giving head, but she knew sucking him would drive him crazy. Considering he was having that effect on her, just by looking at her like he might jump on her and tear her up in the next instant, she felt compelled to give a little in return. She could be submissive and still take some initiative in the bedroom… or the dungeon for that matter.

Her pussy tingled as she watched him remove the final barrier between her eyes and his cock, a pair of snug black briefs. He kicked them off and stepped closer to her. His cock stood straight out, its ruddy tip mere inches from her mouth. But before she took him inside, she tipped her head and gave her Master a flirtatious smile.

His eyes widened to the size of silver dollars. And then, as she gripped his erection in her fist and swirled her tongue around the head, they narrowed to slits.

Oh yes, it was fun to be naughty.

He dug his blunt-nailed fingertips into her shoulders when she opened her mouth wide and took him in as deep as her overactive gag reflex would allow. She used her hand and mouth in unison, moving forward and back in a slow but steady pace. If his sighs and groans were any indication, he was fully appreciating every lick and suck.

Meanwhile, her body was heating up like a blast furnace. Her heart was pounding so hard she could feel it knocking at her ribcage. Air rushed in and out of her lungs in short, staccato gasps and her muscles were starting to tremble. Heat had pooled deep inside, where it churned and simmered and boiled. Her pussy was empty. She wanted him inside her so much it hurt.

She couldn't say who was in worse shape -- Miko or her -- when he jerked back, pulling his cock from her mouth.

He looked at her with fierce eyes then motioned behind her. "Do you like to be spanked, kitten?"

Truth be told, she had no idea whether she liked being spanked. At the moment, it sounded damn good. She responded with a, "Yes, Master," then turned around and leaned her upper body over the support. Kneeling with her ass in the air, she felt alive and completely at her Master's mercy. It was sexy beyond words.

He stroked her ass first with firm hands. His fingertips slipped between her ass cheeks and teased her anus before gliding up higher to tickle the small of her back. "You are so obedient and trusting. I hadn't expected that from you, honestly. I thought you'd be more resistant."

"Me too," she managed to mutter. The things that man's hands could do to her!

"Spread your knees apart." He used his foot to push at her inner thigh. She shifted positions slightly, spreading her legs as far as she could. "Oh yes." His voice was closer now, maybe six inches from her right shoulder. Little tingles and tickles danced up her spine. "I can smell how much you want me," he whispered. "That is the most delicious scent in the world." He audibly inhaled. "I can't get enough."

She shuddered. Her pussy clenched tightly around burning emptiness.

He pulled her ass cheeks apart. "I want you more than anything."

Take me.

"I want to fuck you until you lack the strength to remain kneeling, until every muscle in your body is quivering and your brain has shut down and your insides are all twisted and looped around themselves. And then I want to fuck you again. This hunger. It won't go away. It's getting stronger and stronger. I don't know how much longer I can deny myself."

"Don't."

"You don't understand. If I lose complete control, I'll bite you. I can't do that. Not yet."

She twisted her upper body to look at him. He was holding a whip in his fist. The long leather straps cascaded down over his forearm. Her gaze locked on that whip for a few stuttering heartbeats before climbing north, to his face.

"Does this scare you?" he asked, lifting the whip.

She watched him comb his long, tapered fingers through the leather straps. "A little."

"Usually the anticipation of the pain is worse than the reality of it. I'm not just talking about in a dungeon, either."

"Yes."

"It's normal to be anxious. That's what gets the blood pumping, the endorphins rushing. That can be good or bad. In this case, it's very good. I want to build expectation." He pulled his fingers through the straps again. Then he gave his wrist a quick flick, sending them flying toward her fanny, they struck with a quick and light snap. The pain followed, a dozen little stings.

She gasped and tensed the muscles of her back.

"Oh yes, very nice. Look how you've raised your ass. You want another? Perhaps a little harder this time?"

The pain from the first strike was already fading. She nodded and stared at his hand, waiting for that quick motion again.

One side of his mouth lifted into a crooked smile. He shook his head. "No, this time I don't want you to watch. Turn around." He motioned with an index finger. "It'll be even more of a surprise if you can't see."

What a delightfully naughty game he played! Trembling now from head to toe, she turned and leaned over the kneeler's center support. She felt every tiny gust of air, heard every breath she took in. Her mouth still tasted of his kiss.

A whoosh of air hit her backside and she flinched, expecting to feel the bite of the whip but it didn't come. Her heart was pounding out a wild conga beat now, and she was tempted to turn around but before she could, the whip struck her ass. She jerked and yelped when the pain shot up her spine. She was shaking now, shaking and on fire and ready to collapse. Every nerve in her body was lit up. She felt like she was about to jump out of her skin.

A third strike landed on her other buttock, sending yet another spike of pain blazing up to her brain. This time she cried out, "Ow!" She was lost to the world, to everything but what was happening inside her.

She felt him kissing her burning flesh, stroking her sopping pussy. His hair tickled her skin, giving her a healthy dose of goose bumps. She shivered, even though she was so hot she was sweating.

"Enough." He walked around the kneeler and stopped directly in front of her. "I know you hunger for more pain but you're not ready. Not yet." He helped her stand up and wobble to a sex swing. She leaned back and waited as he strapped her into it, tied her knees out to the sides and wrists up over her head. The skin of her ass still stung but the burn only added to the already overwhelming mix of sensations charging through her system.

"Have you ever fucked in a swing before?"

"No, Master."

His smile promised her the kinds of delights she'd only dreamed about until recently, and she briefly reflected on how much things had changed over the past several nights. It was so cliché, but she knew her life would never be the same again. Burke and Miko had set her life on an entirely new and thrilling course.

Still smiling, Miko gripped the straps rising from either side of her hips and pulled the swing toward him until the head of his erect cock was prodding her pussy.

Just a little more. A few inches and he'd be buried deep inside.

He gave the straps a swift yank and they were joined completely. His cock slid deep inside. Simultaneously, she moaned and he groaned. Then he set about driving her absolutely insane by alternatively pushing her away and pulling her closer.

Tied as she was, she could do nothing but drop her head back and enjoy the ride. And oh what a ride it was! She was weightless, completely under Miko's expert control and out of her mind with lust. With each rock back and forth, she was brought closer and closer to climax. Tension wound through her body, pulling muscles into tight knots. Heat spiraled out from her center, spreading up over her stomach and chest. Down to her toes.

And then he stopped, pulled out and dropped to his knees.

She knew what he was about to do, but it didn't stop her from giving a whimper of pleasure when he parted her labia and flicked his tongue over her clit.

The bliss was beyond words. He pushed two fingers into her pussy while continuing to stimulate her clit with his magical tongue. Climax came swiftly. It was like a warm wave as it rushed over her body, carrying away all the tension his sweet tormenting had sparked. The spasms hadn't yet eased when he stood up and resumed fucking her. The added sensation of his intimate strokes in and out made her climax last for what felt like an eternity. She blinked open her eyes mere moments before he reached climax. And then, as she watched, the beautiful man making love to her changed into a hideous beast. No sooner did she gasp in surprise than he was back to Miko, the handsome man. He staggered as he pulled out of her and gave her a sated smile.

Had she just imagined that change?

He must've realized something was wrong because his expression sobered. He tipped his head and gave her a questioning look. "Is something wrong, kitten?"

She was still tingling all over and warm from Miko's thorough lovemaking, but the horror of what she'd seen was sending chills down her spine. "I... I think I saw something."

He nodded and silently freed her from her bindings. After helping her to her feet and magically producing a robe, which she promptly put on, he motioned for her to have a seat on a bench. "You know we are a magical people by now."

"Yes."

"What you see, in that brief moment as I reach climax is what we call our Verus Corpus, True Body. Our magic is strong enough to maintain the form you see for all time, with the exception of a brief instant before we climax and at the time of our death. It is only then that you will see me as I truly am, as a monster to your eyes."

It was hard to wrap her mind around the fact that, in truth, she was making love to monsters. Great, tall beings with long, gangly limbs, skeletal bodies and gray-hued skin. Miko's face had changed too. It had reminded her of that hideous deep-sea fish. The one with the blunt-nosed face and mouth full of long, needle-like teeth.

The image was stuck there, in her head. It was frightening and repulsive and even knowing she didn't have to see it again, if she simply kept her eyes closed during that brief instant when the shroud fell away, she wasn't sure if she could get past it.

Monsters. Burke and Miko were truly monsters.

Since she'd first met Burke, she'd barely recognized the fact that they weren't human. She was slowly accepting the fact that when either of them was around, her brain didn't function. There was some kind of invisible erotic bond between them and no matter what was going on, in the world, in her head, wherever, if one of them touched her, she was ready to go at it like rabbits.

And she'd become even more accepting of the perks of being with a man who could drum up a five-course meal or designer wardrobe at the snap of his fingers.

But this... this wasn't fun. It wasn't even mildly annoying. It was spooky.

She supposed she should've expected some kind of negative to the whole dating-a-vampire thing. Something that went beyond the difficulties of Burke having been wrongfully accused of committing a crime. Everyone who walked the earth had a good and a not-so-good side. Why should vampires be any exception?

She supposed it would take some time to accept what she'd seen today. She could tell by the kind warmth she saw in Miko's eyes that he was going to be his understanding self and give her some space.

The man was really a sweetheart. Sexy and commanding in the bedroom yet sincere and kind outside. Perhaps it wouldn't take as long as she thought to get over that scare.

He snapped his fingers and the furniture changed into cozy, upholstered pieces. "I'm sorry I didn't do this earlier. I hadn't had the time to prepare the apartment for you, hadn't expected to have you stay this long." He swept his arm in a wide arc, motioning to the furniture in the room like a model in a game show. "How's this? Better?"

"How about some books? If I'm going to be stuck here all by my lonesome for God knows how long, I sure would like something to make the time go by. Oh, and a nice, cushy bed to sleep in too."

He snapped his fingers again, and one wall of the living room was covered with bookcases. "How's that?"

"Better. But can you tell me why can't you stay here with me? Why do you have to stay away?"

He glanced toward the window and pursed his lips. "Because if I stay, we'll never catch the killer." He looked reluctant as he stepped closer and took her hands in his. And she admitted, she felt a little uncomfortable, having not gotten over the shock of discovering her hunky vamp turned into a hideous monster when they fucked. But she stayed put and gazed into his eyes as he kissed each of her fingertips. "Patience, kitten. When this is all over, we'll be together."

"What about my bills? My club?"

"They are all being taken care of."

"I don't accept charity."

"It's not charity. Consider it a loan if you like. I know how much your business means to you and I wouldn't want it to suffer. By staying here, you're helping me catch the killer. I think that entitles you to something. Wouldn't you say?" he asked, giving her a teasing, sparkly-eyed look.

"I suppose so," she said, not exactly sold on his reasoning, but figuring she'd go with the flow. Sooner or later, if things didn't change, she'd lose her patience. For now, she was willing to wait. "Hurry. Please."

"I will." After giving the back of her hand one lingering kiss, he bent, looking all noble and dashing, like a prince, and carried himself with long, purposeful strides to the door. "We will see each other very soon."

"I hope so," she whispered as she watched him leave.

TWELVE

It wouldn't be long now. He'd finally solved the puzzle, found the missing piece, discovered why his prior attempts to raise his beloved had failed. It had taken him a while.

He now knew what blood he needed, or more specifically whose. A bound *Origo*. That complicated matters a bit, since there was only one *Origo* he personally knew. And she hadn't yet been bound to her Masters. Plus, there was the minor complication regarding what her death would do to her Masters. But he couldn't think of that now. Not with the hunger inside him burning so agonizingly. He needed his beloved. He'd lived without her for too long. The end would have to justify the means.

Unfortunately, he was going to have to do something to help move things along for the *Origo* and her Masters. It wouldn't be easy, considering everything, but he needed them to complete the *Iugum*. And he needed them to complete the *Iugum* before sunrise.

He'd suffered long enough.

* * *

"Sylvie's in danger." Burke dropped the newspaper on the floor and charged for the door, knocking Isabella's hand away when she reached for him.

"Wait!" she shouted to his back. "How do you know this isn't a trap?"

He stopped, turned and nodded. "I don't know that. It could be a trap. But the bottom line is she's not with Dvorak anymore, and if she's not with him then she's vulnerable."

"You're overreacting. Think about it. There's been nothing for nights. No murders. And you never did have any proof that she was the murderer's next victim. Maybe he's left town to track down the next victim? Maybe he's dead. Who knows?"

"Yeah, you could be right. But I can't stand the thought of Sylvie not being with one of us. Do you know what her death would mean to us? What the hell is Dvorak thinking by leaving her alone like that?"

"Exactly!" Isabella said, lifting a hand. "What is he thinking? And why is this in the newspaper? It rings of a setup. They're trying to trap you, use Sylvie to coax you out of hiding. It's all too convenient."

"Fine. So that just means I'll have to be ready for them." He scooped up the paper. "I need to find that ass, Dvorak, and find out where they have her."

"You're being stupid."

"No, I'm doing what needs to be done to protect my *Origo*. If something happens to her…"

"Hey, Dvorak isn't going to want anything to happen to her either. Bound or not, there's a connection between the three of you already. It's just not quite as deep yet. He'll still suffer if she's harmed."

"Unless he can't help it. Unless he can't protect her." He pointed at the article. "Do I need to read this to you again? According to this article, Dvorak's been taken off the case. I need to get to him before he's reassigned and find out what's happened."

Isabella frowned and shook her head. She grumbled something under her breath as she walked past him to the door of their temporary sanctuary, an abandoned store in a strip mall, and headed outside. "I know I'm going to regret this. Let's go," she said on a sigh.

Burke followed her to the rusted pile of bolts they'd bought off of a punk for a couple hundred dollars and they headed to Dvorak's place first. He'd spent the past few nights going back and forth between local nightclubs and Dvorak's house, unable to resist the temptation to try to get a peek at Sylvie. It had been several nights now since he'd seen her. He'd thought the pain of being separated from her would've eased with the passage of time, but it hadn't. It had grown steadily worse. It was now a fierce, excruciating agony, a cramping in his gut and heaviness in his chest that was making it hard for him to think, to function.

Isabella was probably right. This was a trap. But he was in such misery now, he didn't give a damn. If he could just see her. Touch her.

"What're you going to do?" Isabella asked once he'd cut the car's engine.

"I'm going to knock on the door and ask him where she is and what the hell he thinks he's doing leaving her unprotected. That's what I'm going to do. And if he's lucky, I won't kick his ass before I leave."

"This isn't going to be pretty." Isabella followed him up the front walk.

"Yeah, but at least he's been pulled off the case. I doubt Hadrian expected me to come knocking on his brother's door, so there won't be a trap set here. They're probably waiting wherever they've hidden Sylvie. Dammit, I wish they'd catch the bastard who's really committing the murders."

"You and me both."

He rang the bell. Within seconds, he saw a shadow pass across the window. He readied himself for a battle and, senses alert, took a step back from the door. "Watch my back," he whispered.

"Got it covered," Isabella answered.

Miko looked like he'd seen Dracula himself when he opened the front door. "What the hell are you doing on my porch?"

Burke didn't give him time to react. He charged at him like a pissed off rhino, shoving him back until they were both in his living room. Burke held Miko pinned against the wall. Their noses were nearly touching.

He could smell Sylvie on his skin. In agony, he dragged in several deep breaths. "Where is she? And what the hell do you think you're doing abandoning her with no protection?" he demanded on a growl. He had to give Dvorak credit. For a guy pinned against a wall by a vampire who could rip him like tissue paper, he was calm, icy cool.

Miko lifted his chin and glared. "What the fuck are you talking about? She's safe."

"If she's not with you and she's not with me, she's not safe."

One side of Miko's mouth curled into a cocky smile. Damn, he wanted to smack that fucking grin off Dvorak's face. "You've lost it, friend," Miko said.

"No, but I will lose it if you don't tell me where she is. Right now." He punctuated the last two words with a hard shake of the bastard's shoulders. "There's a fucking killer out there."

"Yeah. Why don't you tell me about him? Huh?"

"No, why don't you take a ride with us? Since you don't seem to be in a hurry to get rid of me. Is Hadrian on his way in with a fucking army?"

Miko shrugged. "No."

"Yeah. And I'm the Pope. Let's go." He took Miko by the shirt and shoved him toward the door.

"Where are we going?" Miko asked as he strolled through the doorway.

"How about we do a double date?"

"Okay. This'll be the last date you'll be on for a long, long time, once my brother gets his hands on you."

"We'll see about that."

* * *

Someone was at the front door. Sylvie knew that someone was not just any someone either. This someone was special. This someone was making her hot and they hadn't even opened the door yet.

Curious. Very, very curious, indeed.

Neither Burke nor Miko had stirred this kind of reaction in her, at least not without touching her. Was something going on that she didn't understand? Had the bond between Miko and her somehow strengthened after their last lovemaking?

Expecting to find Miko on the other side of the door, she hurried to it, but it swung open before she reached the middle of the living room.

She halted mid-step and nearly fell over.

Burke and Miko. Together. No wonder she was on fire!

She did something she hadn't done in many years -- she squealed like a little girl who'd just been told she could shop till she dropped at Toys-R-Us. Then she hurled herself at the guys, determined to show them both exactly how thrilled she was to see them.

Miko slammed the door at the precise instant Sylvie landed in Burke's arms.

She cupped Burke's gorgeous face in her hands. "Are you okay? Is everything all right? I'm so glad to see you." She didn't wait for him to respond before peering at Miko. "You came here together?"

"He sort of kidnapped me," Miko admitted, sounding sheepish. His face was the shade of a ripe tomato.

She adored that face.

Compelled to soothe Miko's bruised ego, she took one of his hands in hers and squeezed it. She met his gaze. He didn't just look embarrassed. He also looked troubled. Deep furrows cut across his forehead. "What's wrong?" she asked.

"Nothing."

She tipped her head back to look at Burke's face. Unlike Miko, Burke was smiling.

"I think he's just sore because I'm not in handcuffs yet," Burke said. "He expected Hadrian and the gang to be here."

"Operative word -- yet," Miko murmured.

"Come on, boys. I might've been dreaming, but I was hoping we could all make nice." She gave Burke another squeeze around the waist then released him and turned to Miko. "I know what you're worried about, but I promise, Burke's innocent."

Miko crossed two thick arms over his chest. The black shirt he was wearing now stretched taut over his muscles. Yummy! Her body decided it was party time, despite the serious subject matter of their discussion. "Doesn't matter. He's a convicted felon --"

"The so-called trial was a sham!" Burke barked back. "My court-appointed lawyer didn't know what the hell he was doing. Did he even graduate from law school, I wonder? Or did he buy a degree from www.degreesforsale.com?"

Miko shrugged. "I don't hire them."

Sylvie, who was so ready to jump both their bones, heaved the sigh of a woman who'd had enough testosterone. There was only one thing on her mind at the moment, and it had nothing to do with playing referee to bickering boys. The need to have them both naked and on top of her was almost beyond bearable.

Didn't they feel the same thing? That same desperate urge?

She glanced into Burke's eyes. Oh yes, he was feeling it. The holdout was Miko, no doubt because of his guilt.

A sassy thought whipped through her mind and she instantly reacted to it. This might be her only chance to have both Masters in the same room, especially if Miko continued to refuse to help Burke.

The agony of being apart from them would be eased, if only temporarily, if she could distract them from their differences for a little while. She was quite certain there was one way to would accomplish that. The average red-blooded American male forgot most everything when he was toe-to-toe with a naked woman. Why wouldn't two red-blooded vampires?

It was worth a try.

While Miko continued grumbling and Burke lobbed smart comebacks, she stripped nude. As she slowly peeled away one piece of clothing after another, the fire in their voices faded and the flames in their eyes flared.

Oh yes, it was working!

Both vampires were standing wide-eyed and gape-mouthed by the time she'd shed the last piece of clothing. Neither of them seemed to possess the mental capacity required to string together a sentence at the moment.

It was all good.

The two men looked at each other, seeming to be doing that male sizing-the-other-guy-up thing. The tension in the room was thick as liquid concrete. Sylvie stood her ground and waited.

"If we complete the *Iugum*, we're all fucked if you're executed," Miko said, as he pulled off his shirt.

"I know." Burke followed suit, kicking off his shoes and shucking his pullover. "This is why you have to help me. I'm innocent."

Miko was standing there, looking perplexed, his hands at the front snap of his pants.

Sylvie couldn't help noticing they weren't using magic to undress. Why?

Burke mirrored Miko's pose. "You and I both know there's no way we're going to leave here without completing the *Iugum*. Look at her! Just look!" Burke motioned toward Sylvie, whose face heated at the wild expression on his face.

Oh, who cared why? She dropped to her knees and lowered her head. "My Masters." She almost giggled when one of them growled.

"You did this on purpose."

It sure sounded like Miko's anger was losing steam.

"No... okay, maybe. But who could blame me? I couldn't fucking stand it anymore. I'd been away from her for too long. I was going nuts. Literally. But I'm innocent. I swear it. We'll complete the *Iugum* and then we'll find the real killer. You and me. Together. And you'll be a hero when it's all over, for finding the real killer and taking him down."

She trembled as she waited, her gaze on the floor. Her entire body was shaking with the anticipation of what was to come. She didn't know exactly what to expect. It wasn't every day that a girl did the We-gum or whatever it was called with two absolutely scrumptious, handsome, thoughtful, strong and sexy vampires.

Considering everything, she figured it was bound to be mind-blowing.

There was a long, drawn out moment of silence and she guessed Burke and Miko were giving each other another stare. She lifted her eyes to check.

Burke turned a second later and still half-dressed strode toward her. He stopped directly in front of her, effectively blocking her view of Miko. "You haven't had her and then lost her like I have. You don't know what it's like." He palmed her cheek and snapped his fingers. Once again, the room's furnishings changed. The bookshelves and comfy couches were gone and in their place were the assorted wooden bondage structures. "You are my life," he said, reaching down and palming her cheek. He took one of her hands in his and pulled her to her feet while tracing her lips with his thumb. "I had no idea how hard it would be to stay away. How excruciating. I need you, Sylvie. I must have you."

She smiled and nodded, grateful for his gentle touch and the warmth she found in his eyes. "I want to be with you and Miko. Together. For always. It's been so difficult."

He pulled her into a tight embrace. One of his hands rested on her head while the other pressed on her lower back. She smiled, inhaling the scent she'd missed so much over the past few nights -- of Burke, of man and passion and crisp night air -- and wrapped her arms around his waist. Even with her eyes closed, she sensed Miko approaching. He was behind her now. Her spine tightened as little pleasant tingles raced up and down.

Miko kissed a path down the center of her back then gripped her buttocks in his hands. While she shuddered against Burke, at Miko's touch, she tipped her head up to beg for a kiss. Burke obliged without her having to ask. He slanted his mouth over hers and gave her a slow, sensual kiss that left her breathless and dizzy and aching for more.

Miko's touch became more bold. His fingers slid between her buttocks and teased her anus, her pussy. Slick juices pulsed from her vagina, coating the insides of her thighs. Her knees turned to molten marshmallow. She started sinking, relying entirely on

Miko and Burke to keep her from landing on the floor like a dropped sack of flour.

Burke swept her into his arms and carried her to a wooden table. He lowered her to the flat top, polished to a gloss. A set of four cuffs hung from long chains suspended from the ceiling.

With their help, she settled on her back. Burke kissed the breath right out of her then lifted her arms and secured them up high, over her head. As he stood beside her, Miko eased her knees apart. She could see the hunger on his face, in his eyes, as he looked down at her.

She was quite certain her heart was going to explode. Or plain stop working. One or the other.

Her head was spinning but she didn't want to close her eyes. Watching Miko and Burke move, their muscles ripple and bulge as they lifted their arms. It was mesmerizing.

Huge, happy sigh.

Miko lifted her ankles and pushed her feet back, forcing her to bend her knees. Now her pussy was open and fully exposed to him, and she couldn't be happier. Being the gentleman he was, Burke decided this was a good time to produce a vibrator and use it to tease her nipples. Little zaps shot through her body. Heat gathered between her legs. Tension coiled in her belly. She quivered and moaned.

"You don't know what you're asking us to do," Miko said, teasing her slit with a fingertip.

It wasn't easy, but she responded. "Yes. I do."

Miko took his hand away and she whimpered. "No, you really don't understand. To complete the *Iugum* would mean to bind us together. You will live as long as we do, but should any of us be killed -- executed -- the others will die too."

Despite the fog of desire clouding her judgment, she recognized how serious this Binding stuff was. She knew she had no business making a decision this weighty while tied up and on the verge of ecstasy, but the illogical part of her -- which happened to possess firm control of her at the moment -- demanded she complete the Binding as soon as possible.

A few years ago, she'd had meningitis. The pain in her head had been so horrific she'd begged the doctors to make the pain go away. Every second of pounding pain was like a lifetime of agony.

This was no different. With two of them there, together, the misery was amplified. The blood in her veins felt like acid. Her skin felt like it was on fire. She needed them to make it go away. She wanted to feel normal again. She wanted to be happy. She wanted to be happy with Miko and Burke. And she wanted to make them happy.

"I can't stand this anymore. Make it stop," she begged. She lifted her head and looked at Miko. "Please." When his gaze moved to the left, she turned her head to Burke. "I know I don't fully comprehend what this means, but I know I need to finish it. I need to be with you and Miko."

Burke nodded and stroked her cheek. Then he unfastened her wrists and together they walked to a low, narrow bench. He pushed her onto her knees and while she knelt before them, the two vampires undressed completely.

They were both gloriously built, their bodies like fine marble statues sculpted by the greatest master of all time. She was in awe of the fact that they would be hers, and only hers, forever. And she would be theirs.

What had she done to deserve such a wonderful gift?

Miko sat on the bench. His cock was erect, thick and long and hard. Her pussy throbbed at the thought that it would soon be buried deep inside her.

Burke, who stood beside her, handed her a tube of lubricating jelly and pointed at Miko.

She knew what he expected her to do. Still on her knees, she scooted closer. Then, with Burke behind her whispering sweet words of encouragement in her ear, she flipped the top off the lube, squeezed some of the cool jelly into her hand and closed her fingers around Miko's cock.

Miko audibly inhaled when she slid her hand down to the base and back up again, and Burke murmured, "That's it, baby. Oh yes."

Miko's face was flushing a deep crimson and his stomach muscles were tight, forming defined planes, cut horizontally by two lines and vertically straight down the middle. She'd always had an appreciation for the sight of a well-defined stomach. Miko's was as near to perfect as they came. Burke's was nearly as scrumptious.

Just because she had to, she stood up and traced the line of hair running from his bellybutton down to his cock. That was one of the sexiest parts of a man, that and his upper back. She had to swallow several times, the drool was coming fast and furious.

As she bent over, Burke caught her hips in his hands and started kissing her bottom. That inspired her to stay put right were she was and perhaps have some more fun with Miko's to-die-for bod. She continued pumping her hand up and down his cock while kissing and nibbling her way around the territory surrounding his genitals, upper legs, stomach. His skin was slightly salty but it smelled sweet. The combination of taste and scent, along with the tickly kisses Burke was planting all over her ass and lower back were enough to make her shiver with delight.

"In order to complete the *Iugum*, you must take us both at the same time," Burke murmured.

Two men at the same time? Was that even possible? She shuddered. Did that mean one of them would have to fuck her in the ass?

"We must both be inside you when we bite." Miko's eyelids lifted. His eyes shone with a strange golden glow, like a cat's that had been struck with a flashlight beam. "We are nearly ready for you now." He reached out and grabbed her shoulders.

Burke pushed her from behind, forcing her to turn to the side. "The lube."

She handed the tube of jelly to him and watched, mesmerized, as Burke dispensed some into her other hand. He pressed his palm against the back of her hand and he didn't remove it when she replaced her one hand with the other. His fingers twined between hers as she glided it up and down to spread the lube.

Miko visibly quivered. He dropped his head back, letting it rest against the wall behind him.

"Yes, love. That's it." Burke released her hand and guided her to turn to face him. His gaze locked with hers, he nodded. "Take him in your ass. All the way in."

The breath she'd been about to inhale lodged itself in her throat. She was really going to do this? Take two men at once?

Ohmygod!

She looked over her shoulder and reached behind her to hold Miko's cock. Then she shuffled backward, her legs wide, straddling Miko's legs and the bench, and positioned herself over his cock. It pressed at her perineum, and the skin burned fiercely, but she found comfort and encouragement in Burke's eyes. He held her at the waist and helped hold her weight as she slowly, painstakingly lowered herself a fraction of an inch at a time.

Miko's cock filled her ass and then some. A flash of liquid heat coursed through her body when she'd taken him in entirely, and she cried out. She needed Burke's cock.

Miko wrapped his arms around her and pulled until her back was resting against his chest. While she lay there, waiting and in sweet agony, he slowly rocked his hips. His cock moved inside her and she nearly came. The promise of ecstasy lingered just out of her reach.

"This is it, love. You'll have what you've ached for all this time. Your suffering will be over." Burke lifted her knees and positioned his cock at her vagina.

Miko pinched and pulled at her nipples, sending torrents of pleasure pain pulsing through her body.

"Please," she begged, her body about to go up in flames. "Now, Burke. Now!"

He smiled and slowly pushed his cock inside her.

"Oooohhhhh!"

The sensations were beyond words. The fullness in her ass and pussy, the crazy currents of energy charging through her system like bolts of electricity. The way everything seemed so much more intense -- touches were almost painful, sounds nearly loud enough to bust her eardrums, her vision crystal clear, despite the dim lighting.

Burke withdrew his penis and then thrust deep inside again, and Miko growled beneath her, his voice seeming to express what she felt. Her eyelids were too heavy to hold up and her eyes were blurry with tears. She closed them and let her head fall back onto Miko's shoulder. All she wanted to do was feel, to let the incredible sensations they were stirring in her body carry her far away.

They were both moving inside her now, and oh the joy! Burke stroked her clit, round and round, drawing slow circles over her sensitive flesh. Miko pinched and tugged at her nipples. Their cocks worked in unison, driving slowly in and out of her body until she was on the verge of climax.

She cried out. The sound was nearly deafening. The soles of her feet cramped as she climaxed. Her pussy and ass contracted around Miko and Burke's cocks in a swift rhythmic spasm.

Then she felt it, the sharp pain of their bites. But instead of stealing her pleasure, it increased it. She reached out blindly, grabbed Burke and dug her nails into his skin. Wave upon wave of wild erotic heat charged through her body like blasts from a blow torch. Still spasming from her climax, she trembled and clung to Burke, wishing the sensations would never ease, yet knowing she'd die if they didn't.

This was beyond anything she'd ever imagined. It was beyond comprehension. Beyond words. Beyond thought. It was both beautiful and horrifying at the same time. Erotic and terrifying.

When they stopped sucking, it all stopped. The pulsing heat. The spasms of her climax. She felt exhausted and shaky and muddle-headed. It took Herculean effort, but she managed to drag her eyelids up so she could look at Burke.

He was still inside her, but he'd stopped moving. He was gazing down at her with the sweetest, most peaceful expression.

She felt very much the same -- content. At last. Sated. At peace. Yes, she'd done the right thing.

He slowly withdrew from her before helping her off of Miko.

She was barely able to stand. Her knees were softer than ice cream left outside on a July afternoon. She stumbled, catching herself before she fell.

Miko cradled her to him, and with Burke beside her, he walked back to the bedroom and laid her down on the bed. And then, as she lay on her back, her body relaxing and her mind still, the two men settled on either side of her.

She was complete at last. Complete and content.

She hoped this feeling would last forever.

* * *

It was nearly finished. There was one more step to the *Iugum* and then Sylvie would be a fully bound *Origo*.

He would have to be patient a little longer. It was getting more and more difficult to wait, but some things couldn't be rushed. Soon he would have his love. Soon.

Making sure to remain in the shadows, he watched and waited.

THIRTEEN

Sylvie Durand woke up as the meat in a hunky, alpha vampire sandwich. She was still tingly, giddy and weak from their earlier lovemaking. A happy little tremble shook her body at the memory. She'd had two men at once. Two! Who would've ever thought it? Certainly not her.

To think it had all started just a few nights ago, after a man was murdered in her bar, Carpe Nocturne. Immediately after discovering the poor guy in her office, his blood drained from his body, she'd learned vampires were real -- gasp!

The shocking discoveries didn't end there. Next, she'd discovered she was some kind of mate (an *Origo*) to a pair of vampires -- another gasp! Burke Langton was a vampire on the run from the law for a series of brutal murders he didn't commit. And Miko Dvorak was an officer with a super-secret vampire police force.

And finally, she'd fairly quickly discovered that her libido had a mind of its own whenever her hunky vampires entered the room. Her body insisted she complete this bizarre Binding ritual -- called the *Iugum* -- that involved making love to both her vampire Masters at the same time. Last night, she buckled to the agony, which had taken the form of this awful pounding, burning pain that felt like a full-body toothache.

At least for now, the pain had eased. Sweet relief.

She stared at her first Master's handsome face, committing his features to memory. Burke Langton had the most delightful mouth this side of paradise. And he looked adorable when he was sleeping, sweet and sexy. His eyelashes were uber-long, the shade of coal. His cheekbones and jaw line hewn in hard angles. His skin was the deep olive tone that perfectly set off the deep ebony of his wavy hair.

A work of art.

Miko Dvorak, her second Master, was sleeping behind her. As he changed positions, spooning tightly against her back, his dick prodded her bottom. She was tempted to arch her back and welcome him inside. The only things stopping her were the bazillion questions running through her head, now that her brain was finally working again, and the absolute lack of energy making her feel like she'd swallowed an entire bottle of sleeping pills. When she lifted her arm to brush away a strand of hair hanging over her face, it felt like her limbs were carved out of solid concrete. Too much work. She let her arm drop back to the bed. It fell like a dead fish.

"We're not finished with the *Iugum* yet," Burke said, his eyes still closed.

"We're not?" She wasn't sure how she felt about that little tidbit of information. A part of her was relieved. She was not only uncertain of what she thought about this binding stuff but also feeling like something her neighbor's cat had dragged in. Now she had to wonder if it was because of her half-*Iugum*-ed state.

"We had to wait to finish," Miko added. "You must make the decision with a clear head, not while in the midst of a Binding Fever."

Now, that was thought-provoking. She shifted positions, rolling onto her back to allow her to see both men. "Binding Fever? That's what they call that agony? I swear, I thought I was going to die."

Both men gave her a sympathetic nod, reminding her of twin bobble head dolls. Hunky, handsome bobble head dolls.

"So, uh, do I dare ask? What's left?" she said when they didn't elaborate.

"We both fed from you, which is why you feel so tired and weak." Miko took one of her hands in his and stroked the back with his thumb. His touch was like feathers. Soft and teasing. Tormenting. "Now you must feed from us."

"Feed?" She knew she was scowling but she couldn't help it. "As in drink your blood?"

"Yes."

She shivered, and not because she was cold. She didn't eat rare meat because the sight of those bloody juices gave her a serious case of the squicks. How would she manage to consume blood? And not animal blood, but people blood? Vampire blood. Her throat constricted, her gag reflex threatening to kick in. "And if I don't?"

"You'll eventually grow stronger." Burke sat up and snapped his fingers. In the time it took to blink an eye, he was fully dressed in a pair of black pants and a snug black T-shirt that was this close to being obscene it fit so perfectly.

"But the Fever will return eventually as well." Miko mirrored Burke's actions. Although he ended up in a pair of blue jeans, his shirt was identical to Burke's. And it looked just as good too. "I'd be willing to bet the Fever will be worse, now that we've fed from you."

"I'm thinking the same thing," Burke said.

Okay, she was getting the picture. Granted, earlier she'd said such noble things about wanting to be with these men forever, being willing to make whatever sacrifice was necessary to become one with them. They'd been heartfelt. She did want to be with Burke and Miko. But blood? They'd never mentioned her having to drink blood. Ew! And ew!

All this talk about the Binding raised a few questions. What exactly would happen after she drank their blood? What did this Binding mean?

Gosh, would she become a vampire? Would she be forced to keep a liquid diet for all eternity? Ack! Would she turn to dust if she went out in the sun?

As much as she adored Burke and Miko, she wasn't sure she was ready for such a huge change. She was suddenly very thankful they'd waited to complete the final step until after she'd had some time to think.

Yes, for an onlooker, it might seem a little late to be asking these questions. If she'd seen this in a movie or read it in a book, she would've been skeptical. But the pain had been so overwhelming, she hadn't been able to think of anything but finding relief. At the point when it had been the worst, there was no saying what kind of awful things she might have done to receive even a temporary break from the agony. Thankfully, she hadn't been forced to test herself. But, she could see how someone evil might use the pain -- or more specifically the promise of a cure -- to his advantage.

Miko's suggestion that the so-called Fever would return certainly didn't sit well with her. "Couldn't we settle for tomato juice instead?" she offered. "Is there a less permanent arrangement we can make? I need some time yet to figure this stuff out."

Both men shook their heads, grave expressions on their faces.

She heaved an intentionally loud and long sigh. "It was worth a try. Hey, how about some clothes for me too?"

Burke snapped her a cozy velour outfit and T-shirt then sat beside her and took her hand in his. "This isn't an insignificant decision, and although it's being made under some pressure, you need to think it through thoroughly. There are both benefits and drawbacks to being a bound *Origo*."

"And they are? Give me the bad stuff first. I'm the kind of girl who likes to hear the bad news before the good."

"The most significant drawback is if something happens to any one of us, then it happens to all of us," Miko explained.

That statement confused her. "In what way? If you get a toothache, then I will too?"

"In a matter of speaking, yes," Miko said. "If you are hurt somehow, then we will also feel your pain. If you are killed, we will die with you."

A huge glaring light bulb flipped on in her head. "And if Burke is executed for murder then I'll die too?" A second light blinked on. "And so will you."

Miko's expression darkened even more. "Yes."

"So why aren't you telling me this is a bad idea?"

"Because I can't influence your decision. It's not right... and I want to complete the *Iugum*," Miko admitted in a softer voice. His eyes were full of confusion and turmoil and a deep line cut between his eyebrows. "God help me, I want it more than anything."

She wanted something really bad too -- to touch him. She also longed to tell him she wouldn't go through with the *Iugum*. To save his life. But she knew she lacked the strength to resist.

Already, the hunger or fever or whatever was returning. Her blood felt hot as it pumped through her body. Like boiling acid. And little razor sharp spikes of awareness shot up and down her spine.

Her Masters were touching her. They were close. They both smelled wonderful, and oh boy, how they looked!

A lump had gathered in her throat. She swallowed hard to force it down and blinked away the stinging in her eyes. "You want to complete the Binding? Even if it means you might die?"

"We are your Masters, and no matter what you decide, we will remain your Masters." Burke cupped her chin and gazed deeply into her eyes, like he was trying to delve into her very soul. She both welcomed the erotic, unsettling probing and bristled against it. Could he see her secrets? Her darkest fears? "Don't let the worry of losing us sway you. We're not going anywhere."

Had she said she was worried? Maybe she hadn't, but it was something to think about. The whole death issue, of course, took precedence over any other concerns -- sunlight and diet, saying goodbye forever to her adorable, scrumptious vampires. She broke eye contact with Burke to look at Miko. "Will you help him? Will you help us find the real killer? Or do you still believe Burke's the murderer?"

Miko's gaze shifted to Burke then darted back to her. "I've begun to re-evaluate the evidence and there is the possibility that Burke is innocent."

Sylvie didn't hesitate to show Miko how happy she was to hear that. She threw herself at him and flung her arms around his neck. Luckily for her, even though she'd taken him by surprise, he was quick to recover -- as it seemed most vampires were. He stood quickly, holding Sylvie so that her toes barely skimmed the floor. She showered his face with sweet kisses in between thank yous.

But within seconds, each kiss started getting longer. And each thank you got quieter until eventually, something inside her snapped. She fell into full-blown lust mode and could think of nothing but how to cram her tongue down his throat.

Who needed to talk right now?

Miko kissed her back for a few minutes and then seemed to find his head -- the big one on top of his body. He gently pried her off and gave her a bleary-eyed smile. "We need to decide what we're doing before it's too late." His face was a deep scarlet, the shade of one of her favorite dresses.

Burke chuckled and she was tempted to give him a little taste of the medicine she'd just dosed to Miko. As if he'd read her mind, he sobered and crossed his arms over his nummy chest. "Miko's right. As I understand it, it is our legal -- not to mention moral -- responsibility to make sure you comprehend all the possible consequences for your decision before you do anything."

"Is that the lawyer in you talking? Or the man?"

"The man. I've never dealt with an *Origo*, in my fake law practice or otherwise." He winked. "Frankly, I'd always assumed they were legend. Little did I know." He chuckled again and he and Miko exchanged knowing glances. "I'm relieved to see that Miko's looking into the case against me, but you should still remember that there's always the possibility that one of us could be harmed or killed. And since we'll be psychically bound for all time, we will always be vulnerable."

"So what's the good news? I've heard the bad. Or haven't I heard it all?"

"That's about it. I think." Burke looked to Miko for affirmation, which Miko delivered with a nod.

"I haven't read much about *Origos*," Miko said. "But I think that's it."

"Good news?" she prodded.

"The good news is you'll be immortal," Burke said with a smile. Dimples poked into his cheeks on either side of his mouth. Dimples! She was inspired to heave another sigh, this one of pure bliss.

Then she remembered what he'd said. Immortal? Like live forever? Did that mean she would be a vampire? Would have to become nocturnal and drink blood? What kind of job could she hold down if she had to work from sundown to sunrise? "How exactly does that immortal stuff work? Will I have to avoid sunlight, sleep during the day, and snack on vagabonds?"

Burke shook his head. "No. You won't turn into a vampire. You will remain human. Consume food. Drink whatever you like. But you will not age and you will not get sick."

Now that was good news indeed. Not age? She'd be perpetually thirty-something? She'd never go through menopause? Or get arthritis or osteoporosis? She'd never get thick like her grandmother? Or start growing hair in places she didn't want to think about?

Forever thirty. Hmmm… Yes, that was one heck of a benefit. The cons were pretty bad, but the pros sure did sound great.

"And my fountain of youth is within you two?" she asked, growing giddy. "I'll just need to do this once? Drink your blood?"

"Only once," Burke said.

"And only a small bit. A drop or two," Miko added.

Only a drop or two? That didn't sound so bad. That wasn't more than a lick. Not a gulp. She could handle that.

So, the decision was either face certain death as a human or unlikely death as an immortal? Not much to think about when it was put that way.

"So, do I need to sign some kind of disclaimer first?"

Both men gave her the kind of smile a guy might give his doctor upon hearing he won't have his testicles removed sans anesthetic.

"There is no paper to sign," Burke said, positioning himself directly in front of her. "At least none that I know of. Since I don't think either of us has witnessed the *Iugum*," he added, glancing Miko's way, "we'll have to wing it."

Miko nodded and stood beside Burke. "I don't think there's any official forms we must submit to the United Magical Nations."

"Okay." She eyed their necks. Really, did they expect her to literally bite them? It wasn't like her teeth were made for that... well, kinda. She'd consumed her share of meat in her day, but never raw. Her chompers were strong. She'd practiced good oral hygiene all her life. "Uh, what's next then?" Her stomach did this funny little squirmy, flip-floppy thing. Blood. Ick.

The two guys looked at each other then simultaneously said, "I'll do it. Oh."

Do what? she wondered.

Miko pointed. "The wrist, you think?"

"Yes, that makes the most sense," Burke agreed. "I can bite yours and then my own."

"No, no. I'll bite yours and then my own."

They were fighting over who gets to bite whom? Would she ever understand vampires?

"Here's a thought. Why don't you bite yourselves?"

They looked at her like she'd grown two heads.

Why was that such a bad suggestion? It wasn't like they had a thing about biting themselves. They'd each offered to do as much a second earlier... granted, after biting the other guy.

Finally, Burke grumbled, "Fine," and chomped on his wrist.

That was so not an appetizing sight. "Yikes! Could've given me some warning," Sylvie murmured as she struggled not to gag.

She made sure to keep her gaze focused on a much more pleasant sight -- the brown shag carpet -- while Miko took care of his arm. *Breathe in through the nose. Out. In. Out. How will I get through this?*

Within seconds, there were two wrists hovering under her nose, both with two tiny tooth pricks in them and a ribbon of blood running from the holes.

The blood was a deep crimson and she'd swear it looked thicker than normal, not that she'd spent hours and hours staring at blood. It kind of oozed from the wounds, sluggish like molasses dripping from an overturned spoon. Her stomach did another flip-flop, this time threatening to lurch up into her throat.

If only there were an easier way for a girl to gain eternal youth, like sell her soul to the devil.

She closed her eyes and tried to visualize something more appetizing, like a triple-fudge brownie sundae with all the fixings. Oh yes, much better. Saliva collected under her tongue.

Her eyes still closed, she reached out, caught one hand in her fingers and pulled until it was up by her mouth. Then, with her thoughts on all things chocolate and good, she pressed her lips to the skin and slipped her tongue between them.

The taste was salty like seawater and bitter like coffee left out overnight. She fought the urge to vomit, pressed her mouth firmly to the arm, and sucked. The salty, thick liquid seeped into her mouth slowly, like a milkshake sucked through a skinny straw. When there was enough to swallow, she contracted her throat to force it down.

Her eyes watered.

She released the hand she'd been holding and reached blindly for the other one. Once she had a hold of it, she repeated the same process, breathing in through her nose in slow, deep breaths to counteract her gag reflex. This was one girl who'd never win *Fear Factor*. Heck, she got nauseated from watching the show.

After forcing down the second swallow of vampire blood, she released the other hand and blinked open her eyes.

When was it going to happen, whatever it was?

Sylvie felt nothing. Or rather nothing extraordinary, that would suggest she was now eternally thirty-something. There was no gripping pain or lights or ringing in the ears. Neither was there a huge surge in energy or sudden super-duper strength. She wondered if they'd done something wrong.

She shrugged. "Well, that was sort of anti-climactic. I don't feel any different. Did we goof something up?"

"Well, hell," Burke murmured.

Miko shrugged. "I doubt it."

"How can we test it?" she asked. "Anyone have a friend who's sick? They can sneeze on me."

Both men shook their heads. Burke was looking like he was deep in thought. "I think I'll call Isabella. She'll know if we did something wrong."

He had his phone in his fist in a snap, but before he'd punched a single number, she had gently plucked it from his grasp and was setting it on the nearest horizontal surface she found.

She was in the mood to celebrate -- *Origo* style.

FOURTEEN

Sylvie had just paid a visit to the fountain of youth. This was for real! She'd never have a saggy ass or boobs. No floppy arms. Or drooping chin.

And best of all -- no disease.

Burke was quick to catch on to her festive mood. He scooped her into his arms, spun her until she was dizzy and then carried her to the bed.

How she adored her vampires! She nuzzled his neck as he lowered her to the bed, inhaling his nummy bad boy vampire scent. He tugged her jacket's zipper down, pushed the garment's sides apart and tickled the inch of tummy exposed when the hem of her T-shirt inched north. A coat of goose bumps sprang out all over her upper body. Her nipples tightened to sensitive peaks, straining against the snug knit material of her shirt.

It did not surprise her to find Burke had failed to provide her with a bra when he'd snapped her into clothes. Not that she was complaining. Especially after he pinched her nipples through the thin cotton.

Sweet agony.

Smiling, she briefly wondered why Miko hadn't jumped into the action yet. But she quickly decided it wasn't worth worrying about. At the moment, nothing was worth worrying about.

It was time to just lie back and enjoy.

Burke slid his hands beneath her bottom, wedging his arms between the bed and her backside, and sliding them upward until he found the back of her knit pants. He tugged them down, over her buttocks, her legs, her feet. They went sailing across the room.

She giggled, realizing, of course, that as she'd expected she had no underwear on.

He grimaced. "What's so funny? You know what? You need to be spanked." As if to punish her, he sat on the bed, positioned her on her stomach, draped over his lap, and gave her fanny a light smack. The sound reached her ears a split second before the sting registered in her brain. She yelped, not so much because it hurt, but because it caught her by surprise. Then, because she liked it, she wagged her hips back and forth, an invitation for another.

He was quick to respond. The strike was as hard as the first one. But the next several became progressively softer until he was gently caressing her stinging flesh. His fingers slipped into the cleft between her buttocks, teasing her anus. Then, those naughty digits slid down lower, to tease her pussy and clit.

She wrapped her arms around his leg and gritted her teeth against a shudder. Burke knew exactly how to touch her, how hard to strike to produce just the right amount of pain to drive her crazy. And then how gently to touch her to drive her even more mad.

Warm wetness pulsed from her pussy to slick the insides of her thighs. She rocked her hips up and back, eager to rub away the wicked ache his tormenting was stirring between her legs. "Fuck me," she pleaded.

"Gladly." He eased her off his lap, undressed and then sat on the foot of the bed, coaxing her onto his lap. She knelt with her knees positioned on either side of his hips, her pussy hovering over his erect cock. He held it in his fist, pumping up and down until a pearl of precome collected on the tip.

Burke nibbled on the tickly spot just below her armpit, producing a quiver of pure, indulgent pleasure.

Miko came up behind her, pressing his stomach against her back, and sliding his arms around her sides until he had his hands closed over her breasts. She let her head fall back against his chest, closed her eyes, and surrendered to the powerful men stroking and kissing her to oblivion.

Life as an *Origo* was oh. So. Goooooooood.

Burke held her hips, supporting her weight as she slowly impaled herself on his thick cock. A moan rushed up her throat. With his penis buried deep inside, she wrapped her arms around his neck and slowly circled her hips like a belly dancer, grinding her slick folds against his pelvis. His fingers dug into her soft flesh. He dropped his head forward and nipped her collarbone, murmuring sweet promises against her warming skin.

Now, this was the way to spend an eternity! She had to be the luckiest woman alive. Once, she'd figured she'd never find the right man for her. Now, she had not only one Mr. Right, but two. And they were both so very right.

While Burke lifted her hips, pulling her up until only the tip of his thick erection remained inside, Miko kissed a searing path down her spine. Fingertips teased her anus. Burke's hips rocked upward, once again thrusting his penis deep inside her. Over and over he drove into her, and over and over she murmured, "Ohmygod, ohmygod!" Miko kissed and tickled and teased. Pulses of heat rushed through her body. Pounding, urgent desire drove her to the brink of release.

And just as she was about to soar over the crest, Miko caught her hips between his hands, pulled her roughly off Burke's cock, positioned her so that she was bent over Burke's lap and entered her from behind.

Oh yes, this two-guy thing was for her.

She rocked back and forth, slamming into Miko's groin, the sexy slap of her ass striking him adding yet another sensation to the flurry already driving her to madness. Her deep breaths became little panting gulps. Her heart pounded against her breastbone, and the telltale flush of heat swirled in her stomach.

"Yessssss!" she screamed, giving herself over to an intense orgasm. But before the delightful pulses of bliss had eased, a loud bang sounded at the door. Miko jerked away, spun around and snapped his fingers, instantly dressing himself and her.

"What the hell?" Visibly confused, Burke jumped to his feet. He snapped his fingers mid-stride as he raced to the door, magically donning a pair of jeans and a shirt. "What's going on? Hang on!" Just as he was about to reach the door, it flung open.

"Shit!" Miko cursed, lunging in front of Sylvie, who suddenly realized she was standing dazed and motionless as a deer caught in the headlights of an oncoming semi. He backstepped, taking her with him as a horde of men stormed into the room.

Although Miko's bulky bod blocked her view, the slamming and scuffling, shouting, crashing and thumping told her things were getting ugly fast. At the sound of Burke cussing, she tried to inch around Miko's right side to sneak a peek. Was he okay? What was going on?

Had Miko known what was about to happen? Had he intentionally stopped the Binding from working, so that they wouldn't die if Burke was killed?

Two men had Burke pinned to the floor, flat on his stomach. Because of the angle, she couldn't see his face, but what she could see sickened her. The two men were battering his head, shoulders and back with black metal rods.

He went completely still.

Was he dead? Oh God. Her insides went ice cold then blazing hot. Someone screamed, someone female.

Miko spun around and, sweeping her into an embrace, crushed her against him. It was then, as the shrieking grew muffled, that she realized it had been her. She clamped her eyes closed, wishing it was as easy to shut out the image of Burke lying still as death from her memory. She shuddered. Tears ran unchecked from her eyes, coursing down her cheeks and dripping from her chin.

"Excellent work, Miko," someone said.

Excellent work? She wanted to spit at whoever had said that. This wasn't good work. It was terrible. They'd just beaten an innocent man unconscious. A man she loved.

Unable to hold back the rage, flared hotter by the added hurt of knowing Miko had somehow contributed to what happened, she wrenched herself free from his embrace. "Bastards!" Spinning, she kicked the man closest to her. Her foot made contact with his knee and there was a satisfying crunch, but she didn't bother looking to see what -- if any -- injury she might have caused. At the moment, her focus was on Burke.

The two creeps who had beaten him senseless were now hauling him to his feet, but his head hung limply. His body flopped as they dragged him toward the door.

"Burke! Ohmygod!" It was hard, but she fought her way between several men to get to him. She caught his hand in hers and squeezed. *Be alive. Just be alive.* "Burke?"

Nothing. His hand was cool and lifeless in hers. His head remained slumped forward.

The men holding him yanked, forcing his hand from hers. Desperate, she lunged forward, to grab any part of him she might reach. Arm. Hand. Leg. Whatever. But a split second before she touched him, someone caught her from behind, jerked her arms back.

"Miko?" she screamed. "Ouch!"

Whoever had her was holding her tightly, to the point of pain. Panicking, she twisted her upper body, trying to see who was holding her. Whoever it was, he now had both wrists held in one steely fist, had wrapped an arm around her waist, and was rushing her toward the exit.

She just knew she didn't want to go outside with whoever was manhandling her. Frantic, she dug her heels in and fought to free her hands. Didn't help. She jerked and kicked. Nothing. She screamed and fought.

Despite her thrashing, she was forced outside and into a black car with tinted windows. Finally, while fighting for her life -- kicking, punching, clawing -- she caught sight of the man who'd smuggled her outside. She didn't recognize him.

"Why?" she whispered, breathless. "Where are you taking me?"

"Miko asked me to take you to his car so you wouldn't be hurt," the man responded calmly. "Sorry I had to be so rough, but you were fighting me, and I didn't want to take any chances you were going to get in the middle of something again. You got this close to having your skull crushed." He gave her a friendly, reassuring smile. "Miko'll be out as soon as we wrap things up inside." At the sound of a voice on his radio, the man shut the car door, turned and ran back toward the building.

A split second later, another man approached the vehicle. This one she recognized immediately. It was the man from the bar, the one who'd been there with Miko. She wished she could remember his name but she was drawing a blank.

He pulled open the door and motioned for her to follow him. "Something's happened. I need to protect you." When she hesitated, he added, "It's okay. Everything's going to be okay." He leaned forward and unfastened her seatbelt. "It's just a temporary thing, until we can sort out the facts."

A sickly chill swept through her body, followed by a wave of nausea. She wrapped her arms around herself to hold back the shudders wracking her body. "What happened? Is Burke okay? And Miko?"

"They're both fine. But there's been another threat on your life and Miko felt it would be better to get you out of here immediately." He led her to another car, identical to the one she'd been sitting in, opened a rear door for her and shut her in before taking the driver's seat. "We have another safe house not far from here. I'm going to drop you off there, and he'll follow as soon as he can." He started the car, and pulled away from the apartment building.

"Okay." She had a niggling feeling this man hadn't told her the whole truth, but she wasn't exactly in the position to demand any more information. She'd have to wait for Miko.

He'd get a good grilling. The way she saw it, things were looking really bad. For all of them. But especially for Burke.

The niggling feeling morphed into a serious case of the jitters when she noticed there were no handles to open the back doors. Locked in. Like a criminal.

"How far away is the safe house?"

Bringing the car to a stop in a parking lot, next to a big white van, her unofficial chauffeur twisted, giving her an empty smile she assumed was meant to reassure her. "Everything's going to be okay. Trust me."

* * *

Miko sensed something wasn't right about sixty seconds too late to do anything about it. He'd been too distracted by the chaos to keep a close eye on Sylvie, but now that the proverbial dust had settled, he could think of nothing but finding where she'd gone.

If she was hurt, he'd never forgive himself.

It had only taken a little over a half hour for Miko to put a stop to the senseless beating his fellow officers had launched on his bound mate, secure Burke, and take him down to a waiting vehicle for transport back to Burke's homeland in eastern Europe.

Miko still hadn't pieced together all the facts in Burke's murder case. But it would have to wait until he made sure Sylvie was okay.

It was too soon to panic. He didn't see Hadrian at the moment. He guessed his brother had probably just escorted her outside where she'd be safe.

If only he'd been able to protect her from the trauma of watching Burke's capture. There'd been no other way. The decisions he'd had to face. Impossible choices between love and duty. Heartrending.

Miko rushed out of the building, his gaze sweeping the scene outside as he ran. There were several unmarked *Excoluni* vehicles scattered about in the parking lot. He headed for the closest one, inhabited, as it turned out, by an old friend of his brother's, Tom Cizak.

"Have you seen a woman? About this tall with long blond hair?" he asked the officer.

"Yeah. She was a little shaken. Hadrian put her in his car, I think." He motioned to the car parked closest to the street.

Thank the gods. She was safe. The burning in Miko's gut eased. The fact that he'd reacted so strongly to her disappearance bothered him more than a little. He'd had no reason to suspect something bad had happened to her. She'd been surrounded by *Excoluni* officers he trusted with his life, not to mention his brother. Yet he'd been damn close to panicking. Why?

As he approached the vehicle, the driver's side door swung open and Hadrian stepped out. Brows lowered and mouth twisted in confusion, Miko's brother slammed the door shut. "What's up?"

Miko motioned to the car. "I just wanted to make sure Sylvie's okay. She was pretty upset."

Hadrian's brows scrunched even lower. "She's not with me. Petrov told me you asked him to take her to your car."

Now, that confused him because he did not remember saying any such thing. "Really?" He glanced over his shoulder at his car.

"Yeah. I was about to take her with me, but decided, since I had to go back to the station to make preparations for the prisoner, I'd better find someone else to babysit her. I didn't think twice about letting her go with him. Dyre Petrov has been a friend to both of us for years…"

"Sure. Okay." Ignoring his brother's continued reassurances, he turned, waved a farewell and headed for his car. His heart thudded heavily in his chest, a reassurance that she was probably still alive. At least for now.

He was overreacting. Hell, maybe he had told Petrov to take her to his car. Things had been so crazy, he'd probably shouted at least a half dozen different commands without even thinking about them. In a crisis, he'd learned to operate on auto-pilot. To act and react without thinking too much.

Approaching his car, he glanced up, catching the vehicle transporting Burke turning out of the parking lot, headed for the closest underground *Excoluni* facility, about an hour's drive away. Time was running out for Burke -- and possibly for both Miko and Sylvie too. The jury was out yet on whether they'd succeeded in completing the *Iugum*. Because he hadn't felt the effects of Burke's beating, he suspected they hadn't. But since Burke had not been killed, he couldn't be absolutely certain. Injuries were temporary, only slowing a vampire down a little. Within minutes, broken bones, stab wounds and ruptured organs could be healed. Perhaps that was why Burke's bound mates had not felt any pain from his injuries?

He almost hoped they hadn't completed the *Iugum*.

If he failed to clear Burke's name in time, and if they'd succeeded in completing the Binding, they'd all die. The clock was ticking. At most, he figured they had another twenty-four hours.

First things first, however. He couldn't concentrate on investigating the string of murder cases Burke had been suspected of until he knew for a fact that Sylvie was safe. Now within feet of his car, he ducked down to peer in the window.

Empty.

His heart skipped several beats before launching in a wild gallop.

Maybe she was lying down?

He jerked open the door and searched the front seats then did the same with the back.

Empty.

His knees wobbly, he sat in the car and depressed the call button on his radio. The little voice in his head had warned him something wasn't right. That nagging voice was now screaming. He called Hadrian, and Hadrian assured him Sylvie had to be okay. There'd probably just been a misunderstanding.

He could hear the guilt in Hadrian's voice.

Knowing his brother, he was blaming himself.

He placed a call to Petrov, who said he had indeed walked Sylvie to the car, but had been called away immediately afterward. He had no idea where she might have gone.

Had she simply taken a walk? By herself? In the dark? When she was worried about Burke?

He couldn't see that being the case, but just to make sure, he drove around the parking lot then circled around the block. It was a residential area. No convenience stores for her to duck into. No grocery stores.

Did she have a friend in the area?

He tried to recall their conversation as he'd driven her to the safe house. No, he was pretty sure she'd never been to this part of town. But desperate, he looped around several more blocks. When that turned up nothing, he called Hadrian to see if he'd learned anything yet.

Nothing, but he promised to keep trying. Miko could tell his brother was nearly as worried as he was.

Growing more desperate by the moment, he called Szader, the officer who was driving Burke's car. He heard Burke speaking in the background as they talked but couldn't make out his words. Next, he heard a lot of commotion, shouts, tires screeching. The tooth-jarring sound of metal striking metal at high speed, and then Burke's voice on the radio, "Where are you?"

Oh, shit.

He was not going to communicate with a wanted felon on the radio. A felon who'd just done something to an *Excoluni* officer.

What the hell was Burke Langton thinking?

FIFTEEN

What the hell had Miko been thinking? He'd let Sylvie out of his sight? Lost her!

Burke cussed under his breath for the desperate act he'd been forced to commit to get free -- he'd attacked an *Excoluni* officer. Shitpissfuck! Now he couldn't deny he was a felon.

But what choice had he been given? Sylvie was missing. He couldn't trust Miko like he thought. What if he'd been right all along in assuming the murderer had been after her? And what if the bastard had her right now?

If anything happened to her, he had no idea what he'd do.

He punched the vehicle's gas, speeding through a yellow traffic light. Most likely, Miko was still somewhere in the vicinity of the safe house, searching the streets for Sylvie. That's where he needed to head first.

He couldn't afford to keep this car for long, especially since he knew there was a GPS chip planted on the vehicle. At best, he figured he had an hour before someone with the *Excoluni* realized something was wrong. Sooner if the officer he'd bound and gagged somehow found a way to escape and phone in.

He glanced at the officer's radio, which he'd chosen to keep so he could monitor communication. It seemed, at the moment, no alarms had been sounded. Yet.

It took less than twenty minutes to return to the safe house -- luckily he hadn't been taken far before picking the handcuffs and convincing the *Excoluni* officer transporting him to pull over. The short drive, however, hadn't allowed him enough time to cool off. The minute he spotted Miko's car, slowly rolling down a residential street about a half mile from the safe house, a pulse of rage spiked in his gut.

He jerked the wheel, maneuvering the car into a tight one-eighty then pulled up behind Miko's vehicle. His mate's brake lights glowed red. Both vehicles' doors swung open simultaneously, and both men exited, charging at each other like pissed off bulls. Miko's face was nearly the same shade as his previously illuminated brake lights. The heat burning Burke's neck, ears and cheeks suggested his were equally inflamed.

Miko shot Burke death-daggers from his eyes. Burke returned them. "What the fuck!" they shouted in unison.

Burke then launched into a tirade about Miko's lack of testicles, and Miko came back with a rant about Burke's lack of a brain. Insults were traded... then shoves... then punches. Before long, they were both breathless and sore, battered and bruised. But at least the heat of their rage had been cooled.

Catching his breath, Burke clenched and released his bloodied fists. His knuckles cracked and popped, the pain just intense enough to make him grit his teeth.

He knew they'd both expected it to come to this. They had never been on the same team, yet they'd pretty much chosen to ignore it -- up until this point. Couldn't anymore. Miko was the law. He lived the law. And he lived by the law.

Burke, on the other hand, had once had a great deal of respect for the law, but not any longer. His esteem had disappeared when the law -- and the organizations representing it -- had turned against him, despite his innocence. Justice was a myth. When it came to crime and punishment, finding the guilty party wasn't as important as playing to the demands of politicians in the UMN. The *Excoluni* was a puppet organization.

The sad truth was it didn't matter whether he was innocent or not. A judge had determined he was. Some bastard who had only one priority -- winning his next term on the bench -- had determined what facts would be presented in his case. A lowly citizen of the UMN, given no *real* legal representation, was powerless to change the fictitious reality that power-hungry piece of shit had created.

It was amazing the way the truth could be stretched and reshaped by the manipulation of facts.

"What did you do to Szader?" Miko snapped.

"No need to get all pissy. He's still alive. I just bought myself a little time."

"I should take you in. You know that, don't you?"

"If you do, then Sylvie's as good as dead."

"You don't know shit. Dead? What makes you think she's in danger? She could have gone to a friend's --"

"You don't believe that any more than I do," Burke interrupted. Dvorak didn't honestly believe that, did he? "Come on. Use your fucking head. She would've left a note, a phone message, something to let us know where she was."

They traded more hostile glares. Miko was the first to break eye contact. He combed his fingers through his hair and dropped his gaze to the ground. "Yeah."

"I say it's time you made a choice."

Miko lifted his eyes and slowly nodded. "It's been a long time coming."

"You can't straddle the fence. Either you're with us, or you're with them."

Miko leaned back, resting his backside against his car. He toed a stone, sending it skipping across a puddle before landing with a plunk in a deeper patch of water a few feet away from the car Burke had stolen from Szader. "My career's been everything to me. My purpose. My life."

"Yeah, well, I learned a career isn't the solid foundation I once thought it was. It can drop out from under you at any time, and then you fall. Hard."

Still staring down, Miko simply nodded.

Burke sensed Miko's struggle, read it in his mate's set shoulders, dark expression and distant eyes. "You never know if or when something might happen. Relationships, people, they can be just as shaky and unreliable, I suppose. But they sure make for a more pleasant, more meaningful base. We might have a lot of differences between us, and maybe we'll never fully settle them. But we share a very powerful and unique bond."

Miko finally met his gaze. "Our love for Sylvie."

"Yeah."

Silence.

Burke pressed Miko, knowing his decision could very well determine how this whole thing ended for all three of them. "What's it going to be, Miko? Your ego? Pride? A career that could let you down tomorrow? Or us?"

"I've wanted to be an *Excoluni* officer for as long as I can remember. My father. My brother…"

"For some reason, I don't think it's as important to you as you think."

After another brief silence, Miko admitted, "You don't know. I don't know. Maybe."

"We're not going to save Sylvie if we don't work together. Working together means you're going to have to betray your *Excoluni* pals, the guys you've trusted and respected since your first day. Can you do it?"

"What about you? You're going to have to trust me. Fully."

"Not liking it, but that's the way it is."

Miko nodded. "That goes for me too."

"Let's see what we can do when we're truly playing on the same team."

"I say we go back to the safe house and see if we can find any clues. She didn't just vanish. There's got to be something."

"Good idea." Burke motioned to Miko's vehicle. "You drive."

* * *

After enduring a nerve-wracking ride in the backseat of an unmarked cop car like some common criminal – an unpleasant if not downright terrifying experience -- Sylvie was hardly relieved when she caught sight of their final destination. The words ghetto, slumlord, and dilapidated sprang to mind immediately.

Granted, she supposed it would be a little farfetched to expect a public safety organization -- human or otherwise -- to set her up in a five-star hotel. But still. Sheesh. They could do better than this place. Was it even safe?

She followed him into the ramshackle building with the boarded up windows, peeling paint and rotted front porch. The hinges groaned loudly when he pushed open the front door, revealing an interior as neglected as the exterior. He slammed the door closed behind them, eliciting a shudder, and motioned for her to continue straight ahead, through a living room inhabited by a single ratty couch which had clearly been abused by more than its share of transient cats.

Another shiver zigzagged up her spine. This place gave her a serious case of the willies. Since her vampires had been able to give her last safe house a facelift with a simple snap of the fingers, why did this dump have to be so ugly? Weren't all vampire types magic? Maybe Mr. Big Shot hadn't had a chance to fix the place up yet?

"Uh," she hedged, eyeballing the dirty walls and filthy linoleum floor in the kitchen as they headed toward the back of the house. Surely she wasn't expected to consume any food stored or prepared in that filth. "This place could use a little TLC, doncha think?"

"Apologies." Her escort gave her a reassuring smile, which didn't exactly do its job. "This was the only remaining safe house we have in the area. You won't be here long."

"Glad to hear that." Her toe caught on a curled tile and she stumbled, catching herself on outstretched arms, hands flattened against a closed door. Upon contact, the latch released, the door swung open, and she tumbled into a bathroom so grimy, she gagged. Twisting, she jumped to her feet and lunged forward.

Her host had one hand on the door. Was he about to shut her inside? Why would he do that?

She shivered as she stomped down a narrow passageway. "Okay, not trying to be a whiner, but oh my God. I'm going to get the plague. You've got to do something about this place," she ranted as she shoved by him. "It's gotta be condemned. I'm wondering if it's even safe. Black mold's deadly, you know. You could at least give me some hand sanitizer. And where are we going?"

"The bedrooms are in better shape." He hurried past her, halting outside another door. He twisted the knob and pushed open the door, revealing a room the size of a closet.

"Better shape? Says who?" Her gaze hopped from the wall, painted the most obnoxious red color ever, to the twin-sized bed, lacking bedding of course, to the boarded up window. The carpet's grungy nondescript color reminded her of boogers. It was all too gross for words.

Before she could voice her opinion about the state of the bedroom, Mr. Big Shot gave her a swift shove then slammed the door shut.

What the hell? Closed inside this dump? He had been trying to shut her in that nasty bathroom. Did he think she was going to run?

She clambered to her feet, knowing something was really, really wrong, and lunged for the door. Locked. Scared, confused and pissed, she pounded with her fists. "Hey! Open up!"

No answer.

Well fuck! She was getting really tired of being locked up. What did these vampires think? She was going to head out for a little stroll in the moonlight? And if they thought Burke was the killer, and Burke was now in their custody, why did they need to hide her away anyway?

What the hell was going on?

Miko was going to have some explaining to do. And that other guy, the one who'd locked her in this shithole -- he'd just better protect his dangly bits.

She was about to proclaim open season on his groin.

* * *

Burke was in hell. He'd long hated having dragged Isabella into this mess. She was now wanted for aiding and abetting a convicted felon.

She was a great friend, a dear woman who deserved so much better than what she'd received in the last several months.

And now he'd inadvertently hurt Sylvie too.

God help him, maybe the Binding had been completed, because the torture he suffered now... Agonizing. He'd never possessed a soul. He'd never been complete, fully human, in the most positive sense. Never experienced the kind of bone-deep regret he felt right now. If he didn't know better, he'd swear he had a soul. And it had been put through a shredder.

Death would be welcome relief.

He loved Sylvie. Loved. A man without a soul. He'd always thought it was impossible.

"Since I was slightly indisposed, I couldn't exactly keep a close watch on Sylvie," Burke snapped as they pushed open the door to the apartment. His gaze swept around the room, now completely empty. The only sign of the earlier struggle was a single scuffmark on the scarred wooden floor.

"If it hadn't been for my intervention, they would've killed you. And then where would Sylvie be?" Miko stood in the hallway outside, down on one knee inspecting the stained carpet.

"We don't know that they'd have killed me. Yet. Do we?" Burke toed the floor, kicking up a cloud of dust. "Dammit, how will we find her? I was flat on the floor. I saw Szader and of course Hadrian. Who else?"

"There were several agents inside. But there could have been someone else outside, waiting."

Burke headed for the window, shoving aside the battered blinds to peer down to the parking lot below. "How would they know what was about to happen?"

"Overheard?"

He glanced over his shoulder. "One of the *Excoluni*?"

Miko gave his head a decisive shake. "Absolutely not. Impossible."

171

"Aren't you trained to consider every possibility? Even the impossible?" he challenged. The blinds slipped through his fingers and fell back into place with a metallic rattle. "Who was the last man to see her?"

"Petrov escorted her to my car."

"Then we will talk to him. There's nothing here." Burke pushed past a bewildered looking Miko and hurried down the stairs without a backward glance.

Who is the detective here?

* * *

Several hours later, Sylvie had not only developed a seriously full bladder, but also a really pissy attitude. Thus, when the door to her prison cell was finally opened, she had a tough time deciding which pressing issue she needed to deal with first -- the urgent need to pee or the equally pressing compulsion to make one asshole pay for his sins.

The need to pee won. But it was a temporary concession. She gave Mr. Big Shot Whatever-his-name (Was it Adrian? She couldn't remember, but she did recall meeting him at the club) the cold shoulder as she shoved past him. "That was just wrong."

"Your safety is our only concern."

"Heh, right. That's why you brought me to this deathtrap. There's more germs in this dump than a cesspool, the roof is about to fall in on us, and there are more holes in the floor than Swiss cheese. Puhleez." She found a larger bathroom at the end of the hall, and after giving him yet another scowl, closed herself in and took care of business.

There was, of course, no running water. Therefore, she could not flush. She could not wash. It left her feeling icky, itchy and dirty. And more annoyed.

The instant she opened the bathroom door, she launched into yet another rant. "This is unacceptable. What kind of second rate organization houses innocent victims in roach infested, filthy accommodations that aren't fit for vermin? Come on! Snap, for chrissakes. Do something about it." At his bewildered look, she illustrated with a literal finger snap. "You know? Snap?"

"Not sure what you mean by that."

"Uh… You can't snap?"

"Of course I can, but what's that got to do with the safe house?" He snapped his fingers, but absolutely nothing happened.

Interesting. So, the snap didn't work for all vampires? How about that? Then again, did she know for a fact that this guy was a vampire?

A flurry of questions followed. Why were Burke and Miko able to do magic and this guy couldn't? Did he know Burke and Miko possessed magical powers? What did it all mean?

"Sorry. I guess I thought you were magical. Silly me."

He eased her down the hall with a gentle press on her lower back. "Oh, I can. But it takes a little more than a gesture to invoke a spell." He directed her a little more forcefully toward the kitchen.

"I see," she said, intentionally dragging her feet. "Where are we headed? Do I need to be worried about anything? You know, while I was in the prison cell, I had some time to think. Why do I need to hide if you caught the killer?"

"Hmmm. It's a little complicated." He reached around her and opened a door, which she quickly realized led to the basement.

Oh. No way.

A coat of goose bumps popped up all over her back and this funny, tickly sensation pricked her spine, little creepy spider feet. "Why do I need to go down there?" She was getting a bad vibe about this.

As crazy as things had been when she'd been on the run with Burke and then hiding with Miko, she'd never once felt this squicked out. She'd never been afraid they were going to hurt her. Quite the opposite, she'd felt safe, protected.

She guessed this guy was a big shot in the vampire secret police, but he gave her a bad case of the willies. There was no way he was convincing her to go down into that basement. Something was wrong here. She didn't want to know what that something was.

Twisting, she planted an elbow in his gut then sprinted in the opposite direction. But before she'd gotten very far, something hard and heavy slammed into her from behind, flattening her to the floor.

"Dammit, I don't have time for this," her assailant whispered, his voice trembling. "I have some blood and an assortment of body parts to harvest."

A split second later, just as she was about to belt out a scream, everything went black.

SIXTEEN

Miko knew he shouldn't be smiling, considering the situation, but he couldn't help himself. Burke really thought he was something. Yet, at the same time, his insides were being ripped apart. Sylvie was missing. He -- a man who hadn't questioned his ability to do his job in several centuries -- was suddenly wondering if his life was on the right track. He'd always dreamed of being an officer with the *Excoluni*. Further, once he had joined the force, he'd never questioned his ability to be a damn good officer, just as his father had been.

Until now.

Since the first night he'd met Sylvie, everything he'd believed about his life, himself, his priorities, had been in question. Was he a good officer? Did he want to be? What was important anymore?

He hated to think he'd spent his entire life to this point chasing rainbows.

On Burke's heels, he headed back to his car. But just before reaching the vehicle, he took a quick detour. He hadn't taken the time to inspect the ground where he'd been parked earlier, a mistake. He was getting sloppy.

With the wind having picked up, he expected anything that might have been left behind gone, swept away. But it was worth a look, anyway.

What he found was a large puddle about a foot away from where his car had been parked, and three sets of footprints. Three people had passed through the water, leaving a wet trail going to and from the vehicle.

One set of prints was noticeably smaller than the other two -- it had to belong to Sylvie. The others were both similar in size. The tracks were identical in pattern, suggesting both men wore the same size and type of shoe. He stooped down, to get a better look at the trail heading away from the car.

The footprints were dry, and the mud around the puddle showed few tracks. But what remained was enough. Hadrian had led Sylvie from his car. To... somewhere. Maybe another vehicle?

He'd lied.

Why?

"What do you have there?" Burke asked from behind him.

Miko pointed at the evidence. "My brother knows more than he's telling."

"What makes you say that?"

"He's always had troubles with his left leg. See the way the left footstep is scuffed? He sort of drags his foot as he walks. Has done that as long as I can remember."

"Well... damn." Burke scowled. "Why would he keep secrets from you?"

"Maybe he thinks I'm helping you? And since he thinks you're the killer..."

"Yeah. Maybe. Could he be using her as bait? To get to me," Burke offered.

"Why would he do that? She was missing before you escaped."

"True."

"I need to talk to him." Miko jumped to his feet and hurried back to his car, Burke mirroring his strides beside him.

"I'm sure you're right," Burke said as he slid into the passenger seat and pulled the door shut. "He's just trying to keep her safe."

"Yeah." Miko shoved the key into the ignition, started the car and threw it into gear. He couldn't get to Hadrian's fast enough. To his credit, Burke didn't complain when Miko sped through not one, not two, but three red lights. Nor did he comment on the hairpin turns he took at speeds that should have earned him a ticket for reckless driving.

The car's tires skidded on wet pavement as he hit the brakes in front of his brother's temporary home, a townhouse in a nondescript building. Before he left the car, he gave Burke a warning glance. "Wait here. Keep your eyes open."

"Sure."

Running, he approached the building. Hadrian's car wasn't in its marked slot in front of the townhouse's entry. Chances were he wasn't home. He knocked anyway but wasn't surprised to get no answer.

Now what? Did he want to risk taking Burke to the command center? It could be a trap. He did a one-eighty and sprinted back to the car.

Before Burke could ask the questions etched all over his face, Miko raised an index finger and went for his phone. He tried Hadrian first, and got his voicemail. Next he tried Petrov. Dyre hadn't heard from Hadrian in a while.

Although Miko didn't dare risk asking, he sensed Petrov had not heard about Burke's escape yet. Petrov did, however, say that he thought he'd spied Hadrian approaching Miko's car earlier. But he hadn't thought anything of it.

Something was really nagging at Miko about all this. Specifically, he was having a hard time understanding why his micromanaging, uber-efficient brother had pulled a Houdini so quickly after Burke's capture. Normally, he would be breathing down everyone's neck, demanding paperwork and preparing for their return trip home. What the hell was so important?

He hit the speed dial key for Hadrian's number. This time, when he got his voicemail, he left a message. "Hey, I have my reports. Where are you?" Then he punched in the command center's phone number. No answer. He shifted the vehicle into gear and drove to the command center -- housed in a warehouse located in the rear of an industrial complex -- explaining his worries to Burke as he drove. As a safety measure, he left Burke at a nearby motel before heading to the complex. A wise decision. Hadrian's car was parked in front of the building. Miko laid his hand on the hood as he walked by.

Hot. His brother hadn't been at the command center for long.

Preparing himself for whatever might happen, Miko pulled open the door.

His brother wasn't there. Cizak had driven his car back to the command center for him. That same man had some very shocking information to share with Miko about his brother.

Cizak had been secretly watching Hadrian for the past few weeks, and had developed his own theory about the string of murders they were investigating. Of course, at this point, he still had no proof to support his suspicions. Therefore, he hadn't been able to take any action against Hadrian. But he'd been watching, waiting for Hadrian to make a mistake. He explained he regretted not telling Miko what he suspected earlier, but he hadn't wanted to risk it, since he couldn't be sure he could trust Miko.

Could Cizak be right?

Struggling with disbelief, Miko dashed out to his car, leaving Cizak back at the command center, hoping he'd keep Hadrian distracted if he returned.

If what he'd heard was true, Sylvie was at another safe house, about fifteen miles away.

And Hadrian was the killer.

* * *

When Sylvie had been four or five -- she wasn't really sure how old she'd been at the time -- she'd faced a demon head-on. That monster hadn't been a literal being with claws and scales and teeth, but a figurative one.

Hopelessness. Despair. Desperation.

She'd never denied the fact that those awful years had shaped who she was and how she reacted to situations as an adult. Day after day, night after night, spent hungry, dirty and scared, begging for money from passersby under the protective cover of a freeway overpass had taken its toll.

As a child, she'd spent years constantly fearful of being scooped up by a social worker and taken from the only adult she trusted, the mother who she now knew had had no business becoming a mother. Years narrowly escaping the leering eyes and groping hands of men who'd offered her brief relief from hunger by doing the unthinkable.

Thanks to the pressure, she'd more or less skipped childhood, maturing to adulthood long before she'd reached puberty. As her mother's mental illness progressed, Sylvie stepped into her place, becoming the parent. Her mother's mind slowly deteriorated until she was like a child, entirely dependent upon Sylvie for her every need.

But it all changed one chilly, rainy night in the spring. Sylvie woke up to the sound of screeching tires. A dull thud followed. Then silence.

It didn't take long for Sylvie to realize what had happened. Her mother had wandered into the street and had been hit by a passing car. There were no police cars, no ambulances. Only whispers, rain and darkness, terrible emptiness.

That emptiness had become a part of her over the years. It was always there. A cold spot inside. She'd tried filling the void with food, work, alcohol, studying, friendship, sex, exercise. Sometimes the cure-of-the-week would give her some temporary relief, but over time, the empty feeling would return and she'd be on the hunt for the next treatment.

Carpe Nocturne was her most recent temporary fix. Or at least she'd thought it was, until she'd met her vampires.

Whether it was the magic or something much deeper, they did something for her that nothing and no one had done before. Yes, the pain of the Binding had been agonizing. But now that it had eased, and she'd had time to just lie there in the dark and think, she realized that she felt complete, whole, for the first time ever.

Ironic, since she was pretty sure she was about to die.

She was spread-eagle on a chilly concrete floor, wrists and ankles in shackles. Heavy chains locked to the cuffs held her arms and legs in position, despite her struggles. There was no way she could escape. Not a chance.

To think her life was about to end like this.

She was alternately petrified and in complete denial. This wasn't really happening, right? It was some kind of hallucination. Or a dream. Nightmare. She'd simply overdosed on junk food and fallen asleep with the television on.

If only.

Although she'd completely lost track of time, she sensed the end was near. The bastard who'd kidnapped her had brought her down here unconscious, chained her to the floor. And just as she'd regained consciousness, explained exactly what he intended to do. In horrifying detail.

She wasn't heartless. Hell, in a way she could appreciate the reason why he was going to such extremes. The woman he loved had been taken from him, cruelly, unjustly. And he simply couldn't live without her. It was a tragic story, the kind she'd read many times in her favorite romance novels.

Unfortunately, it seemed that she, being an *Origo*, was the cure to his heartbreak. Her blood would revive his dead lover.

Why couldn't she just donate a pint? It was so unfair.

From her spot on the floor, she could see the corpse, positioned like Sleeping Beauty on a flat stone pedestal that in a bizarre way reminded her of a church altar. A band of strange engraved symbols circled the upper edge of the platform. Part temple, part storage room, the basement in which they both lay was very dark, with walls painted a deep burgundy. Floor-to-ceiling wooden shelves lined one wall. There were also some kind of symbols painted on the floor. It was all so… gothic. Creepy yet fascinating at the same time.

Up above, she heard a thump. Instantly, her heart rate launched into high speed, sending hot blood pounding through her body. She twisted, cocking her head to the side so she could see the stairs.

Was this it? Had her time run out?

Oh, God!

A coat of sweat slicked her skin. She pulled on her restraints, even though she knew it was useless trying to break free. This whole time she'd held some hope she'd somehow escape. But, as the door at the top of the stairs swung open with a spine tingling creeeeek, the last remains of her hope were wafting away.

A rush of chills swept through her body. Her stinging eyes filled with tears, and pleas for mercy rushed to her mouth. To hell with pride, with romance, and tragedy. She was going to plead, beg, cajole, whatever it took. As long as she had breath, she'd talk. Her words were all she had anymore.

She didn't wait for him to descend the stairs. Eyelids pressed tightly together to stem the flow of tears, she pleaded, "Please, I realize you love her, but you can't do this. It's wrong to take someone else's life. You know it --"

"Sylvie! Thank God we found you."

The rest of her unspoken plea jammed in the back of her mouth. Emotion rushed up her throat and out in an incoherent cry. Miko? He'd found her?

He dashed down the stairs, ran across the room and dropped to his knees. His dark gaze swept up and down her chained body before settling on one of her bound wrists. "What is this?" He curled his fingers around the cuff circling her right arm and pulled. His scowl deepened. He snapped his fingers. Nothing happened. He cussed, "Bastard!"

"He's going to kill me. To bring that corpse back to life. It's some kind of spell or magic," she blurted. Her gaze hopped between Miko's red, stress-filled face and the door at the top of the basement stairs. "Is he up there?"

"No. I don't know where he is." Miko jumped to his feet and started searching the room. "Did you see where he put the key?"

"Key?"

"To the bindings."

"No. I was unconscious."

"Dammit." He charged from one wooden shelf to another, knocking dusty boxes full of who-knew-what to the floor. Muttering curses, he dug through rattling contents until he'd run out of boxes and shelves to search.

Then, he turned his attention to the dead body. "What the hell are you doing, Hadrian? My God! Is that your girlfriend? She's been dead…" He approached the stone altar slowly, hands fisted at his sides, rage pulling the muscles of his shoulders and arms into tight, trembling ropes. "What the fuck?"

Sylvie's breath caught in her throat. She'd never seen a man more angry, confused, conflicted. He sniffled, swiped at the tears running from his eyes, and ran his hand along the upper edge of the pedestal, fingering the engraving. "I didn't want to believe it."

"What time is it?" She hated interrupting him, but even more than before, she sensed time was running out.

Miko checked his watch. "Almost four in the morning."

She'd been lying there for hours upon hours. "Oh God! We need to get out of here."

Catching the panic in her voice, he started searching the altar for the keys. An excited yelp and raised fist indicated he'd found them.

He dashed back to her, dropped to his knees at her feet and fumbled with the locked cuffs, releasing her left then right ankle. She worked the blood back in her limbs by shuffling her legs while he freed her wrists. Her head swam as he hooked his elbows under her armpits and lifted her to her feet.

"What about Burke?" she asked as she shuffled up the stairs behind him.

"He's safe." Miko knocked the door open, then turned and caught one of her hands in his. "We'll all be together soon."

"Thank God." Relieved, she ran through the dilapidated house with Miko, her sight focused on the door, freedom, safety, finally the happiness she'd waited a lifetime to find. "How'd you find this place?"

"I had some help." He opened the front door, and together, hand in hand, they ran across the weedy front lawn to his car, parked on the street. He helped her into her seat and slammed the door.

But then, as she sat frozen in horror, she watched her kidnapper sneak up behind an unsuspecting Miko. She hit the window with her fists, desperate to warn him. She screamed. Pointed. Gestured. But he didn't react quickly enough. One second he was standing there, staring at her through the car's side window, the next he was gone. The kidnapper was in his place, his face a deep scarlet, his eyes narrowed to slits as he glowered at her.

Horrified, she scrambled with wildly trembling hands for the car's power lock button, but in her panic unlocked the doors instead. When her door flew open, she shrieked and threw her body backward, slamming the back of her head against the steering wheel. Dazed, she started kicking, aiming for any part of her would-be killer she could strike. He grappled for her feet, cussing when he lost hold of them.

Sure that this was her last chance at escape -- at survival -- she caught the steering wheel in her hands and held on for life. He'd caught her legs again, had her by the ankles and was yanking hard, trying to drag her out of the vehicle. She screamed as loud as she could, hoping by some miracle someone might hear her and come to her rescue.

The sweat coating her palms was making her grip on the steering wheel loosen. She gritted her teeth and tightened her hold. But even as she did, she knew it was only a matter of time -- a very short time, at that -- before his strength won over her desperate determination.

The short time ended up being even briefer than she'd hoped.

It took one hard jerk, and he pulled her halfway out of the car. She screamed again and stretched, rolling onto her side to try to catch a hold of the steering wheel again. But it was too late. Before her fingers had closed around it, she was sliding out of the car and landing flat on her back on the ground.

Instinct took over. She thrashed wildly, arms, legs, body. She twisted and rolled, punched and kicked. But for all her effort, she received little in the way of reward. The killer had her pinned to the ground within moments, his butt parked smack dab on her stomach. Under his weight, she struggled to catch her breath. Tears blurred her vision. She lacked the lung power to shout. Her strength was slipping from her.

It was over. She'd lost.

But just as she'd all but given up, Miko knocked the killer off her, sending him rolling to one side. While the two men battled, throwing punches hard enough to knock out a world class champion boxer, she scrambled to her feet and scampered back to the car, crawling across the passenger seat to wiggle herself behind the steering wheel. The keys were dangling from the ignition. She started the vehicle, hesitating, one hand hovering over the gear shift, her foot resting on the brake.

What to do? Drive away, leaving Miko to fend for himself? Or wait?

As if he sensed her struggle, Miko turned to give her a shooing gesture. "Go!" he shouted. "Now!"

She depressed the brake and shifted into drive. Yet, she couldn't make herself drive away. At the moment, he wasn't winning the fistfight. In fact, he was darn close to losing it. And while she could admit he was taking a beating to keep the kidnapper distracted long enough to allow her to escape, she simply could not abandon him like a chicken.

If only Burke were there to help!

Another slug to the face sent Miko staggering backward. He stumbled and fell to the ground. The kidnapper didn't let up. He kicked Miko, beat his head, shoulders, chest.

Crying, Sylvie jerked the steering wheel and gunned the gas, steering the car straight at the bastard. He was too close to Miko for her to run him down, but she was hoping she might be able to slam him with the car door. Or at least distract him long enough to let Miko escape.

Anything was better than sitting there like some stupid, helpless sissy. She stopped the car mere inches from the kidnapper and kicked the door open with all her might, catching him with it in the hip. The force knocked him aside but didn't hit him hard enough to give her the time she needed to get to Miko.

Miko was struggling to sit up, but the blows to his head had taken their toll. He moved sluggishly, clumsily, like he'd downed an entire bottle of tequila.

Meanwhile, she slammed the door closed and locked it to keep the kidnapper from getting his grimy paws on her again.

Visibly furious, he spun around, dragged Miko to his feet, and jerked him back against him. More monster than man, the kidnapper glared at her. "I'll kill him."

"If you do, then you'll kill your lover," she screamed through the window. "We're bound. If he dies then I die. You need me alive. That's what you said."

Hatred flared in the man's dark eyes. At that moment, she had to question whether he just might kill Miko, regardless of the consequences.

How did a man who lived to uphold the law, justice, all that was good, go so bad?

"You bastard, Hadrian," Miko shouted, struggling to break free from his captor. "He won't kill me. I'm his brother. Don't believe a word he says."

"Wouldn't I?" Hadrian produced a knife from somewhere and pressed it against Miko's throat. Miko's eyes revealed the depth of his shock.

That… that awful person was not just Miko's superior, but his brother? The one he'd talked about, bragged about? Compared himself to?

She could only imagine how painful it must have been for Miko to have someone he loved and admired so much do what he had. At that moment, her gaze tangling with Miko's, her doubt about Hadrian's intention completely evaporated. Poof. Gone. Whether it was insanity from extreme grief, or rage, or mental illness, Hadrian was not firing on all cylinders anymore. Brother or not, he would kill Miko.

And, if the Binding had been completed, she'd die too. Sure, there was a possibility it hadn't been. But did she want to take that chance?

The answer was no.

"Get out of the car," Hadrian demanded.

She flipped the lock and pulled on the latch, but before she had the door open enough to get out, Miko kicked it shut. "The Binding's not complete," he blurted.

Something flashed in Hadrian's eyes. For the briefest of seconds, the hand holding the knife dropped. Miko took full advantage of the opportunity. Within a blink, he was free from Hadrian's grasp and was lunging for the car.

Seeing where this was going, Sylvie stomped on the brake and shifted the vehicle into gear. But as Miko dove into the back seat, Hadrian lifted the knife and plunged it into Miko's back.

Sylvie felt the scream tear from her throat.

SEVENTEEN

His brother. Miko could hardly recognize the man he'd known his entire life. It was as if something -- a demon? -- had taken over his body. Gone was the boy who'd teased him relentlessly as a child. Fraternal twins raised in Eastern Europe by loving, indulgent parents. The so-called older brother -- Miko's senior by mere minutes -- Hadrian had pushed him, encouraged him, challenged him as they'd attended a small college in France.

Hadrian had been accepted into the *Excoluni* several years before Miko, and had quickly progressed up the ranks. But once Miko had been accepted, working under his brother's command, he'd demanded Miko perform his very best every day. Two brothers determined to do their father proud.

Hadrian. His mentor. His hero.

Miko wondered, was there any hope of rescuing the brother he loved? Or was he gone forever?

Then again, Miko wondered as he took in his current situation -- injured, bound tightly, gagged, gloves preventing him from performing magic -- would he even live to make that attempt?

He'd told Burke to give him one hour. If he didn't return to their designated meeting point, he was to prepare for the worst.

Ironically, if Burke followed that timeline, they'd probably all be dead.

For the first time since they'd started working together, he hoped Burke would defy his direct order.

* * *

Three, two, one. Time's up!

Burke didn't give a damn what Miko had said. He'd waited longer than he'd intended in this dump. It was time to find out exactly what was going on.

Miko had been very tightlipped about what he'd learned over the course of the last several hours, but Burke had sensed something was very wrong. Miko had simply given Burke a gun with vampire-killing bullets, a cell phone, a piece of paper bearing an address, and a set of car keys. Before he walked out of the motel room he'd rented under an assumed name, he told him if he didn't return by five a.m., he should go to the address prepared for the worst.

Of course, Burke had no intention of waiting that long.

A knock sounded at the door.

Isabella.

He checked the peephole before opening the door. "Glad you could make it."

"Wouldn't miss this for the world." As usual, she was dressed in black, her hair pulled into a tight ponytail. There was only one change in her appearance -- the former red hue of her hair had been replaced by a deep mahogany.

She adjusted the black bag hanging from her shoulder, pushing the strap higher. "You look like hell."

"Yeah, well." Burke heaved a weary sigh. "At least I think it's almost over."

Scowling, Isabella reached a flattened palm to his cheek. "You... love them, don't you?"

He nodded. "I had no idea it would be like this. My insides feel like they've been shredded, incinerated, and then stuffed back inside."

"Miko and Sylvie will be okay." She adjusted the strap of her bag on her shoulder for a second time. "This stupid thing is heavy. I brought everything you asked me to."

"Let's go."

Despite Isabella's insistence they take her car, Burke went with the car Miko had supplied him. After making a stop at a nearby gas station for a map, they drove the short distance to the address on the paper. When he slowed the car in front of the building, Burke was instantly overcome with bone-deep, nauseating dread. What kind of place was this? Why would anyone bring Sylvie here? What kind of hell was he about to walk into?

He gave Isabella a warning glance as he drove around the block then past the building a second time. He wasn't sure he wanted to take his friend into that shithole, placing her in even more danger than he already had over the past few months.

It could be a trap. Maybe Miko's *Excoluni* pals had convinced Miko that he should be captured?

Deep inside, he doubted Miko would, after all this time, betray him. But he couldn't deny it was possible.

Car parked a safe distance away, Burke loaded the gun but left the safety on. His heart thumped against his breast bone as he exited the car, weapon in his fist. Sweat beaded on his forehead, his temple. Dragging one slick palm down his leg, he motioned to Isabella to arm herself, and tipped his head toward the house. "Tell me I'm not going to regret getting you into this."

"You're not going to regret getting me into this," Isabella parroted. A glance caught her giving him a toothy grin. "I'm here for you. Always have been."

"Thank you."

"Don't mention it. But remember our agreement. When your name's clear, I'm heading home and you're selling me the house."

He smiled at their inside joke. As long as they'd known each other, Isabella had wanted to own his house in Valtrusy, a quaint town in the Czech Republic. Of course, thanks to the criminal case, which stripped him of everything he owned, he didn't legally own the property anymore. The UMN didn't recognize geographical boundaries. It didn't matter where on earth a crime was committed. By law any member found guilty of murder lost every material possession he had. But he'd promised that if he were ever able to clear his name, and regained ownership of his property, he'd sell it to her. For a fair price, to be negotiated at a later date. If he had it his way, that fair price would be exactly one dollar. "You got it."

Smiling, she handed him an elastic band for his hair. He accepted it, setting the gun on the car's trunk to gather his hair into a low ponytail. His hands trembled as he struggled to perform a task that had always been second nature.

Then, the gun back in his hand again, his dearest friend at his side, he moved toward the ramshackle house with caution. Every nerve in his body prickled. The hairs on his nape stood on end. He could hear the blood pounding through his head. The sound echoed in his ears.

His conscience screamed dire condemnations in his head. Miko might have walked into this place of his own free will, but Isabella? Sylvie? He wouldn't be able to live another day if something happened to either of them.

When he reached the house, ducking behind a scraggly pile of twigs that might have once been a beautiful rose bush, he turned to Isabella and shook his head. "I can't let you go in there. I don't know what we're walking into."

"Fuck you," she snapped. "I'm not sitting out here filing my nails while you're in there fighting God knows what."

"But --"

She silenced him with a lifted hand. "Nuh uh."

He knew there was no way she'd listen to reason. "Stay behind me, at least."

She gave him an eye roll. "Whatever you say, boss." Then she winked. "I'd rather look at your ass anyway. Have I ever told you that you have a great butt?"

"No." Brows furrowed, he twisted at the waist to get a look at his rear end. Then he met her gaze. "Are you flirting with me?"

"Hell no! But I can appreciate a nice body when I see one. I've never kept my appreciation of your finer assets to myself."

So, why couldn't he recall a single time when she'd commented on his butt -- or any other part of his person -- before? Granted, there'd been that time of the "experiment," when they'd toyed with the idea of becoming more than friends. But as quickly as that notion had risen, it was cast aside. They were definitely not compatible. There'd been no funny business since then, not a look, word, twinkle. "Ooookay."

"I'm just in a weird mood, I guess."

"Yeah. Weird." He turned around, focusing his attention on the window. There was a split in the plywood covering it. He peered through the crack. The glass behind was cloudy and smudged with filth, and a torn curtain limited his vision, but he could see inside. The window, positioned on the side of the house, faced the neighboring multi-family structure to the west. It provided a fairly good view of several rooms inside -- kitchen, living room, dining room. Because the exterior was cloaked in heavy shadows, the dim lighting inside was adequate enough to illuminate a single shadowy figure moving in one of the rooms. If he had to guess, Burke would say the person was male.

Miko? Who was inside? And if that was Miko, where was Sylvie?

The person headed toward the back of the kitchen, disappearing through a narrow doorway. The door closed behind him.

Figuring it was now or never, he motioned to Isabella then sprinted around to the front door. He tried it. Locked. Knowing Isabella would get the door open in half the time it would take him, he waved to her. She shuffled past him, lock pick at the ready. Within seconds, the door inched open. Burke stood back, peering around the door as it slowly swung in. Isabella stood against the front of the house, about five feet from him. Their gazes met for an instant. He lifted the gun, switched off the safety and tiptoed into the house.

Silence. Empty. Filthy. Carefully, slowly, he moved deeper into the house, heading toward the rear where he'd seen the mystery person moving around. He heard muffled voices. Below them?

Basement.

A tingle pricked his spine and a fresh coat of sweat slicked his face and palms.

A board creaked under his weight when he stepped toward the basement door. He froze in place, his breath wedged in his throat.

The voices below were silenced.

Burke lifted his foot slowly and placed it a few inches to the right, this time testing the board before settling his weight on it. He did the same with his other foot, impatient with his painstakingly slow progress, but worried he'd alerted the killer. Without the element of surprise, he had few advantages over the bad guy.

He reached the door without a killer filling him with silver bullets. Relief. He gave himself a few seconds to gather his frayed nerves before taking hold of the doorknob. He twisted the circa 1950's cut crystal handle a fraction of a degree at a time until the latch clicked.

He swapped a worried look with Isabella before pushing the door open. It struck something hard. An instant later, a man blasted through the door, slamming into Burke and knocking him to the ground before he'd had time to react.

Everything blurred. Someone's fists slammed into his face. The back of his head struck something hard. He tried to turn his head to the side and block the blows, but he couldn't move his arms. Sounds of scuffling and skin striking skin, the crunch of shattering bone, filled his ears. A grunt blasted from his chest. Cool darkness seeped into his pores, gathering like a toxic cloud in his head. He struggled to fight it, but the cold intensified, nearly overwhelming him. He focused on Isabella's distant voice, a whisper in the night. Followed it, out of the shadow, the frigid emptiness.

"Burke! I need your help. Hey, let me out of here, you fucking bastard!"

"Isabella?" He heard himself speak. That was his voice, wasn't it?

Light pierced the black world that had closed in around him. Painful, agonizing, blinding light. A searing ache blasted through his body in wild, relentless waves.

In the darkness was respite. Soothing cold. Peace. He wanted to surrender to it, but Isabella's screams kept pulling him toward the light.

He wasn't very happy with her at the moment, especially when another crush of white-hot, throbbing pain pounded through his body.

He blinked open his eyes. He was on the kitchen floor. Alone.

A muffled shriek.

He slowly turned his head toward the sound but saw no one. Muddy-headed, he moved his hands, legs. So far, so good. He rolled onto his side and levered his upper body off the floor. The pounding in his head intensified. He sandwiched it between his flattened hands, squinted, and slowly stood up.

The world tipped and whirled as he moved, but he continued, driven by worry for Isabella, Sylvie and Miko. He licked his parched lips, tasting blood. Was it his own?

His gun. Where'd his gun go?

The room spinning around him like he was on a runaway carnival ride, he turned a complete three-sixty, searching the floor for his lost weapon. Nothing.

Why did that not surprise him?

He searched for an alternate weapon, something hard he could use to beat some Hadrian ass. He'd recognized the *Excoluni* officer sometime after the bastard had pounded his nose flat.

Of course, the fact that he'd been attacked by Hadrian Dvorak led him to a devastating conclusion -- Miko could be a part of this. His own mate might have intentionally led him into a trap.

No. He didn't want to believe it. Not after what had happened earlier. They were on the same team now.

What if Miko hadn't known what he was facing when he arrived? What a shock it must've been -- discovering his own brother was somehow tied to the murders. Was in some way responsible for his *Origo*'s kidnapping.

He had to find Miko. He had to find them all.

He swept up a broken broom handle tucked between the refrigerator and the wall and headed back toward the basement stairs. Whatever was going on, it was happening down there.

He had no idea what kind of hell he was about to walk into, but he was ready to give the devil a little taste of his own medicine.

* * *

The stench of those candles, it was enough to make Sylvie's eyes water. What the hell were they made out of?

Come to think of it, she didn't want to know.

Her belly was twisted into a tight knot, the awful smell only making the nausea that much worse. The chill of the floor cooled her back, sending shivers up and down her spine, while her heart sent scalding blood pounding through her body.

He had a strange looking knife in his hand. It reminded her of that scene in *Braveheart*, the awful one at the end. She was about to feel the same thing -- the agony of having her insides cut out.

Terror ripped through her body. She dragged in desperate breaths between muffled sobs. As she had a hundred times before, she started yanking on the chains holding her arms and legs, gritting her teeth at the pain. The skin around the bindings had no doubt been rubbed raw. Sharp, piercing sensations razored up her arms and legs every time she moved them.

Stilling, gaze focused on the man holding the knife overhead murmuring words in a foreign tongue she didn't understand, she made promises to every deity known to mankind that she'd live a better life, contribute to every church raffle in her neighborhood, and pay a weekly visit to every church, temple and mosque she could locate. If only she might be spared.

She'd long ago accepted death as inevitable. Everyone died -- everyone, that was, but vampires. And their *Origo*s. Only she would discover immortality was truly possible and then find herself slaughtered brutally, the lamb whose blood was shed to redeem a dead person.

It was almost too bizarre to believe.

The man turned to her. Her eyes filled with tears. She tried to be strong, but terror completely obliterated every bit of pride and courage she had clung to.

He was coming closer.

His face was a blank canvas, completely devoid of emotion. His dark eyes glittered, the light of a nearby candle reflecting on the surface. Inside, the depths were like the furthest regions of outer space. Empty. Cold. Nothingness.

He lowered the crescent-shaped blade and hooked it in her shirt. The metal was cool against her skin. Her stomach muscles tightened. She jerked when he gave the blade a swift yank, cutting through her top. The material fell to the sides, leaving only her bra between his evil, empty eyes and her skin.

Trembling, air sawing in and out of her lungs as if she was sprinting up a mountain slope, she tipped her head to look at Miko. He sat in a chair, his arms tied behind him, his ankles strapped to the chair legs with duct tape. More tape covered his mouth, yet he still managed to shout, to rock the chair. Unlike the man standing over her, preparing to remove her insides like some demented surgeon, his eyes were filled with emotion.

Their gazes met as the blade pierced her skin. Instinctively, she flinched. Her eyelids shut out the agonizing sight of Miko struggling to escape to save her. "It's not going to work. We didn't complete the Binding," she said for the bazillionth time. "If you kill me now, you kill your chance of bringing her back."

A puff of air struck her skin and she flinched. There was a thump, then a clatter. Lots of scuffling. Some angry shouts.

She opened her eyes. "Burke," she whispered, turning to watch him fight the killer. The rage she saw in his face shocked her.

Within minutes Burke had the killer flat on his back, the wrist of the hand holding the knife pinned to the floor. "What the hell, Hadrian?"

"You wouldn't understand. You've never loved a woman."

"Yes, I have. I do." Burke lifted Hadrian's wrist then smashed it down. The knife was knocked from his grip, slid across the concrete, stopping next to a pillar candle burning on the floor. "And you're about to kill her."

Burke loved her? He loved her! Tears of joy burned in her eyes, along with the lingering tears of terror that hadn't yet dried.

"Then you know what I'm feeling. The desperation. I can't live without her. I had to do… this. There was no other way. You understand?"

"No. I don't want to understand. I don't want to hear anything. I just want you to pay the way I have. You did this to me. Took everything. You bastard." He closed his hand around Hadrian's throat. His knuckles turned white as his grip tightened. Hadrian's face turned a deep cranberry, yet he didn't move, didn't struggle.

Burke released Hadrian's throat and knocked him out cold with a single punch to the face. He flipped the would-be murderer over onto his stomach and hogtied him before coming to check Sylvie's cut.

Expression dark with barely repressed rage, he ran his fingertip down the wound, a gentle, soothing touch. "I can't believe he almost succeeded." He kissed away the tears streaming from her eyes, and the pain on her stomach, wrists, ankles. "Where's the key?" He glanced at Miko, who was shaking his shoulders and head. "I need to go find Isabella." He stood, found the knife then rushed to Miko and pulled the tape from his mouth.

"If you get the gloves and give me that knife, I'll free myself and Sylvie. You can go look for Isabella."

Burke hesitated for only a blink before doing exactly as Miko suggested. He pulled the gloves off, and handed him the knife, allowing Miko to cut himself from his bindings. Then, after giving Sylvie another gentle kiss, he promised he'd return in a minute, as soon as he found Isabella. He ran upstairs.

The instant Miko located the key and freed her from her restraints, Sylvie climbed to her shaky legs and staggered toward the stairs. There was plenty of time for hugs and comfort and marveling about his miraculous healing later. Right now, she just had to get out of that hellish place. She wouldn't breathe easy until they were far away from there. As she passed Hadrian, he lifted his head, startling her. She hopped to one side, kicking over one of the smelly candles sitting on the floor. A few scraps of paper ignited.

"Shit!" Miko looked at her and then at Hadrian, helpless as he was.

She had her own ideas about what that monster deserved, but Miko had the morality of a police officer. She supposed he wouldn't be able to leave him down there to burn to death.

"Get outside," Miko shouted, as he stomped on the spreading flames.

"Come with me," she pleaded from the foot of the stairs.

"I'll be out in a minute. I just can't... he's my brother."

No, he wasn't going to risk his own life for that bastard!

Her heart rushed up her throat. She nodded and tripped her way up the stairs, using the loose wooden railing as support. Because she'd inhaled so much smoke, her lungs were burning, her eyes were tearing and her legs weren't one hundred percent steady.

She screamed "Fire!" as she wobbled and swayed through the house. A cloud of smoke was rolling up the stairs and gathering along the kitchen ceiling. Legs getting stronger, adrenaline doing its job, she ran through the dining room. "Burke?" She turned a corner and dashed across the living room.

The smoke was getting thicker by the second. She reached the front door but hesitated. Run outside to safety or help Burke and Miko? She threw open the door and filled her lungs with fresh air. "Burke! Fire! Miko!"

No one answered.

Clutching the shredded pieces of her shirt to her breasts, she scampered outside, jumped off the porch and ran around the outside of the house. At the very rear, she found the kitchen window. The board covering the window was partially pulled down. She frantically clawed at it, tearing a piece away. She now had a limited view of the scene inside. Miko had his tied brother in his arms and was staggering across the kitchen, toward the side door. Burke had Isabella with him and was running in the opposite direction, toward the front hall. But just as he was about to head out of the room, there was a loud crack, splitting wood. Miko dropped out of sight.

Had he fallen down, or literally crashed through the floor?

God, would this hell ever end? Sylvie screamed and ran around to the side door leading into the house. The knob was blistering hot. She covered it with a scrap of her mangled shirt and twisted, kicking it in.

Burke was long gone. There was an enormous hole in the floor. Red and gold flames danced around the opening. She kept close to the wall and inched back toward the stairs. But before she reached them, Miko staggered through the basement door, collapsing at her feet.

She grabbed his hands and dragged him toward safety outside. Only a few feet. She could do it. Her muscles screamed in protest but she pushed aside the pain. Safety was so close.

The moment she had Miko outside, she joined him on the cool grass. Flat on her back, gasping, her lungs burning, her eyes tearing so badly her vision was blurred, the cut in her stomach throbbing. Her skin felt dry and hot, like she'd fallen asleep in the sun.

But he was safe. She was safe. And the bad guy, Hadrian, she could only guess what had happened to him.

"Sylvie?" Burke called from around the side of the burning building.

"I'm here," she returned weakly.

"Oh, thank God." Burke dropped to his knees and pulled her into a tight embrace. And finally, she felt safe enough to just sit there and enjoy it.

The danger was over. And hopefully, with Miko's help, Burke would get back everything that had been taken from him.

EIGHTEEN

It took at least forty-eight hours for Sylvie to finally accept that she didn't have to hide from a killer anymore. But even two months later, she still hadn't worked through the lingering effects of the trauma she'd endured. She suppressed the worst of her emotions for as long as she could, burying herself in the business of getting Carpe Nocturne back on its feet.

She didn't want to accept the fact that the terror she'd endured in that basement had changed her, perhaps for the rest of her life.

Life had to go on. Right? People who'd endured more pain than she had -- attempted murder, spousal abuse, child neglect -- they pushed on. They grew up, graduated high school, got married, had families. Why was she having such a hard time?

Sleeping was particularly difficult. Nightmares woke her night after night. Burke and Miko stayed with her in her home, putting every obligation off to be with her. Work. Reclaiming the life they deserved to have again. Everything.

They held her as she cried out in the night, murmuring soothing words as she trembled in bed. Nothing was said about their Binding, whether it was complete or incomplete, or about the desire simmering below the surface of her vampires' concern-filled eyes.

They simply waited. Patiently. Supporting her. Encouraging her. Even helping her at Carpe Nocturne. Burke rarely let her out of his sight. He shadowed her everywhere she went, and she was grateful. This was ironic, since she'd always been the kind of woman who bristled at a man's overprotective attention. No longer.

She couldn't step foot into her office without reliving that first night. She could practically see the dead man hanging in her office, could smell the pungent stench of death. Cold, dark places struck cold terror in her. She could see what was happening to her, like she was standing outside of herself, watching. She was letting those bizarre events shape her.

How could she stop that from happening?

Late one night, after closing Carpe Nocturne, she sat in the center of her bed and cried. The bad guy was dead -- the fire had destroyed the house and everything in it. But she was still in so many ways chained to that floor, a victim who couldn't move on. She was tired of being scared. Pissed off at her inability to put it behind her. But she just couldn't. Carpe Nocturne was doing well. The weekly costume parties had taken the failing bar and turned it around. But she couldn't handle working the theme nights. The creepy vampire outfits were just too much for her, despite the fact that she knew Burke and Miko were vampires. That night, she'd been unable to find someone to work the shift.

Burke and Miko traded concerned glances as they positioned themselves on either side of her. Burke rested a single hand on her knee; Miko placed a hand on her shoulder. They watched her cry, determination and anger and a plethora of other emotions playing over their faces. She knew they wanted to ease her pain but felt powerless to give her more than temporary relief.

Finally, as her sobs wore down, Burke spoke, "I think it's time we leave."

What? He was going to leave her? How could he even think of doing that? "No. Please." Panic set her heart racing. The organ thumped against her breastbone. She clenched her trembling hands in her lap, struggling to hide the effect his words were having on her.

"It's for the best." Miko took hold of her chin and coaxed her to look at him. "We talked about it and we both agree. You need to give yourself some time to heal."

"But without you? What will I do? I need you."

"Not without us. We want you to come with us."

Relief took the form of a warm, pleasant sensation that spread across her chest and down her torso. "Where?"

"Back to one of my estates in Europe," Burke said. He inched closer, sandwiched her hands between his. "You can have a new life, a new beginning. Not that I expect all this to go away yet -- the fear and trauma. But I want to give you the choice. I will stay with you no matter what. Don't think for a minute I'm going to walk away from you. I love you." He blinked several times and she realized, from the shimmer in his eyes and the slight tremble in his lips, that he was on the verge of crying too. "Do you want to stay here, continue to build Carpe Nocturne? Or would you rather come away and begin a new life far away from the memories?"

Her heart felt like it had swelled to at least twice its normal size. Contentment. Joy.

There could be no doubt. Burke was telling the truth. He loved her. More than any person ever had, with the exception of Miko. Their love had been like a cloak she wore whenever she left the house. It kept her warm, eased her fears, gave her strength. She wanted to give them the same kind of joy, to get beyond her own neediness and reach out to them.

If they wanted to fly across the world, to Timbuktu or wherever, did she belong anywhere but with them? Did she want to continue like this? Losing herself in ugly memories?

They wanted what was best for her. "Okay," she agreed.

Her vampires sandwiched her between them in a long, warm, soothing hug.

Yes, she was looking forward to starting her life over. The ghosts haunting her wouldn't follow half way around the world. At least she hoped not.

Above and beyond getting past the trauma of her kidnapping, she simply wanted to enjoy life and enjoy the two men who'd become such a huge part of it.

Over the next several weeks, a lot of things happened. She sold Carpe Nocturne to her friend Lisa, packed up the few personal possessions that mattered to her, took a final trip to the charred remains of the house she'd been held captive in, and then boarded a private jet with her vampires. She spent the bulk of the overnight flight in the plane's comfy bed. For the first time in months, she didn't wake up sweating and shaking from night terrors.

Yes, this had been the right decision.

While the private plane should have clued her in to how rich Burke was, it wasn't until they'd landed and driven to his so-called estate that the reality sank in. Burke wasn't just a little bit rich. He was very rich. Like own-a-small-country rich. Because they had to travel at night, she wasn't able to get a good feel for the scope of Burke's real estate holdings, until she stepped foot in his house -- correction, castle. And this was supposedly his country cottage. Oh. My. God!

Clearly, the Langton family had deep roots in the Czech Republic. Burke gave her a brief history lesson about his family as he led her on a tour of the house. It was fascinating, learning how the former socialist government had taken possession of the property for a time and then returned it later. But what intrigued her the most about the house and its beautiful furnishings was the sense of history, of former lives and loves, she felt as she passed through the rooms.

Perhaps that was what she'd long ached for? Having been a child with no roots, no family that she knew of after her mother died, she lacked ties to the past.

She knew she'd heal in this place. Even though it was huge and so gorgeous it looked more like a museum than a home, there was something here that fed her soul.

"Are you tired?" Burke motioned toward the sweeping staircase that arched elegantly around in a wide "c" to the second floor above. His index finger traced the beautiful swirls carved into the wooden railing.

Mmmmm. A little ripple of warmth shimmied through her body. She'd had plenty of sleep on the plane. She wasn't tired. If he did decide to take her upstairs for a tour of the bedrooms, she could think of a few things she'd rather do than sleep. She glanced over her shoulder, wondering where Miko had gone.

Burke answered her unspoken question. "I believe he's upstairs, taking a shower."

Miko in the shower? Now, that called to mind some intriguing images.

Come to think of it, she was feeling a little grungy herself. A shower would be a good thing, especially if she were lucky enough to have some company.

She raised an eyebrow at Burke and he burst into a guffaw that tickled her insides like a flock of butterflies had been released in her tummy. A few parts of her anatomy launched into party mode when one side of Burke's mouth lifted into that wicked grin she so adored.

He scooped her up into his arms, flung her over his shoulder like a caveman hauling off a prize kill, and ran up the stairs. Thanks to her bouncing against his shoulder, her giggles rushed up her throat in broken bursts. Burke dashed through a bedroom she was sure she'd seen in an interior design magazine and threw open the door to an attached bathroom that would make the average girl weep. A sunken jet tub, long stretch of stone counter with framed mirrors hanging above it. Gorgeous tile floor and walls. But best of all, an enormous glass enclosed shower that could hold a half dozen people comfortably, with at least as many spouts spraying water at the one scrumptious body standing inside. Burke didn't bother to snap the clothes off either one of them before throwing open the glass door and carting her into the stall. The water temperature was perfect. It struck her from all directions, soaking her clothes within seconds. But she couldn't care less about a few soggy garments.

She was going to do the wild thing in the shower! Happy squeal!

She closed her eyes and focused on the erotic sensations pummeling her system. The water, caressing her skin as it ran down her torso in warm rivulets. The naughty thrill she received as her vampires ripped her soaked clothes from her body. The sound of rending fabric and murmured promises of wicked fun by the two most amazing men this side of heaven. She cleared her head, mentally shoving aside a few lingering questions she ached to have answered, and instead focused on the moment. How often did a woman find herself in the shower with two gorgeous men who were determined to drive her absolutely insane with pleasure?

Ohhhh! Could this moment last forever?

At one end of the shower was a wooden bench, jutting from the tile wall. Miko coaxed her backward and down, until she was sitting, her legs spread wide. He bent, muscles bunching as he moved, to kiss her shoulder. Burke, still dressed, the knit shirt clinging to his skin and emphasizing his bulk, knelt before her, his eyes taking a tour of her wet, trembling body. He rested a hand on each of her knees, pushing them further apart, and licked his lips. "Damn it, what you do to me. I want to take my time…" He skimmed one flattened palm up over her thigh before stopping at her hip. She quivered at his heated expression, and feeling naughty and brave, reached down to finger her labia.

Both her vampires visibly swallowed as they watched her. She knew how much power she held over them right then. She'd literally forced them to their knees. But at the same time, she ached to surrender to the latent power she witnessed in their bodies. They both had the kind of bodies that inspired wet dreams. She'd gladly swap shower nookie vampire dreams for the night terrors that had been interrupting her sleep for the last few months.

The water made Miko's hair hang in heavy waves around his face. Droplets clung to his eyelashes, nose, lips. He ran his tongue along her collarbone, and she gladly tipped her head to the side to give him greater access to her neck.

Would they bite her again? She wanted them to for some reason. As much as she wanted them to fuck her like they had before, both at the same time. While she'd been struggling the past few months, the guys had refused to make love to her. Burke had said they didn't want to make things more difficult for her.

Obviously, they weren't worried about that anymore, and she was oh, so happy.

While Miko worked his way lower, to her left breast, Burke pushed aside her hand and replaced it with his mouth.

"Ohhhhh!" she moaned, letting her head fall back to rest against the wall a few inches behind her. Her vampires had performed magic plenty, with the snap of their fingers, but now, they were performing magic on her body. With their mouths.

She wrapped her fingers around the edge of the seat and inched her bottom forward, offering Burke easier access to her pussy.

"That's it, yes. Open for us. Take what is yours." Burke simultaneously pumped two fingers in and out of her clenching pussy and teased her clit with the world's most agile tongue. It danced, flicked, swirled. His fingers thrust in and out, somehow stroking that special place inside that sent quakes of pleasure through her body.

Miko's tongue was dancing over her nipple. He pulled it into his mouth, suckling. She arched her back, thrusting her breast forward, and sighed. The agony! The profound pleasure. It was all so overwhelming.

The water, scents of soap and man and sex, the sounds of mouths working over wet skin, all blended inside her body, whirling around and around like a ball of fire in her gut. Miko pushed roughly at her shoulders, forcing her to lean back until her shoulder blades ground into the tile wall. That little act of domination made her insides go all hot and molten. She groaned, blinking into the water spray. A part of her wanted the moment to last forever, another wanted to soar over the pinnacle. Release was just out of her reach, even with two men both pleasuring her. Something was missing.

Burke lifted his head and narrowed his gaze. "I know what you need."

She was quite certain, from the fire she saw in his eyes, that statement was true. He stood, pulled Miko away from her and turned off the water. Then he motioned with a tip of his head. "I think she's ready."

Miko's smile took her breath away. A blend of unspoken promise and raw desire, the expression made her squirm. He pulled her up and maneuvered her between his yummy body and Burke's.

She had to wonder if Burke's castle had a dungeon. The kind he'd magically created in the safe house. The answer, she quickly learned, was yes. Every bit as erotically dark and dangerous as its owner.

She let her Masters lead her inside. "Can I ask a question? Why couldn't Hadrian snap like you?"

"The dark magic." While Burke shed his sopping clothes, Miko lay on his back on a narrow, hip-high wooden table. His expression was wicked, the muscles of his toned stomach and lean, smooth-skinned thighs taut. A bead of precome glistened on the tip of his thick, rigid cock. "Suck me." It was a command, and a plea. Sylvie heard both in his voice.

She bent over him and swirled her tongue around the tip, enjoying the salty flavor of his skin. He smelled so good, masculine and clean. And he tasted even better. His moans of pleasure guided her as she experimented with tongue, teeth and hands. She took him deeper into her mouth, using her hands to pump his shaft.

Burke stroked her fanny, slow caresses that spiked the simmer in her blood to boiling. Heat pulsed down her legs and up over her chest. She groaned around a mouthful of Miko and sped up her motions. This is what she'd always wanted -- to be possessed by two powerful, dominating men. Maybe she hadn't been ready to admit it before she'd met them, but she had stared at her share of group porn pictures.

Two men. One girl. So hot.

Ha, she hadn't known how hot the reality of it was! It was like a nuclear blast. Kaboom!

Burke pulled her cheeks apart and teased her anus and pussy with his fingers. He bent over her back to kiss her shoulders and nape, while stimulating her clit with magical fingers. Miko grasped her hair and pulled, forcing her up and down, fucking her mouth.

She wasn't going to last long. She wanted release. Now. She couldn't plead, not with Miko's thick cock plunging in and out. Feeling powerless and wonderfully submissive, she whimpered and surrendered, letting her vampires dictate her motions.

Miko stopped her with a tug on her hair and forced her upright with a push to her chest. From behind, Burke guided her into position, her legs straddling the bench, her pussy hovering over Miko's hips. He pressed between her shoulder blades, bending her forward at the hips, gripped her waist and eased her down until Miko's cock was buried deep inside.

The air left her lungs in a slow sigh. Up, down, he supported her with his hands as she rode Miko, yet her thighs began to burn from her position. The pain wasn't enough to distract her from the pleasure her two vampires were giving her, though. Miko pulled and pinched her uber-sensitive nipples. Burke produced some lube from somewhere, spread it over her anus and slowly inched inside.

Oh, glory!

"Open, baby. Take me in."

Her perineum burned as he breached her hole, but the pain was oh, so good. She groaned, tossed her head back and relaxed, taking him deep. Miko's thrusts slowed, falling into the same pace as Burke's. The combined movements of both cocks, gliding in and out, coupled with the guys' softly uttered words of encouragement, and the tormenting touches of two sets of hands, sent her over the edge. A powerful orgasm blasted through her body just as her vampires found their own releases. Their cum filled her pulsing pussy and anus, lubricating her. They quickened their pace, taking her harder, faster. A second orgasm coursed through her body. Her pussy and ass milked their cocks until every drop had been expelled and she lacked the strength to stand.

Burke lifted her off Miko and took her hand, kissing each fingertip.

"Now, my love, it's time for you to make your final decision," Burke said, as he led her to the center of the room. "I wish we had more time. But we don't."

Her gaze focused on the floor. Four chains were connected to steel rings affixed to the floor, just like the ones she'd been tied in when Hadrian had tried to kill her. The lingering heat simmering in her blood chilled. Ice shards pricked her insides. The resemblance was too creepy. Why was he doing this now? Exposing her to something that would scare her, instead of turn her on? They'd just shared the most amazing experience, and she was still tingling all over. Now she was ready to run screaming for the nearest exit.

Did these two have the world's worst sense of timing or what?

"I learned there's a reason why our Binding didn't take effect," Burke said while easing her onto the floor. "Something was missing."

"Then it really hadn't taken? The Binding?"

Miko circled her before stooping down to pick up one of the leather cuffs attached to a chain. "Only partially. Just enough to ease the pain."

"Partially? How does one become partially bound? Isn't that kind of like being partially pregnant?" she snapped, resisting Burke's effort to force her to the floor. "What are you doing? Are you crazy?"

Burke muscled her onto her butt. "Not unless you want to equate loving you with insanity."

"I don't know. That's a close one," Miko quipped.

"Gotta agree with you," Burke said.

"This is no laughing matter," she shouted, struggling to break free from Burke's tightening grip. Her mounting panic took the form of an invisible belt of ice. It wrapped around her chest like a constrictor and squeezed the air from her lungs. "Stop."

Miko gave Burke a warning glance then settled on one knee beside her. "If you don't want to complete the final step of the

Iugum, we can stop. Nothing has to happen if you don't want it to. But I think it's only going to help you to do this -- to face up to your fear."

"That's the final step? I have to conquer a fear?"

Miko took her hand in his and gently stroked the back. The innocent touch, a small show of concern and support, eased her panic somewhat. "No, it's more like pass a test of love."

"A test? I'm not fond of tests. Maybe we don't need to complete the *Iugum*? We're not hurting anymore. Right?"

"That's an option."

"What'll happen if we don't?" Her vampires swapped who's-going-to-break-the-news-to-her looks. She did not like the vibe she was getting. "It's that bad?"

"I guess it depends on how you want to look at it," Burke answered.

"Okay, Mr. Vague, what's that mean? Am I going to die?" She decided Miko might be more forthcoming, and turned a questioning glance his way.

Miko shook his head. "It's unlikely."

That sounded like good news. So what was the big deal? What weren't they telling her? "Is that awful pain going to come back? So far, it hasn't. Thank God. That has to mean something right?"

Miko released her hand, which almost made her whimper. It had been such a sweet gesture. "Sure. It means something."

"Then what?" she prodded. "I need to know. What are you holding back?"

"I contacted someone local here, to find out exactly how the *Iugum* works, and why our Binding didn't fully take." Burke settled next to her on the floor. He stretched his long legs out in front of him. "I also asked what the consequences would be if we went no further."

"Yeah, yeah, I kind of got that. So, what's the deal? You're killing me here."

"I'm trying to break it to you easy."

"Forget that."

"Okay." He sent Miko yet another one of those looks. "We didn't want to pressure you. We wanted to let you take the time you needed. But we didn't know... Neither of us have ever met an *Origo*. We didn't know there were certain rules..."

"What kind of rules?"

"There's no way we could have known before we left the United States," Burke added. "The elder I consulted is very ancient and does not use modern technologies..."

"What are you trying to tell me?"

Miko sighed. "Because we brought you here, to our homeland, if we don't take the final step by sunrise, you'll become a vampire."

"Oh."

Both her vampires stared at her like they expected her to freak out. She briefly considered doing just that. But instead, she bit her tongue and tried to sort out the facts.

She was a semi-bound *Origo*. She'd gone as far as she had for several reasons. First, to escape that awful, gnawing pain. Second, because she really liked the idea of being forever young. Immortal. She'd never get sick. Never age. But mostly, she wanted to be with her vampires, Burke and Miko. She loved them.

There'd been a time -- not so long ago -- when she'd accepted the fact that her past had made it pretty much impossible for her to love another person. Human or otherwise. Her mother's death, the life-or-death existence on the streets she'd endured for years, and the many years spent later being shuffled from one foster home to another had taken their toll. Her heart had been hardened. Her ability to trust severely impaired.

She'd even kept friends at a safe distance, including Lisa. To let anyone get really close, to mean something, was to risk losing them. She could not survive another loss like that, even if she had immortal blood coursing through her veins.

But then Burke and Miko had come. Yes, initially her attraction to them had been all physical. They were both beautiful men. What red-blooded woman wouldn't find them attractive?

Next, she experienced a sense of needing them. For protection. Despite all the crazy things going on around her, they made her feel somewhat safe. That was one emotion that was completely foreign to her. She liked it. A lot. Soon, she started missing them when they were gone. This wasn't a little twinge of missing but a gut-deep, painful kind.

Finally, somehow she found herself loving them. She sold her bar. She walked away from the life she'd known. And she hadn't done those things just to escape the pain of her past, but because she couldn't imagine living a day without her vampires.

Maybe she could live with becoming a vampire. It would take some getting used to. But why would she go that route?

She loved Burke and Miko.

Now, she had to prove it. To Burke and Miko. To herself.

NINETEEN

Sylvie took several deep breaths to slow her out-of-control heart rate. Adrenaline had her feeling dizzy, jittery, out of breath. Her senses were over-reactive, sounds, smells, touches so intense they were almost painful. She nodded to Burke and Miko, swallowed a huge lump in her throat and let them ease her onto her back on the floor.

"Trusting is one of the most essential aspects of love," Miko said while fastening one leather binding around her wrist. "Do you agree?"

"Yes," she whispered.

"Can you trust us?" Burke moved to her ankle, lifting it to slip a leather cuff around it.

"I want to."

"That's not the answer we need," Miko said, reaching for her other arm.

Tears burned beneath her closed eyelids. "It's not easy for me to trust."

"Why? Can you tell us?" Burke pleaded, before securing her second ankle. "What happened to you, Sylvie?"

"Life happened. It taught me that trusting other people was stupid. Because people die. Move away. Decide they don't want you around. Whatever."

"We aren't going to die," Miko said.

"Or move away."

"And we definitely want you around for a long time."

Despite the fact that she was once again tied down spread-eagled like she had been in that awful place Hadrian had taken her, she had to give her vampires a teary-eyed smile.

Burke stroked her cheek, his love for her shining in his eyes. "The chains aren't really what are holding you down. You know that, don't you?"

"Yeah."

Miko's eyes shone with love too, as he also smiled down at her. "Are you ready to say the words that will finally break the chains?"

She was surprised by how easily they came. "I trust you. I love you. I want to be with you forever."

Burke and Miko bit their wrists and each let a single droplet of blood fall, striking the center of her forehead.

Unlike before, their irises turned deep, blood red. It was the most bizarre sight she'd ever witnessed. And yet, she wasn't afraid.

It was going to work this time.

The bindings fell from her ankles and wrists and magically dissolved into a swirling mist. The white cloud whirled around her. The circling wind started slowly but gained speed until it was howling like a tornado. Within seconds, the center of the cyclone was directly over her forehead, the narrowest part hovering less than an inch from her. She wanted to flinch, to move away, but Burke and Miko told her to remain still in calm, soothing voices. There was nothing to fear. The wind was magic. It wouldn't hurt her.

It touched her, a soft caress like a summer breeze. She closed her eyes, letting the wonderful sensation relax her. Behind her closed eyelids, images flashed through her mind. Memories of Burke and Miko in strange historical costumes, doing things like riding horses across green fields, sailing wooden ships. A barrage of emotions swept through her -- sorrow, joy, confusion, loneliness, despair.

And then there was only peace. Quiet contentment.

Her vision cleared. She looked at Burke, at Miko. Their eyes were normal again. Their love for her shown clearly now, as if some kind of fog had been cleared.

She sat up and sank into Burke and Miko's embrace, thankful for what she'd learned, and for the gift they'd given her -- freedom from the chains tying her to the pain of her past.

"Now, are you ready to finish what we started earlier?" Burke clapped his hands, rubbing them together eagerly, sexual promise glittering in his eyes.

A whole other kind of sensation pulsed through her ? a simmering sensual heat. A very wonderful erotic warmth, coupled with pure joy that made her feel so light she could literally take flight like the birds.

* * *

Miko had never known such profound joy existed. Having lived for centuries without a soul, he'd learned to accept the way he was. He'd also learned to hide from the emptiness, distracting himself with work. He still loved his job with the *Excoluni*, and in fact was looking forward to the challenges of his new position -- the one formerly held by his brother, Hadrian. But he now could put his job in its proper perspective. No longer would he live to work. There were two other reasons to wake up in the morning -- Burke and Sylvie. They were much more important.

Someday, however, he hoped to find out what had changed his brother. He could appreciate Hadrian's grieving for the loss of his girlfriend, now that he had experienced love firsthand. Yet it wasn't exactly the same. Hadrian and his girlfriend hadn't been bound mates. Hadrian couldn't love her. At least not in the purest sense. Perhaps he'd loved her as a soulless man could? And just maybe that imperfect love had destroyed his brother?

Answers. He would get them. But he would not let his quest for them rule his life. The man Miko had respected was gone. Nothing would bring him back.

* * *

Burke signed the final document and slid the stack of papers across the table's glossy surface.

The agent from the title company checked the signatures, nodded and set a signed check before him. "Very well. Best of luck to you both." He stood, shook hands with Burke then turned to do the same with Isabella, after handing a set of keys to her.

As soon as he left the room, Isabella beamed at Burke, keys in hand. "I wanted to pay more, you know."

"You paid enough." The full price she'd paid hung between them, unspoken words. She'd sacrificed her job, home, friends. She could have lost even more. Thankfully, she hadn't.

She raised the key ring. "You can still change your mind."

"No, never."

"You're too damn stubborn for your own good."

"Nah. Just too damn stubborn for your good."

She gave him a watery smile. "Come visit me?"

"Soon."

"I'm going to redecorate. The estate's so… medieval. It's needed a facelift for centuries."

He knew damn well she had no intention of changing a thing. She was, after all, a medieval woman at heart. "It's yours now. If you want to put in shag carpet and mirrored disco balls, that's your choice."

She lifted a single delicately groomed eyebrow. "Hmmm. That is a thought." Leaning forward, she pressed a kiss to his cheek. "Thank you. For everything."

"No, thank you. For being my friend when I needed one most." He watched her leave the office, knowing she would finally have the life she deserved. No more struggling. He plucked up the check, reading the figure printed on it. One dollar and no cents.

He had paid his debt.

And he had received the most wonderful gift of all, even more precious than the money, houses, freedom he'd fought for.

He had finally experienced love.

BONUS CONTENT

Please turn the page for a special sneak preview of DANGEROUS MASTER, the third book in Tawny Taylor's Masters of Desire series. Available now.

Private Investigator Mandy Thompson knows how to dig beneath the surface and uncover secrets about other people. But the tables are turned when she enters the erotic lair of Master Zane and finds herself revealing her most intimate sexual fantasies. Within this world of dark and dangerous passion, she gives in to her desire for extreme pleasure. She is no longer in control. Her body craves the sensual ecstasy only one man can give her. All she can do is surrender to her master. . .

This was getting old.

Mandy had spent the last few weeks pretending to be a new submissive at a local bondage club, while watching mostly-naked men and women of all ages, shapes, and sizes be chained up, tied down, spanked, paddled, flogged and caned. At first, it was pretty damn sexy to watch. But gradually, it lost its appeal. She just could not understand why they did it. What purpose did it serve? How could they mistake pain for pleasure?

She needed to wrap up this case and move on. She'd put in hours upon hours and had nothing to show for it. She was beginning to think her client was never going to get the proof she needed to win her case. And Mandy was going to lose her reputation as the bulldog of Detroit.

Mandy yanked at the creeping hem of her mini skirt and shimmied through the thick crowd gathered at the far end of the public dungeon. This place wasn't the best for her purposes. There was a no-penetration rule in place, and that rule was strictly enforced. There were security guards ensuring that nobody stepped out of line, and that all play was safe and consensual. Her hope was that she'd score an invitation to a private party somewhere else, a gathering like Zane's.

Zane.

She'd thought about him a time or two since that night. He'd popped up in a dream every so often. In those dreams, he did things to her that she never would have guessed she'd like. She'd wakened in the middle of an orgasm more than once.

No man had ever done that to her before.

But, and this was a big but, he was more than she could handle--outside of a fantasy. She reminded herself of that fact every time one of those dreams had her second-guessing herself.

If only he wasn't so...darkly dominant. Intimidating. Fiercely gorgeous.

A pleasant buzz of energy zapped through her body as she pictured his face in her mind. What a face. What a body.

No, she wouldn't wish him to change, not at all. It was that dark dominance, that sense of danger, that made him so damn sexy. He was the ultimate bad boy.

Someone tapped her shoulder.

Thinking it was Sarah, who'd scampered off to talk to a fellow domme, she spun around.

It wasn't Sarah.

"Hello," Zane said.

"Hi." Mandy's mouth went instantly dry. He was here. Zane. God, it was him. And he was looking just as good, if not better, than he had in her dreams.

He leaned over her and murmured in her ear, "I've been watching you." She wasn't sure how she felt about that. "And I know what you're doing," he added.

"Do you?" She wanted to get away from this man. No, she didn't. She wanted to lean in closer, draw in his scent, and feel his heat burn over her body.

He slid an arm around her waist. "Come with me." Not waiting for her to decide whether or not she wanted to, he started weaving through the crowd, pulling her along. She followed. Her mind screamed silent warnings. But her feet kept going. They left the dungeon, following a long, dark corridor that ran behind it. They stopped at the end.

He turned her so she was trapped between the wall and his bulk. She tried to decide whether she needed to scream for help or listen to what he wanted to tell her. She looked up into his dark eyes. They looked intense but not terrifying.

No, she wouldn't scream. Not yet.

"What do you want?" Her voice sounded small. She felt small too. He was so tall, so big. And, more than that, he gave off a powerful presence, an energy that made her feel powerless and vulnerable.

"You like to watch. It makes you wet."

"Um." A gush of heated cream dampened her panties. He was right, in some respects. She would much rather watch than participate.

He leaned closer, closer still. His breath was sweet, his body warm. "Watch me."

A shudder swept through her body. Hell yes, she'd like to do that. But. But...He lowered his mouth to hers, brushed his lips across hers. The door behind her swung open and she practically tumbled into the room. He grabbed her upper arms, steadying her as she regained her footing. Her gaze lifted to his. Dark eyes locked to soft blue. Mandy's heart did a funky pitter-patter-thump in her chest.

Zane motioned behind her. "Won't you have a seat?"

"I shouldn't."

Zane tipped his head slightly. "Shouldn't, but you want to. You will."

She'd say one thing for this guy, he didn't lack confidence. "No, I don't think I will." She twisted her body to break out of his loose hold. She saw then what was behind her.

A man, nude. A gorgeous man. Kneeling. Head tipped down. Hands resting on smooth-skinned thighs.

ALSO BY TAWNY TAYLOR

Rescue Me (writing as Sydney Allan)
Darkest Fire
Darkest Desire
Dark Master
Decadent Master
Dangerous Master
Wicked Beast
About Monday (writing as Tami Dane)
The Real Werewives of Vampire County (writing as Tami Dane)
Blood of Eden (writing as Tami Dane)
Blood of Innocence (writing as Tami Dane)

ABOUT TAWNY TAYLOR

Nothing exciting happens in Tawny Taylor's life, unless you count giving the cat a flea dip -- a cat can make some fascinating sounds when immersed chin-deep in insecticide -- or chasing after a houseful of upchucking kids during flu season. She doesn't travel the world or employ a staff of personal servants. She's not even built like a runway model. She's just your run-of-the-mill, pleasantly plump Detroit suburban mom and wife.

That's why she writes, for the sheer joy of it. She doesn't need to escape, mind you. Despite being run-of-the-mill, her life is wonderful. She just likes to add some... zip.

Her heroines might resemble herself, or her next door neighbor (sorry, Sue), but they are sure to be memorable (she hopes!). And her heroes -- inspired by movie stars, her favorite television actors or her husband -- are fully capable of delivering one hot happily-ever-after after another. Combined, the characters and plots she weaves bring countless hours of enjoyment to Tawny... and she hopes to readers too!

In the end, that's all the matters to Tawny, bringing a little bit of zip to someone else's life.

You can email Tawny at tawny@tawnytaylor.com or visit her website at http://www.tawnytaylor.com.